FATHER of the BRIDE

Lennox Grey

ISBN: 978-1-968115-90-6 ebook

ISBN: 978-1-968115-13-5 paperback

This is a work of fiction. Names, characters, places, and incidents are either products of the author's imagination or are used fictitiously. Any resemblance to actual persons, living or dead, events, or locales is entirely coincidental.

Dedicated to the ones who can spot me anywhere. You know my voice, even when I change the mask.

CONTENT NOTE

Listen...

You're about to dive into explicit sex, heavy drinking, divorce drama, manipulative exes, paparazzi scandal, and a generous dose of "oh no they didn't."

There's also some light BDSM (safe words, choking, the works). If that's your thing, *fantastic*.

If not... might I suggest a Hallmark paperback instead?

You've been warned.

On a more serious note...

There is a flashback scene where someone passes away from cancer. Having walked through this in my own life, I know how tender and triggering that can be. My hope is that it reads as respectful and brings a sense of peace rather than pain.

PLAYLIST

The soundtrack to Sevynn & London's chaos, lust, heartbreak, and reclamation. Best served loud.

1. **Wicked Game** – Chris Isaak

2. **Earned It** – The Weeknd

3. **Love Interruption** – Jack White

4. **Lay It Down** – Lloyd

5. **Glory Box** – Portishead

6. **Take Me to Church** – Hozier

7. **Cherry** – Lana Del Rey

8. **Heavy in Your Arms** – Florence + The Machine

9. **After Dark** – Mr. Kitty

10. **Sex on Fire** – Kings of Leon

11. **Blue Jeans** – Lana Del Rey

12. **Closer** – Nine Inch Nails

13. **Dangerous** – Big Data (ft. Joywave)

14. **Sweetest Taboo** – Sade

15. **Believer** – Imagine Dragons

Five Years Ago

It was too quiet. No beeps. No whirring. No steady hum of machines to fill the void and distract me from the truth. For weeks, I'd trained my ears to those sounds. I clung to them, because as long as they kept going, so did she. Now, with the machines gone, the silence was deafening.

Sarah lay small in the hospital bed, her breaths shallow, fragile, each rise and fall of her chest slower than the last. The life that used to blaze out of her —laughter, sarcasm, warmth— was flickering, dimming.

Simone was curled in the corner chair, drowning inside her hoodie, face blotched red from crying. Sixteen years old and staring at her mother like maybe if she focused hard enough, she could will her chest to rise higher. I wanted to take that look away from her, to shield her from this moment. But there was no fixing what was coming.

I wasn't ready. I would never be ready. How the hell was I supposed to do this alone? Live a life without her beside me?

Yesterday had given me false hope. She woke up, and she was almost herself again, bright and soft smile. A surge of energy, they said. One last good day. I'd let myself believe it was a miracle, that maybe we'd turned a corner. But miracles, I was learning, weren't for people like me.

"Come here, my loves," Sarah called, her voice stronger than it had any right to be, holding her hands out to both of us.

I sat down beside her, taking her hand in mine, pressing her knuckles to my lips, memorizing the feel of her skin, the rhythm of her pulse.

"It's a pretty day today," she murmured, looking toward the window, like the sunlight streaming in was just for her.

"It is," I whispered back, my throat tight.

Her gaze drifted between us. First me, then Simone; eyes vacant but steady, the kind of look that pierced through bone and went straight for the soul.

"I know this is going to be hard for you both," she whispered. "But you're going to be okay. More than okay. I'm going to make absolute sure of it."

The words clawed at my chest. I forced a smile, though it trembled at the edges. "Oh yeah? How are you gonna do that?" My voice cracked on the tease, a pitiful attempt at playfulness, desperate to keep her anchored here, to keep her talking, anything but the silence creeping closer.

Her lips curved faintly, worn thin with exhaustion, but still carrying that spark of mischief she never lost. That spark that had always drawn me to her.

She turned to Simone then, her smile softening into something wide and radiant, like she was pouring everything she had left into our daughter. She reached up with trembling fingers and smoothed a curl from Simone's damp cheek. "You're so beautiful," she whispered. "Inside and out. Don't you ever forget that."

Simone let out a broken sob, clutching at her mother's hand. "Of course, Mommy."

Sarah's thumb brushed across the inside of Simone's wrist, a tender caress, then she pressed her lips there as though she was sealing something unseen into her skin.

"She'll have a bridge," she breathed, eyes flicking toward me before finding our daughter again. "Like your daddy. A London Bridge. Right here." She stroked the spot, her smile trembling now. "She'll take care of him. Of both of you. I'm going to send you to him. You'll take care of him?"

Simone's head shook fiercely, tears spilling unchecked. "I don't understand," she cried. "No one can take care of us like you, Mommy. No one."

My chest caved in at the sound of her voice, at the way her words rang true, because how could anyone take her place? How could anyone ever hold us together the way Sarah always had?

But she only smiled again, serene, her hand still pressed to our daughter's wrist. "You'll see," she whispered. "One day, you'll see. It's fate."

She was gone within the hour, not passed on yet, but a shell. Barely breathing, and we watched. And waited. Until she took her last breath.

1 | SEVYNN

This must be the most beautiful forty-two-year-old man's back I've ever seen.

If Michelangelo had sculpted him, David would've been laughed out of Florence. The man's built like a god; muscles stacked and defined, as if God had a moment of pure vanity and decided to show off.

His shoulders taper into a back carved like marble, leading down to an ass that deserves its own fan club. And the thighs? Sweet merciful Jesus. Thick, thunderous, heroic.

Thighs that could crush watermelons or weak-willed women. Lucky for me, I currently qualify as both. Yes, I now identify as produce.

And here I am, brushing my fingers down his arm while he sleeps. Stroking his biceps like some pervy TSA agent searching for contraband. Which is wildly out of character for me, by the way. I've never been a one-night-stand kind of woman. I've barely even been a "wink at the bartender" kind of woman.

My résumé had one lonely bullet point: Jaxon Moore. My husband. Well, ex-husband, technically, since the implosion a year and a half ago that could've rivaled a Fourth of July finale.

Fireworks everywhere, except the kind that burn your eyebrows off and leave your life in smoldering ruin.

So, what the hell am I doing here? Laying in a stranger's hotel room. Wrapped in hotel sheets that now smelled like bourbon and questionable life choices. Touching a man I barely know like he's mine. Feeling reckless and stupid and… twenty-one again. Except this time, I come with stretch marks, adult-onset cynicism, a mortgage, and a drawer full of overly used vibrators.

Here's the deal: my oldest son, Derrick, is getting married in four days. He's twenty-three. That's problem number one. Not the age or the marriage itself; I trust his judgment. Derrick's level-headed in a way that still shocks me, considering who raised him. I've only talked to his fiancé Simmy, a couple of times on the phone, but she seems lovely. Sweet. Thoughtful. But Derrick's young. So young. And the closer we get to the wedding, the more the mom in me spirals. Is he ready for this? Am *I* ready for this?

So, I did the logical, responsible thing: I flew into Chicago early, Mother of the Groom duties locked and loaded. The plan was simple; settle my nerves, check into the hotel a day ahead, maybe treat myself to a massage from a sexy masseuse with powerful hands, and a glass of wine, or three; before the chaos swallowed me whole.

And then the universe laughed in my face.

Cue: Jaxon Moore, my ex-husband, swaggering onto the same damn plane with his twenty-two-year-old pregnant girlfriend.

Boy, does the universe have a sense of humor. A cruel one.

And as if that wasn't enough, my body decided "fight or flight" really just meant "trip over absolutely nothing in the middle of the aisle and eat carpet." One second, I was booking it toward the back; the next I was sprawled like a crime scene, palms burning against that godforsaken industrial carpet.

When I looked up, there they were. Jaxon and his too-young, too-perfect girlfriend. Both staring. Not smug, not smirking—which I could've handled, honestly. No, it was pity. And that... was so much worse.

Heat rushed up my neck, shame burning hotter than the recycled plane air blasting through the vents. And then came the chaos. Voices rising, overlapping, a blur of *"Are you okay?"* and *"Miss, can you stand?"* Hands reaching, too many hands—strangers crowding me, tugging me up, faces too close, concern thick and suffocating. The sounds swelled, metal overhead bins clicking shut, boarding announcements droning. Every noise crawled straight into my skull, jagged and sharp.

My chest cinched, breath snagged shallow and quick. My body turned traitor, panicking, and drowning in open air.

The next thing I knew, I was locked in the tiny airplane bathroom, hunched over the sink, gasping like I'd run a marathon on broken lungs. The mirror reflected a pale, wild-eyed stranger back at me as the flight attendant pounded on the door. "Ma'am, we need you seated for takeoff."

But I couldn't. God, I couldn't. My chest was a vise, each inhale like trying to suck air through a straw. The walls pressed closer, plastic and chrome, the hum of the engine roaring like it knew I was breaking.

By the time the worst of it passed—not calm, not even close, but dulled into something I could *almost* control—I splashed water on my face and forced my spine upright. The mirror was cracked at the corner, a jagged line slicing through the reflection of my mouth.

I practiced smiling anyway. It didn't reach my eyes. It never does.

When I opened that bathroom door, I walked out like dignity itself was stitched into my bones, even if every nerve ending in me was still shrieking like an alarm bell. My hands shook, my chest was sore from the fight with my own lungs, but my chin stayed high.

And God help me, the only thought pounding through my skull as I slid back into my seat was this: *The second this tin can lifts off, I'd happily unbuckle, march to the emergency exit, and fling myself into the sky without a parachute. At least then, the freefall would've been mine.*

So maybe crawling into bed with this ridiculously gorgeous man wasn't recklessness. Maybe it was survival. Or CPR for a heart that had been on life support for months. Or maybe it was just the universe finally tossing me a bone.

Pun extremely intended.

But let me back up a bit. Jaxon, my now ex-husband, came crashing into my life when I was fifteen and he was seventeen. He was the golden boy of our Raleigh high school: varsity jacket, cocky grin, the kind who could make a teacher forget her own lesson plan just by walking into class. And I was the girl who thought getting noticed by him meant I'd hit the jackpot.

Except life doesn't hand out jackpots. It hands out pregnancy tests.

I got pregnant in my early teens. Teen mom alert. I had Derrick at fifteen, and our second son, Marley, only ten months later. Irish twins.

While everyone else my age worried about prom dresses and SAT scores, I was worried about diapers and how to keep colicky babies quiet long enough to finish my algebra homework.

While my friends were sneaking out to kiss boys in cars, I was sneaking out to Walmart at three in the morning for formula.

Jaxon and I went from high school sweethearts to shotgun wedding partners to parents before we'd even figured out who we were. He was my first kiss, my first everything, and for a long time I told myself he'd be my forever. Turns out forever had an expiration date.

Jaxon, of course, landed on his feet. He always does. Somewhere between Derrick and Marley, he got scouted for a Calvin Klein ad. Yep. My husband in nothing but boxer briefs, ten stories tall, looming over Times Square while I was home folding laundry and praying the kids would nap longer than twenty minutes.

I was an only child, and my dad died before I was old enough to even hold on to a real memory of him. Mom? She wasn't exactly built for motherhood — or maybe she just didn't want to be. Losing him broke something in her, and instead of pouring what she had left into me, she poured it all back into herself. By the time I was twelve, she'd vanish for weeks at a time, leaving nothing but a little cash for groceries and a note that said *be good.*

So, I learned early how to walk to the store alone, how to answer the questions with a smile.

Where's your mother?

"Oh, she's on the other aisle."

"You just missed her."

It wasn't true, but it kept people from looking too closely.

So, no…it's not surprising that I got pregnant young. Not that it's an excuse, but when you leave a girl to raise herself, mistakes are bound to happen.

It was then just me and my best. My best effort. My best guesses. My best shot at piecing together a family out of scraps. When Jaxon came barreling into my life, I thought I'd finally found someone to fill that gaping hole. Spoiler: it just left me patching new holes with the same old thread.

Not that I didn't land on my feet eventually, it just took me a hell of a lot longer. Because I was the mom. The caretaker. The one juggling diapers and bills while moonlighting as Jaxon's unpaid PR manager, scheduler, therapist, and crisis-control hotline. My entire twenties were sacrificed on the altar of making sure he looked shiny and untouchable while I was running on fumes, caffeine, and the same damn bottle of dry shampoo.

But I got there. Somehow, between soccer practices, tantrums, and making sure the golden boy never looked like he had cracks in his armor, I clawed my way up. I finished school. I worked my ass off. I hustled every hour I wasn't folding laundry or making lunches. Eventually, I built a following of over twenty-three million on TikTok. Yes, million. With nothing but recipes, late-night cooking rants, and videos of me cursing at my oven like it owed me money.

And then? I flipped it. I turned that little corner of the internet into an empire.

Now I own three restaurants.

The first is in Raleigh, my hometown. My first baby. I named it *Sevynn* because what the hell else was I gonna call it? That place nearly killed me opening night. Plumbing disasters, produce arriving half-rotten, and my sous chef getting arrested the day before launch. But somehow, it survived. And thrived.

The second is in New York City, because I clearly hate myself and thought opening in Manhattan would be fun. It's called *Ironcrest*, sleek and sharp, the kind of place where Wall Street assholes try to order off-menu and I politely tell them to fuck off, but with a smile. That one got me my first Michelin star and a seat at the big-kid table.

And then came California; San Francisco, to be exact. *North Current*. My West Coast baby. Light, coastal, inventive. My *"I can do this shit on both coasts"* flex. That one landed me my second star and a James Beard.

So yeah. My salary doesn't just whisper independence, it screams it from the damn rooftops. I don't need a man to pay my bills. Hell, if I felt like being petty, I could buy the house Jaxon lives in and charge him rent.

Luckily, I'm not a total masochist. I've got a team of insanely talented people running the day-to-day, which means I only have to travel about one week every other month to check in, meet with the staff, and remind everyone that, yes, the crazy woman on TikTok is also their boss.

The rest of the time? I let my brain spin. New menus, new concepts, new cities. A pastry shop? A wine bar? Maybe a dessert-only pop-up where we throw cake at the customers if they complain? (Kidding, mostly.)

I'm always chasing the next adventure, the next way to outdo myself. Because once you realize you can build an empire from midnight cooking videos and a half-busted kitchen, you start to believe you can do just about anything.

So, as it turns out, resilience looks pretty damn good on me.

Meanwhile, Jaxon's modeling campaigns snowballed. Modeling turned into commercials. Commercials turned into movie extras. And then, four years ago, he landed his grand debut in a feature film as the brooding detective who rips off his sunglasses to say, *"Let's get this party started."* Oscar-worthy? Not unless they hand out statues for "Best Use of Cheekbones." But hey, his jawline did get its own fan club and at least one very dedicated Tumblr page.

And Jessica? His now-pregnant twenty-two-year-old girlfriend? She was the makeup artist for his latest film. Of course, she was. Young, dewy skin, a winged eyeliner sharp enough to kill a man. A walking reminder that no matter how many Michelin stars I earned, I couldn't compete with the currency of youth.

So, when Jaxon and Jessica were caught on the balcony of a Vancouver hotel mid-shoot…half-naked, sucking face like they were auditioning for a bad soap opera; the internet did what it does best. My humiliation had a clickbait title before

I'd even finished my morning coffee.

"Silver Fox Star Trades In Longtime Wife for Makeup Girl."

"From Calvin Klein to Cougar Crime Scene."

I didn't even need to read the articles. The headlines alone did the damage, sharp little daggers dressed up as puns.

Derrick and Marley dropped everything and flew home the second it hit the news. My boys. They hovered, they sat guard; they played watchdogs against a world that suddenly felt too sharp, and way too loud. And I did what moms do best, I patched the holes, even while I was bleeding out. I smiled. I joked. I swore I was fine.

But then they left—Derrick back to Chicago for law school, Marley down to Tulane in Louisiana. Once they were gone, the silence swallowed me whole. The house wasn't a home anymore; it was a mausoleum of what used to be. No clatter of keys tossed onto the counter. No half-empty cereal bowls sweating milk in the sink. No muffled bass line thumping through the walls at midnight. Just me. Four walls. And the hollow outline of a marriage I'd spent half my life duct-taping together.

Call it weakness, call it desperation to keep my family intact, I took him back after that. We tried counseling. He swore it was a one-time thing. I believed him. Yeah...I know. He did all the things: flowers, notes on my pillow, texts to check in, little gestures like proof of devotion.

And then the women started coming forward.

At first, I told myself it was noise. Static. Wannabes chasing fifteen minutes of tabloid fame. But then came the proof.

Screenshots. Hotel receipts. Photos in places I'd been told were "just business trips." Timelines that overlapped entire chapters of my life, like cracks spiderwebbing through a sidewalk. The kind you don't see until suddenly you're flat on your ass wondering how you missed it.

Each week, a new headline. Each headline, another twenty-something grinning into the camera like she'd won a prize. Like my marriage was her party favor. And every single one of them chipped away at me, splinter by splinter, until there was nothing left to hold together.

One even stretched back twelve years. Twelve. Which meant that while I was carting kids to soccer practice and scraping burned mac and cheese off the stove, he was out rehearsing lines for a role he apparently nailed—faithful husband. Guess he really was Oscar-worthy after all. Because I had no fucking clue.

That's when the truth finally sank its teeth in: I hadn't been abandoned eighteen months ago. I'd been abandoned years ago. Long before the divorce papers. Long before the boys left for their own lives. I just hadn't noticed, because I was too busy raising everyone else, Jaxon included, to realize the bed beside me had gone cold a long time ago.

The divorce was finalized six months ago. That's when the decree was signed. I, of course, found out through the tabloids that he and Jessica never really ended things. They were still having an affair while we were in counseling, while he was "checking in."

There was even a TMZ video — sold for a handsome sum — of him leaving a restaurant with me, turning the corner, and scooping her up into his arms. Kissing her before they slid into his car.

So, yeah…it took months for the frenzy to die down. Eventually the vultures found a shinier carcass, another family to pick apart. They flapped off, leaving me with the scraps. But the thing about Jaxon's mess is it never really disappears — it lingers, resurfaces, trickles back at the worst times.

And now, with Derrick's wedding days away and both families convening in Chicago? The headlines have started creeping back. Little reminders, sharp as paper cuts, that I'll never outrun his shadow.

So yesterday, I did the only thing I could. I checked in early. I tried to breathe. I told myself I just… needed a minute.

And by a "minute," I meant five shots of tequila the second the clock blinked past noon, a plate of bar nachos I don't even remember ordering, and my very bedazzled Kindle, the one Marley gifted me for my thirty-eighth birthday last month. Hot pink. Rhinestones. Sparkling like a Vegas showgirl every time I pick it up.

So, as you can imagine, I wasn't exactly mentally *prepared* when the very tall, very attractive, very bend-me-over-the-bar-and-fuck-me-right-here kind of man stepped straight into my line of sight. His mouth was moving, saying something I absolutely could not process because my vagina was panting like a dehydrated puppy.

"Looks like you're here on the same escape plan," is what it *sounded* like he said, in a voice so deep and gruff it rattled through my ribcage and set up permanent residency there.

I looked up, and my jaw dropped. Not a cute romcom dropped. Not dainty, oh-how-charming dropped. No, this was full-on *unhinged,* mouth-wide-open, probably-some-drool escaped kind of dropped.

Because holy. Actual. Hell.

The man looked like he'd been custom built to ruin me. Broad shoulders under a fitted white shirt, sleeves rolled to reveal forearms that deserved their own Olympic category. A jawline sharp enough to straddle and ride into the sunset.

And those eyes—green, fierce, glinting like he already knew every filthy thought sprinting through my brain.

Salt-and-pepper hair, perfectly undone—like he'd just rolled out of bed, except on him it looked deliberate. Styled by the gods. And the beard—short, scruffy, unfairly perfect.

If there were a glossy subscription catalog called *Hot Older Men You Should Never Trust*, he'd be the cover model. Hell, he'd *be* the entire centerfold, and I'd lick it.

He sank into the chair across from me, and when he leaned back, it was like the entire lounge shrank to fit around him. Broad shoulders stretched the T-shirt. His forearms rested on the arms of the chair, thick with muscles and ridged with veins like roadmaps. And wrapped around each bicep and forearm—three stark black bands, bold ink that begged a story. Soldier? Survivor?

And tall. God, he was tall. Sitting across from him, I automatically sat up straighter, like I'd been caught slouching in church.

He lifted his own Kindle and gave me a grin that shouldn't have been legal in Illinois. *"Last Patient of the Night,"* he said casually, as if he hadn't just dismantled my entire ability to form words. "What about you?"

When my voice finally creaked its way out of my chest, I betrayed myself. Against all laws of dignity, against the internal script I'd rehearsed in my head, I blurted the truth. *"Morning Glory Milking Farm."*

Oh. My. Fucking. God.

Not *The Teacher*, like I'd promised myself I'd say if anyone asked. Not something literary and respectable, something that screamed *yes, I'm a cultured woman who reads books with embossed covers.* Nope. My mouth went rogue and served up my monster-smut-of-the-week to the hottest man I had ever laid eyes on.

His brows rose, just a fraction. The corner of his mouth curved like he was trying, failing, not to laugh. Then it happened: the laugh. Rough, warm, whiskey-over-ice kind of sound that slid under my skin and melted me from the inside out. He tipped his head back, Adam's apple bobbing, and I was done for.

"Holy shit," he said finally, shaking his head with a grin that could absolutely ruin me six ways to Sunday. "You win. Hands down. You definitely win."

And there I was—deer in headlights, clutching my glitter-bomb Kindle to my chest like it might sprout wings and carry me out of the hotel lounge before I died on the spot. "Great," I muttered, heat creeping up my neck. "Glad my public humiliation doubles as entertainment."

"Entertainment?" He leaned forward now, elbows braced on the table, those tattooed forearms catching the lounge light. "Sweetheart, you've just set the bar for every conversation I'll ever have in this place."

And just like that, heat pooled low in my belly. Because this wasn't small talk. This was trouble. Big, broad-shouldered, smirking trouble.

"London," he said, offering his hand across the tiny table, palm open, patient.

"Sevynn," I managed, slipping mine into his. My skin was clammy enough to qualify as a biohazard, but he didn't flinch.

"Beautiful." His grip was firm, steady, a slow kind of confidence that felt like it could hold me together if I fell apart. He let go, but not before giving me one last glance over the rim of that grin. "The name's pretty, too."

Aaaaand, my ovaries broke into a standing ovation while the rest of me tried to pretend I wasn't seconds away from swooning face-first into the nachos.

"I'll leave you to your... *milking*," he said with a crooked smile, leaning back, ankle crossing over his knee, Kindle lifted like he hadn't just disabled my nervous system with a two-minute interaction.

I giggled. Actually giggled. The sound startled me so much I ducked my head to my own screen, even though disappointment pinched low in my chest. Because as much as I wanted to act like I didn't care, God, I kind of wanted the attention.

Let me be clear; it's not that I'm desperate. I've taken really good care of myself; skincare, workouts, the occasional expensive serum when I could justify it. I still get carded to buy alcohol everywhere, which is its own twisted little ego boost. But lately... I've felt that itch. The need to crack myself open a little. To let someone look at me like that again. To be reminded I'm more than just a mother, an ex-wife, or a headline.

Maybe it's because the house has emptied out. Maybe it's because my husband is gone, my kids are grown, and suddenly I've got nothing but time and a very neglected vagina.

The marriage has technically been over for nearly a year, but the sex? That died out damn near two years ago. Jaxon was always on some set, flying off to "shoot on location" (which I now know was code for screwing twenty-somethings). And I was traveling for work, getting the restaurants off the ground, juggling the boys, holding everything together with duct tape and caffeine. We'd become passing ships in the night—except ships at least honk when they pass. Jaxon and I barely managed a nod in the hallway.

So yeah. I wasn't starving for attention because I couldn't get it necessarily. I was starved because the one place I was supposed to be seen, touched, wanted... had gone completely dark.

"Can I get you anything else?"

The server—cheeks flushed like she'd just sprinted the length of the hotel—stood hovering over the Greek god across from me, pad in hand, practically begging for him to look at her. I couldn't even blame her. If I were her, I'd be flushed too.

"Yeah, I'll take, uh..." He plucked the menu from the next table, casual as anything, and the veins running along his hand made my stomach swoop. "I'll do an old-fashioned. And whatever the lady's having."

My head jerked up, panic flaring. "Oh, no. No, you don't have to do that. I'm fine, thanks."

He tilted his head, eyes narrowing—not unkind, but sharp enough to pin me to my seat. "Have you ever had one? An old-fashioned?"

"No, actually." I gave a helpless little shrug. "I've always been more of a shots-or-margarita girl. No in-between."

"Try one with me."

And then he smiled. Jesus. Dimples I hadn't even noticed before carved deep grooves into his cheeks, so unfairly gorgeous they could've had their own gravity. Dimples that could order me around and I'd probably thank them for the privilege.

"Sure," I blurted, heat racing back up my neck. "Yes. Thank you."

"Good girl."

Holy shit. New kink unlocked. The server literally gasped, pen hovering midair as her gaze flicked between us. And I couldn't even blame her either. Because, fuck, *same girl...same.*

2 | LONDON

Good girl? Goddammit. Did I actually just say that out loud?

Fucking idiot.

They both looked at me like I'd just quoted some cringe TikTok thirst trap, and they weren't wrong. Who even blurts that in the middle of a hotel lounge with witnesses? Me, apparently. Forty-two years old, allegedly a grown man.

Smooth, London. Real smooth.

I rubbed a hand over the back of my neck, trying to mask the fact that I suddenly wanted to crawl under the damn table. I'm out of practice with this shit. Way out. It's been years since I've done more than half-assed small talk at a work event or the polite "hello" to someone's mom at a game. I don't know the rules anymore.

And the truth is? I don't know what the hell I'm doing. Not with her. Not with anyone. But for some reason, when I look at her, all I want to do is keep talking. Keep fumbling. Keep trying.

I needed a beat today. Just one. The last few years with Simone have been rough. She's twenty-one, my only kid, and she's getting married this week. To a guy I don't even know, only spoken to on the phone *maybe* three times. It's been pretty much nonstop arguments since the day she called to announce the engagement.

She'd left Durham for college in Chicago two years ago, and I knew she'd been seeing someone for the past year. Serious, from the way she talked about him. Serious as twenty-one can be, anyway. But marriage? Out of nowhere? My brain short-circuited. My heart panicked.

And because I am, in fact, a complete dumbass, the very first words out of my mouth were:

"Are you pregnant?"

That went over about as well as you'd expect. She didn't speak to me for a week. I ended up groveling by paying for her trip to France with her cousins just to patch things up.

Sarah would've handled it better. Hell, Sarah handled *everything* better. She always knew what to say, when to say it, and the exact tone that turned an argument into a compromise. My wife could've negotiated with a terrorist and walked away with a peace treaty and a dinner invite.

But cancer didn't care. It took her five years ago, and since then it's been just me and Simone. Me fumbling through fatherhood, trying to figure out how to raise a girl into a woman without screwing her up worse than she already was from losing her mother as a teenager.

And now, watching her walk straight into this marriage? It feels like failure. Like I missed something vital. Like I'm losing her all over again. Yeah, so what I've talked to the guy a couple of times, the obligatory polite conversations, and he seems solid. But now we're talking forever. And I don't even really know him, but I have to trust her to him, forever.

Maybe that's why I'm here. Why my eyes caught on the woman across the lounge and that smile that hit me straight in the chest. Maybe I just needed someone to remind me I'm not only a dad. Not only a widower. Not only the guy forever playing catch-up with his own life.

Someone to make me feel like myself again.

But it's more than that. There's a familiarity about her. Not the bullshit, "Hey, don't I know you from somewhere?" pick-up line. Real familiarity. Like her face is stamped somewhere in my memory, and my brain just can't place where.

Even from here, she's one of the most beautiful women I've ever seen. And this is Chicago; this hotel is crawling with high-maintenance women hunting for rich pricks. But her? She's not trying. Not decked out. Just comfortable in her own skin, holding that ridiculous, glitter-bomb Kindle like it's all she needs.

And I'm drawn to her. Helplessly. Like there's a string tied to my chest, pulling me toward her.

I tossed back a shot of bourbon, bracing myself before I worked up the nerve to cross the room. Halfway there, I caught the glint of my wedding ring in the glass I still held. Shit. My stomach dropped. I spun on my heel and bolted straight back to the bar.

Cue the same lecture I'd been giving myself for five years: *It's time, London. She'd want you to move on, London. You have to let go, London.*

I'd had that conversation with myself a hundred times. Every time I thought about starting over. Every time I reached for the band. And every time, I couldn't do it. I'd leave the ring where it belonged, on my finger, convincing myself I'd try again tomorrow.

But today was different. Today I surprised even myself when I slid the band free for the first time since Sarah died...and slipped it into my pocket.

I clutched my Kindle, telling myself it'd be the perfect conversation starter. Easier than trying to be charming from scratch. I let myself watch her a minute longer; the way she smirked at whatever she was reading, the way she bit her thumbnail with no idea she was being watched. She was beautiful. Younger, I think. Brunette wavy curls piled up in a messy bun, dark-rimmed glasses sliding down her nose.

She had a couple of tattoos I could make out from here, but one stood out most; two bold lines etched into her neck, stopping halfway down. One arm was covered in a full sleeve, the other dotted with scattered ink. The contrast was insane: this striking, inked-up beauty padding around in fuzzy slippers, leggings, and an oversized T-shirt, like she'd just rolled out of bed and thought, *screw it, I need a drink.*

"Can I get one more, please?" I asked the bartender, motioning with my glass. She'd been making eyes at me since I sat down, leaning in a little too close, asking if I needed *anything.*

"Sure thing, handsome," she said, giving me a smile I didn't want.

Because I already knew what I wanted. And she was sitting across the lounge, being effortlessly beautiful.

I took one more sip of bourbon, just to shut off my mind. My pulse thudded in my throat like I was some damn teenager instead of a man who paid a mortgage and had a kid about to walk down the aisle.

She laughed at something in her book, head tilting just slightly, and it damn near knocked the air out of me. That laugh wasn't polished, wasn't posed. It was messy and real, like she'd forgotten where she was. And all I could think was...God, when was the last time I'd seen joy like that?

So, I stood up before I could talk myself out of it. Every step across the lounge felt heavy, like I was dragging the last five years of grief behind me. But then her head lifted, her eyes caught mine, and just like that... it all got lighter.

I stopped at her table and leaned down just enough to let her hear me over the hum of the room. "Looks like you're here on the same escape plan."

Her jaw dropped wide, unguarded. Not coy. Not cute. And fucking hell, it was better than anything I'd imagined from across the room.

I slid into the chair across from her, trying not to look as nervous as I felt.

"Last Patient of the Night," I said, holding up my Kindle like it was my golden ticket. I gave her a half-smile, hoping it landed somewhere between confident and not-an-asshole. "What about you?"

She blinked at me, eyes wide like a deer in headlights. I figured she'd say something simple, something safe—whatever polite little book club choice she had queued up on that rhinestone Kindle.

Instead, her lips parted, and out it came, clear as a bell.

"Morning Glory Milking Farm."

For a second, I thought I had misheard her. But then her cheeks went crimson, and she snapped the Kindle cover shut so fast you'd think it had caught fire.

Holy shit.

Her eyes went rounder, panic flashing across her face, and it hit me—she hadn't meant to say that. Not at all. Which made it ten times better.

I tried, really tried, to keep a straight face. But the corner of my mouth betrayed me first, twitching up. Then the laugh ripped out of me before I could stop it.

"Holy shit," I choked out between laughs, shaking my head at her. "You win. You definitely win."

The way she stared at me—horrified, mortified, ready to bolt—only made me laugh harder. Not because I wanted to embarrass her, but because Christ, it was real. No posing, no script. Just her being herself, and me being lucky enough to catch it.

And damn, I hadn't felt that in years.

She still looked like she wanted to sink straight into the floor after blurting out her book title, cheeks pink, eyes darting like she was begging for divine intervention. I couldn't stop myself from grinning.

I leaned forward and offered my hand. "London."

There was the slightest hesitation before she slipped her palm against mine. Warm. A little nervous. "Sevynn," she said.

Beautiful. Hell, even the name fit. "Beautiful," I told her. "Pretty name, too."

She's so familiar.

Her lips parted, just barely, like she wasn't sure whether to argue or thank me. That spark in her eyes though? Worth every ounce of awkward fumbling.

I let her hand go and leaned back, raising my Kindle. "Well, I'll leave you to your milking."

That earned me a laugh...bright, surprised, and completely unfiltered. Christ, I liked that sound. I liked that it was mine.

She ducked her head, lifting her glitter-bomb Kindle like it was a shield. I did the same, crossing one ankle over my knee, the picture of casual, even though my pulse hadn't slowed since I walked over.

For a while, we both pretended to read. But I wasn't seeing a single word on the page. I was watching the way she bit the corner of her lip, the way her knee bounced like she couldn't quite settle, the way she stole glances at me when she thought I wasn't looking.

And maybe I should've kept my distance. Maybe I should've just left it at names and Kindles. But sitting there across from her, bourbon in my blood and something restless in my chest. God help me, I finally wanted *more.*

The bartender, now a server apparently, came over, cheeks pink like she'd been watching the whole damn thing. She hovered a little too close to my shoulder, pen at the ready.

"Can I get you *anything* else?" she asked, all syrup and batting lashes.

"Yeah, I'll take, uh…" I grabbed the menu off the empty table beside me, mostly to buy a second to breathe. "I'll do an old-fashioned. And whatever the lady's having."

Sevynn's head jerked up, eyes wide. "No, no, you don't have to do that. I'm fine, thanks."

I leaned in a little, elbows on my knees. "Have you ever had one? An old-fashioned?"

She shook her head, lips curling like she already knew she'd regret admitting it.

"No, actually. I've always been more of a shots-or-margarita kind of gal. No in-between."

Something in what she said slipped under my skin, uninvited, and lodged there before I could make sense of it. Maybe it was the *way* she said it, so casual and playful, like she'd just handed me a piece of herself without realizing it.

"Try one with me." I meant it as a question, but it came out rougher, closer to a command. The bourbon was stripping away my restraint.

Her eyes darted up, caught mine, and for a second, I swore she forgot how to breathe. Then she nodded quickly. "Sure. Yes. Thank you."

And that's when the words slipped out.

"Good girl."

The server actually gasped, pen halting midair. Sevynn's lips parted, her whole body stiffening.

And in my head…one long, panicked string of curses.

I forced myself to lean back, casual, Kindle raised like I wasn't dying inside.

But then, just for half a heartbeat, I caught it. A flicker in her eyes. A spark in the way her breath hitched. And suddenly, maybe that mistake wasn't a mistake at all.

When the drinks finally landed on the table, I realized I was sweating like I'd just run a damn marathon. My collar felt too tight; my palms were slick. I excused myself to the restroom, half convinced I smelled like nerves and did the kind of subtle sniff test you'd expect from a fifteen-year-old sneaking into prom, not a forty-two-year-old man on a casual drink.

Christ. I felt like a teenager on a first date—awkward, overeager, painfully aware of every move I made. My brothers would've had a field day. They've called me "hot and stupid" for years, and I couldn't argue with it. Because here I was, looking like I had my shit together, and inside? I was a mess.

Truth is, I don't know when women are flirting, or when I'm just bulldozing my way through small talk like an idiot. And worse, I couldn't tell if she knew either...or if she was just being polite while I unraveled.

Faking confidence, I squared my shoulders, plastered on something that resembled composure, and made my way back to the table.

She didn't even notice me at first...she was too busy interrogating her drink like a wine connoisseur. First, a quick sniff, nose wrinkling as if she was trying to solve a crime. Then a tentative dip of her tongue, the tiniest frown. Another curious tilt of her head, second taste, lips pursed. Finally, a proper sip...and the way her eyebrows shot up was pure, unfiltered delight.

Fucking adorable.

I slipped back into my chair, hoping my face didn't give away the fact that watching her drink bourbon had just become the highlight of my entire week.

"What's the verdict?" I asked, keeping my tone calm even though I was already grinning like an idiot.

"It's really fucking good," she said on a breath, going right back in for another sip. Then came the sound...low, satisfied, that little *hmmm* that went straight to my bloodstream.

Fuck. Okay. That noise was going to be a problem. A *serious* problem.

"I'm glad you like it," I managed.

I took a sip of my drink, letting the burn settle in my chest before my gaze slipped down. And there they were again...those ridiculous, fuzzy shoes. My mouth twitched, fighting a grin I couldn't hold back.

"I gotta know," I said, leaning in a little, my eyes fixed on them like they were some kind of riddle. "What *are* they? Bunnies?"

Her head tilted, caught between mock offense and laughter, and for a second, I forgot how to breathe.

"Excuse you, sir. They are *clouds*. With faces."

I laughed, shaking my head. "Clouds. Right. My mistake. Obviously, how could I not see the faces?" I gestured with my glass, smirking. "That's some... intimidating footwear. Very authoritative."

She rolled her eyes, taking another sip of her drink to hide the smile tugging at her mouth. "You're impossible."

"Maybe," I allowed, still watching her. Still watching those damn slippers, actually. "But I'll say this much: any woman who can stroll into a bar wearing those and not give a damn what anyone thinks? That's someone I probably shouldn't mess with."

"Damn straight." Her gaze flicked to my chest, quick but not quick enough. "What about you? Did you get that T-shirt from Baby Gap? I mean..." her lips twitched, fighting a grin as she leaned back, glass in hand..."we get it, you have *muscles*."

My brows shot up, laughter breaking free before I could stop it. "Baby Gap, huh?" I looked down at my shirt like I'd never seen it before. "You wound me. This is classic architecture chic. Very exclusive."

"Sure, big guy." She smirked into her glass, eyes glinting. "Bet it came with a free protein shake and a selfie ring light."

Who is she?

I leaned closer, letting my voice drop just enough to make her breath hitch. "You've been staring at it long enough to know the size label, sweetheart."

Her mouth opened; whether to deny it or fire back, I didn't know—but the flush creeping up her neck told me everything I needed to know.

I leaned in just enough that she'd feel the rumble in my chest when I spoke. "Never have I ever checked London out while he was wearing a tight henley..." My voice dropped lower, gravel roughened by bourbon and want. "...then teased him about it."

Her lips spread into this slow and wicked grin as she tipped her glass to her lips. She took a long, measured sip, her eyes locked on mine the whole time, like she was daring me to look away.

The move hit me square in the chest. It was so fucking bold and confident. Exactly the kind of spark I hadn't realized I'd been starved for.

"Good girl," I murmured, the words slipping out again before I could reel them back. The weight of it landed between us, and her eyes widened—just a fraction—but enough to tell me she'd felt it. *She likes that*. Fuck.

I raised my glass and drank, keeping my gaze fastened to hers like it was the only lifeline in the room. "Your turn."

The air thickened, charged. A wild and dangerous hum threaded between us, making the whole world outside this table feel irrelevant.

Fuck. This felt good.

3 | SEVYNN

We were two old-fashioneds in; playing the PG-14 version of *Never Have I Ever* when I dropped the bomb.

"Never have I ever... been to an arcade." I tipped my glass back and took a slow sip, watching him over the rim.

London froze mid-drink like I'd just confessed to murder. His eyes went wide, then he clutched at his chest in mock horror. "Excuse me?"

I burst out laughing, nearly spilling what was left in my glass. "What? Don't look at me like that; it just... never came up."

"Never came up?" He shook his head slowly, as if the universe itself had betrayed him. "You have kids. Sons, no less. How?"

I shrugged sheepishly. "We've gone to malls, sure, but my ex-husband was the one who'd take them into those places. I'd go do girly things. They're just so...noisy."

He slapped his hand against the table like I'd just told him I'd never seen a sunset. "That's not just a gap, Sevynn; that's a tragedy. A childhood crime."

"Dramatic much?" I teased, grinning as he kept up the

theatrics.

"Oh no. This isn't drama." He whipped out his phone, already swiping like a man possessed. "This… is destiny."

I leaned across the table, trying to peek at the screen. "What are you doing?"

"Righting the wrongs of the universe," he muttered, thumbs flying. Then he looked up at me, dead serious, green eyes locking with mine. "I'm finding the closest arcade. And then I'm ordering an Uber. Because clearly, Sevynn, I have the honor—no, the *duty*—of taking you on your very first arcade date."

My cheeks burned, my stomach flipping at the word date. I giggled, waving him off. "You can't just… take me on a date. That's not how this works. Also…" I pointed down at my feet. "I'm wearing fuzzy slippers, London. I can't go in public like this."

"That's exactly how this works." He leaned back, so smug and certain, like he'd already won. "You've been cheated out of air hockey, skee-ball, and neon lights your whole life, sweetheart. Consider this a rescue mission if you don't want to call it a date." He paused, letting it hang, eyes locked on mine. Then his mouth curved into that damn dangerous dimply grin. "No… it's a date."

His gaze flicked down, lingering on my fuzzy slippers, and then slid back up with a grin that made my stomach somersault.

"And for the record? Those," he said, pointing with his glass, "are the sexiest shoes I've ever seen on a woman."

My jaw dropped, a laugh bursting out of me before I could stop it. "You are absolutely insane."

"Insane? Maybe." He shrugged, those damn dimples flashing. "But, I said what I said."

Before I could fire back, he pushed his chair back and stood, towering over me. Then he held out his hand, palm open, command wrapped in charm.

"You're officially mine for the next couple of hours."

The words hit me low in my stomach, sharp and warm all at once. My pulse jumped. For a beat, I just stared at his hand. His very large... very distracting... *fuck me sideways* hand.

The ride to the arcade was quick, but it might as well have been an hour with the way we filled it. London had his phone out, scribbling furiously into his Notes app like a man planning a military operation.

"Okay," he said, brow furrowed in mock seriousness. "Arcade itinerary: one...air hockey, obviously." He gave a quick sweep of his hand, like it was too obvious to waste breath on.

"Obviously," I echoed, matching his tone with a dramatic nod.

"Two. Dance Dance Revolution. Three. Skeeball. Four. Mario Kart. Five. Laser tag, if they have it. You can't argue with the science of fun."

I snorted, leaning over to peek at his screen. "You actually wrote that down? Are you making a PowerPoint too?"

"Don't tempt me," he said with a grin. "I've been known to

go full project manager when the stakes are high."

"And the stakes are...?" I teased.

"Your honor," he deadpanned, then cracked into a boyish smile that made my chest ache. "Your first arcade experience has to be perfect. That's non-negotiable."

He was like a giddy schoolboy, rattling off game strategies and bragging about his high scores. And God help me, he was gorgeous while he did it. Those bright eyes, deep dimples, energy buzzing off him.

I felt like I wasn't just a mom, or an ex-wife, or the subject of gossip columns. I felt... seen.

The Uber pulled up to a squat brick building pulsing with neon. The sign buzzed faintly overhead, casting the parking lot in a wash of pink and electric blue.

When we stepped inside, I froze.

Lights flashed from every corner, neon strobing against the walls, while the air pulsed with digital beeps and bells. The low thrum of bass vibrated up through the sticky tile floor, rattling straight into my bones. Kids shrieked in triumph, tokens clattered into metal trays, and somewhere a claw machine groaned out its taunting mechanical whir.

Instinctively, I reached into my bag. My fingers fumbled through receipts, lip balm, gum wrappers...panic rising with every empty search.

Fuck.

I hadn't brought my noise cancellers.

The realization hit like a sucker punch. Already the sounds were crawling up my spine, burrowing into the base of my skull, pressing in until my skin felt too tight. The edges of my vision prickled, and my jaw locked tight as I tried to cage the rising tide.

Not here. Not now. I forced a breath past my teeth, nails biting into my palms. I wanted to enjoy this. I was going to enjoy this. Just this once, I wasn't going to be the woman who couldn't handle a little noise.

So, I focused on breathing, on taking everything in. I let my eyes dart across the chaos...skeeball lanes glowing in neon, racing pods buzzing like little spaceships, a giant spinning wheel promising prizes I couldn't even name.

I probably looked ridiculous...slack-jawed, frozen in the middle of it all like I'd just crash-landed on another planet.

And London? He didn't move. He just stood a step behind me, watching.

Not the games. Not the chaos. Me. Like seeing me take this in was somehow better than playing any of it himself.

"You look like a kid on Christmas morning," he said finally, his voice low, threaded with a smile.

I turned, cheeks warm. "It's... a lot."

"It's perfect." His smile widened, and before I could argue, his hand closed around mine. "Come on."

"Where are we going?" I laughed as he tugged me through the maze of machines.

"Item one on the itinerary." He stopped at an air hockey

table, already feeding coins into the slot like he'd had it planned from the start. "Time to defend your honor."

He slid a paddle toward me, explaining the rules with mock seriousness. I only caught half of it, too distracted by the way his dimples popped every time he smirked.

When the puck dropped, he moved like a man who'd trained for this moment his whole life. His first two shots were mercifully slow, just enough for me to get the feel.

"See? Easy," he said, as if he hadn't just fired the puck so fast it ricocheted off the wall and straight into my goal.

"Hey!" I yelped, laughing despite myself. "You let me win for two seconds and then went full assassin?"

He winked, leaning on his paddle like it was a weapon. "Honor defended means nothing if you don't have to fight for it, sweetheart."

When the puck dropped again, he didn't hold back. His reflexes were sharp, precise, and he was annoyingly smug every single time the puck zipped past me into my goal.

Finally, I dug in. Shoulders tight, eyes narrowed, I started defending the hell out of my side. He couldn't get a thing past me.

"Well, well," he drawled, grinning. "Look who finally showed up to play."

The second the words left his mouth; my puck slid straight into his goal. I screamed like I'd just won the damn lottery, hopping up and down in my fuzzy slippers, clapping like an idiot.

"I scored!"

"Four to one," he announced in a perfect sportscaster voice, sinking his own puck while I was still celebrating. "A valiant effort, Sevynn. But rule number one..." his grin turned lethal. "never take your eyes off the prize."

I narrowed my eyes, biting back a laugh. "You're enjoying this way too much."

"Of course, I am." He leaned across the table, green eyes glinting beneath the neon. "You're competitive. I like that."

"Competitive?" I scoffed, bracing my paddle. "You've literally been training for this since puberty. I'm just trying not to break a nail."

That earned me one of those dimples. Sharp and unfairly devastating. Once I finally found my rhythm, we were head-to-head. I couldn't shake the feeling he was letting me sink a few shots just to watch me celebrate like a kid on Christmas morning.

Then he scored the final point, the puck sliding into my goal with humiliating ease. "Seven to six," he declared, throwing both hands in the air like he'd just won Olympic gold. "The crown is mine."

I dropped my paddle onto the table and leveled him with what I hoped was my best unimpressed stare. It only half-worked, because the corner of my mouth kept betraying me, twitching upward. "Is it really a win if I've never played before? Maybe you've just taken advantage of me a little."

"Not yet, sweetheart." His voice dipped lower, teasing, dangerous. His grin turned into something that felt less like victory and more like a promise. "We'll make time for that later."

Heat crawled up my neck before I could stop it, and his gaze lingered just a beat too long—like he knew exactly where my mind went with that.

Before I could fumble out a comeback, he tapped the itinerary on his phone. "Item two. Skee-ball." He snagged my hand again, tugging me through the maze of machines like I was already his teammate.

And even though I lost the last round spectacularly, I couldn't stop smiling. We barely made it two steps toward the skee-ball lanes before the sounds hit me like a wave.

The lanes were right next to one of the party rooms, its glass wall rattling with the chaos of a toddler birthday. Kids shrieked at the top of their lungs, high-pitched squeals piercing through the air. Someone banged on the party table, hard plastic against harder plastic. Balloons popped, loud as gunfire.

Then—*crash*.

One of the toddlers bolted straight into a server's legs, sending a tray of cups tumbling to the floor. Water spilled everywhere, the cups skittering and clattering like metal on tile.

My body locked.

The sound of it...all of it...burrowed straight into my spine, curling tight. My breath snagged, shallow, too quick. Lights and sounds crowded in, too much, too close, no way to push it back.

I froze mid-step, one hand braced against the skee-ball lane, eyes fixed on nothing. My pulse hammered in my throat, but my lungs wouldn't catch up.

London's laughter cut off mid-note. He turned toward me, and I felt the weight of his eyes, sharp and immediate.

"Sevynn?" His voice was low and steady, stripped of all the teasing from before.

I tried to answer, but it came out more like a gasp.

He closed the distance in two strides, his hand brushing the small of my back, anchoring me in place. "Hey. Look at me."

But my eyes wouldn't land. Couldn't. My vision skittered, his face blurring in and out like I was underwater. I knew he was there—I could feel him moving in my line of sight, trying to catch me, hold me—but I just couldn't focus.

"Okay," he murmured, voice softer now, the kind of tone that belonged in a dark room at midnight, not a crowded space. "Okay, I got you. Just you and me. Forget the rest. Breathe with me, sweetheart. In... and out. Right here. Just us."

Before I could spiral further, he glanced around and laced his fingers through mine, tugging me gently down a side hall. The noise dimmed with every step until we reached a dark stretch of corridor near the restrooms. It was quiet and mercifully empty.

My back met the wall, grounding me without trapping me. He held my hands in his; thumbs moving in slow, mechanical strokes over my knuckles.

"Eyes on me, sweetheart."

I tried, but my breaths were ragged, shallow. It felt like every pull of air was empty, like no oxygen was reaching my lungs. My chest tightened, and my throat burned. I hated this feeling. I hated it more when it happened in front of people.

Poor broken Sevynn, the cruel little voice whispered. Can't even handle loud noises. Can't even keep it together. So dramatic. Such a drama queen.

"Breathe with me, Sevynn." His forehead dipped closer, voice coaxing me back. "In through your nose. Right now. Good girl. Now out, slow. That's it."

His eyes never left mine, pulling me back into my body every time I tried to disappear.

"Stay here for a minute," he murmured. "Just like that. Keep breathing."

He gave my hands one last squeeze before stepping away. Panic flared, the urge to reach for him strong, but he rounded the corner, out of sight. My chest tightened, and I could feel the tears welling. I bit down on them hard. I didn't want to cry. Not on top of everything else. Not in front of him.

Seconds later, he was back. And in his hands were headphones, the cheap kind you win with tickets. He'd torn the package open on the way.

Without a word, he slid them gently over my head, adjusting until they cushioned my ears. His palms pressed over them firmly, sealing me in. Then he leaned in, close enough that I could see the little flecks of gold in his green eyes. His lips moved deliberately, his chest rising and falling in exaggerated rhythm.

Breathe.

In.

Out.

His gaze softened when mine matched his.

Good girl.

The noise faded. The pressure eased. And for the first time since stepping inside, I felt like I had space in my lungs again.

And all I could think was: no one had ever done that for me before.

4 | LONDON

Her breath was coming too fast. Shallow. Wrong. The second those cups crashed, and the noise swallowed the room, I knew something shifted in her. She froze like someone had flipped a switch, her knuckles went white on the skee-ball lane, her chest rising but not filling. I'd seen that look before; not in her, but in soldiers, in my brothers, in myself. *Panic.*

"Hey," I said softly, moving in before anyone else could notice. My hand brushed the small of her back. Trying to be light and grounding. "Look at me."

Her eyes darted, unfocused, like she was drowning in sound. My chest tightened.

"Breathe with me, sweetheart," I whispered, leaning down so she couldn't look anywhere else but me. "In through your nose. Right now. Good girl. Now out, slow. That's it."

I held her there with my eyes, steady, as if I just kept talking her through it, I could pull her back. But I could see the tears starting, the way her body trembled, and it gutted me.

"Stay here. Just keep breathing like that."

I bolted before I could think better of it, cutting down the corner so fast I nearly shoulder-checked an arcade cabinet. My pulse was hammering, my chest tight like I couldn't get enough air either.

Headphones. I needed headphones. Something—anything—to quiet the goddamn chaos rattling her.

I spotted them hanging behind the glass at the prize counter. I didn't slow down.

"I need those headphones. Right now."

The kid behind the counter blinked, like I'd just asked him for plutonium. "Uh...you can't buy those, sir. You need tickets—"

"Goddammit," I snapped, dragging a hand through my hair. I pulled my wallet out, peeled out two hundreds, and shoved them across the counter. "It's an emergency. My gi—" My throat jammed on the word, my chest squeezing. "My friend. She's out there mid-panic attack, and she needs something over her ears. Now. I don't give a damn about your tickets. Get a manager if you have to, but don't make me climb over this counter, because I will."

The kid froze, wide-eyed. For a second I thought he'd argue. My fists clenched. But then he shoved the box at me and nudged the money back, mumbling, "Take it."

"Good man," I bit out, already tearing into the plastic with my teeth as I ran.

By the time I got back, she was still there pressed against the wall, shaking, eyes glazed and wild. And fuck, I swear my throat burned just looking at her.

"I got you," I muttered, more to myself than her, as I slid the headphones over her ears. My palms cupped them tight, sealing her in, cutting the noise.

"Look at me," I begged, voice low and shaking. "C'mon, sweetheart. Breathe. In...out...that's it."

I exaggerated my chest rising, falling, hoping she'd sync. Her wide eyes locked onto mine, and for a terrifying second, I thought I'd lost her completely; then her breath hitched, stuttered, and finally, *finally*, started to line up with mine.

"Yeah. Yeah, that's it," I whispered, my voice breaking like a goddamn rookie. "Good girl. Just you and me. Just breathe."

And God help me; before I even truly knew her, I already knew I'd burn the whole world down if it meant she could breathe easy.

I kept one hand wrapped tight around hers, thumb brushing soft circles over her knuckles, as if I could smooth the edges of what had just happened. With my other hand, I fumbled my phone out, clumsy from the adrenaline still coursing through me, pulling up the Uber app. My chest still felt tight, like I'd been the one fighting for air.

Even though I had no way of knowing that the arcade noise would set her off, I still felt like a pile of shit. I should've noticed sooner. Should've read the signs. Should've protected her better. She even said that arcades are too noisy, and I didn't catch on.

I didn't let go of her hand as I steered us back toward the exit, the chaos of the arcade fading behind us. Out in the cooler air, she was quiet. Too quiet. Her shoulders curled in, chin tucked, like she wanted to disappear. Embarrassment hung off her like a shadow.

But I wasn't about to let that swallow her.

So, I just kept her hand in mine, rubbing those steady circles over her knuckles, keeping her anchored. Keeping her with me.

When the Uber pulled up, I opened the door and guided her first, still holding on like letting go would undo everything we'd just fought through. She slid across the seat without a word, making room, and only then did I climb in after her.

Our thighs brushed in the small space. Neither of us pulled away.

When we finally made it back to the hotel, she slipped her hand from mine the moment we stepped through the doors. The loss hit sharper than I wanted to admit.

"Thank you. For these." Her voice was barely above a whisper as she held out the headphones, her fingers trembling around the plastic. She sounded like she was right on the edge of breaking.

"Keep them, Sevynn," I said softly. "They're yours."

Her throat bobbed as she swallowed, nodding once. "Thanks." She backed up a step, putting space between us. "I better get back to my room."

I should've let her go. Should've given her the out. But every instinct in me rebelled.

"Sevynn?"

She paused, eyes lifting, guarded but still so goddamn open. "Yeah?"

"Not yet. Please." My voice cracked a little on the word, rougher than I meant. I extended my hand toward her again.

"Come with me. Just...talk with me a little longer."

Her lower lip trembled, like she was weighing the risk of saying yes. But then she slipped her hand back into mine, and the tightness in my chest eased just enough to breathe again.

I led her past the elevator and out to the hotel pool, quiet at this hour, the surface beaming under the sun. We sat on the edge, shoes kicked aside, our feet dipping into the cool water.

"Let's just sit here a while," I said, watching the ripples spread out beneath the glow. "We can just talk. Nothing heavy." I nudged her shoulder gently. "And I'll even order us more old-fashioneds, since apparently, it's your favorite drink now. You're welcome, by the way."

The corner of her mouth twitched, almost a smile, and for the first time since the arcade I felt her relax beside me.

"I'm really sorry about our date, London." She wouldn't meet my eyes; her gaze fixed on the edge of the pool where her toes dragged little ripples through the glowing water. "I should've just... been honest. About why I don't do arcades. I guess..." Her voice cracked, and she gave a weak little laugh that landed more like a wince. "I guess I just wanted to feel normal for a minute."

Her shoulders lifted, tight, like she was bracing for me to laugh or wave it off.

"I thought I had my noise cancellers. They are these little buds I wear most of the time; they make the world more tolerable. But I left them in my room, and then it was just..." She shook her head, cheeks heating, her voice dropping to almost nothing. "It was too much. Too loud. Like my entire brain was on fire. I'm sorry if I embarrassed you. It's so damn dramatic, I know. I've been working on it, hence the earbuds."

Embarrassed me? Christ.

I wanted to find every single person who had ever made her feel like she was "too much" and put them in the ground. Because her admitting that kind of pain, that kind of weight — wasn't weakness. It was steel. It was survival. She wasn't dramatic. She wasn't fragile. She was strong as hell for fighting a war every day in a body and mind that turned every crowd into a battlefield.

And I'd burn the whole world down before I ever let her think she was less for it.

I wanted to tell her that. I wanted to say she never had to explain herself to me, not once. But all I could do was stare, fists clenched against the urge to reach for her.

Her toes skimmed the water, ripples breaking away like she was trying to disappear into them.

I let a beat pass, then another, before I finally said, low but steady, "Hey, Sevynn...you don't owe me an apology. Not for that. Not for any of it."

Her head jerked the slightest bit, like she wasn't expecting me to actually say anything.

I ran a hand over the back of my neck, searching for words I had no business saying to a woman I'd known less than a few hours. "If I'm being honest, I'm glad it was me. At the arcade. In the noise. I'd much rather be the guy standing there with you than anyone else."

She stilled. Just... looked at me. Her eyes searched mine like she was testing for cracks, waiting to see if I was being polite, or if I meant every word.

"Thank you, London." Her voice was soft, fragile but steady. "That's sweet of you to say."

But then her gaze slipped back to the water, and she drew in a deep breath like she was bracing herself. When she stood, I thought that was it. Done. Whatever this was, I'd pushed too far, and she was walking away. My chest caved a little at the thought.

Then, without a word, she peeled her shirt over her head with this slow and unapologetic confidence. My breath snagged in my throat.

Jesus.

Her stomach was tight. She was fucking carved, unreal abs. I don't think I've ever seen a stomach that defined on a woman. The kind you only get from hours in a gym or a fight ring.

And the tattoos—fuck. Black lines across her abs, sharp and bold. I tried not to stare, but to hell with *that*. They made her look even more ripped.

Then, the leggings were gone, and all that was left was black lace. She knows. She has to know. Standing there like that, calm, steady, no nerves. She could break me. And I'd thank her for it.

"Well," she said, tossing her clothes onto the chair behind her. Her eyes met mine, unflinching. "Better make the most of this beautiful pool while we're here."

Before I could even swallow the curse sitting in my chest, she dove. Clean. Seamless. And it made my jaw clench because, of course, she looked like a fucking Olympian even while turning me inside out.

I sat there frozen, watching the ripples fan out across the water, until her head broke the surface on the far end of the pool. She pushed her wet hair back, water sliding down her face and shoulders, and grinned like she hadn't just stripped me of every ounce of control I thought I had left.

My heart didn't stand a chance. *Neither did my cock.*

"Let's go, hotshot," she called, her voice carrying across the water. "You wanted some competition? Welcome to *my* arena."

The corner of my mouth tugged upward despite myself. God help me, she was fire. Wet skin gleaming under the sun, sass dripping from every word. A siren in a hotel pool.

I stood, tugged my shirt over my head, and kicked off my shoes and jeans, my pulse already thundering. "Careful what you wish for, sweetheart," I said, tossing the shirt aside. "I don't lose easily."

Her laughter echoed off the tiles, bright and taunting. "Neither do I."

That was it. I dove, cutting through the water, every muscle burning to chase her down.

When I surfaced, she was already halfway across, powerful strokes cutting clean. I surged forward, catching up stroke by stroke, and when she realized I was closing in, she kicked harder, head tossing back with a laugh that made heat coil low in my gut.

I reached the wall just a split second after she smacked it with her palm, triumphant, cheeks flushed and eyes blazing with victory.

"The crown is mine." She panted; hair plastered to her cheek. "Told you. *My* arena."

I braced an arm against the wall beside her, close enough to feel her breath on my lips, the water running in rivulets down both our shoulders.

"That was only round one, sweetheart," I murmured, eyes locked on hers. "Don't get cocky."

"Round two?" she dared, raising a brow as she swiped water from her lashes.

"Thought you'd never ask." I pushed back from the wall, muscles coiled and ready.

We counted down together—three, two, one—and then she launched forward, cutting through the water fast and clean. But this time I didn't hold back. I drove off the wall with every ounce of power in my legs, thighs burning, propelling me across the pool like I was built for this.

Stroke after stroke, I closed the gap, her laughter bubbling out each time she glanced over her shoulder to see me gaining. She kicked harder, desperate to keep her lead, but the water was mine now.

I slammed my palm against the far wall just before hers, victory surging through me.

Her head popped up, hair dripping down her face, and she shoved at my shoulder. "Cheater!" she gasped, breathless and grinning.

"Cheater?!" I laughed, still panting, chest heaving.

"Yes!" She jabbed a finger at me, eyes narrowed but lit up with mischief. "You have way stronger thighs. That's an unfair advantage!"

I smirked, leaning in just enough, arms braced on the wall, so she was caged in by nothing but air and the thrum between us. "So, what you're saying..." My voice dropped, "...is that you were distracted by my thighs."

Her jaw fell open, that blush climbing high on her cheeks, betraying every denial she might've had locked and loaded.

For a second, she just stared at me, lips parted, breath quick from the race; or maybe not from the race at all.

And then, like the clever escape artist she was, she tore her gaze away and cleared her throat. "About those old-fashioneds," she said, too casual, too fast, eyes fixed anywhere but on me.

I chuckled low, pushing back from the wall, giving her space even though every instinct screamed to close it. "Deflect all you want, sweetheart," I murmured, slicking the water from my hair. "But I'll still order them."

Her lips twitched, fighting a smile, and for once I didn't press. I let the moment hang there; charged, alive, unfinished.

The server finally arrived with our drinks, and I waded back through the pool, glasses balanced carefully in my hands. Sevynn was waiting on the steps, the water lapping around her hips as she idly stirred her fingers through it, lost in thought. The glow of the sun hitting the water shimmered across her skin, turning her tattoos into shifting shadows, like they were alive.

"My lady," I said with mock formality, dipping my head in a half bow as I extended her glass.

She rolled her eyes but took it, the faintest laugh breaking free as she did.

I set my own glass on the edge of the pool, then lowered myself down, settling on my knees in the water between her thighs. The waterline rested just at my waist, her knees bracketing me on either side. The closeness hit me harder than I expected. It felt intimate, too intimate. Like we weren't just sharing a drink by a pool but trespassing into a space neither of us should've had the right to claim yet.

But it felt natural too. Like this had always been inevitable.

"Question eight," I said, tracing slow circles over her knee. "What brings you to Chicago?"

"My son, Derrick… uh…" She paused, lifting her glass for a sip. "He's in law school here. You?"

My mind ran the path that answer could take. *Here for my daughter's wedding. Oh, she's so young. How are you and her mom taking that?* Then the hammer—*Her mom passed away.* Pity would replace this charge between us, and I'd be back to the role everyone saw: the widower, the man just trying to limp through wedding week in one piece.

"I've got a couple of work events." The lie twisted in my gut. I forced a smile. "Question nine. Tell me about your ink."

My fingers drifted over the dark lines etched into her skin. Bold brackets running along her abs, curves of shadow framing her breasts, two stark lines at her throat. Each mark pulled me closer, begging for a story.

Goosebumps broke across her skin where I touched, a shiver racing through her even though the water was warm. She swallowed hard, chest rising, breath catching as if my fingertips had unraveled something she wasn't ready to admit.

"You really want to know?" she asked, her tone caught somewhere between guarded and daring.

I looked up, met her eyes, and nodded once. "Every line."

Her lips parted, just slightly, and I could see the battle play across her face; how much she wanted to keep the story close, how much she wanted to let me in.

"The ones on my abs..." She glanced down. "I got them after my boys were born. My body didn't feel like mine anymore. It felt like it only existed for everyone else. I busted my ass to take it back. Even did a couple of competitions. It was my way of saying *'this is mine again.'*"

I traced them lightly, and her breath trembled out of her.

She tilted her arm, showing the heavy ink that wrapped her bicep, bold and unapologetic. "These are armor. I had them done after the divorce. The designs, though, are old—my grandmother's people wore them as symbols of endurance, of belonging. I wanted that strength. Every stroke, every line...it felt like I was stitching myself back together. Stronger. Harder to break."

Her wrist turned, and I caught the fine detail of the bridge etched there. She smiled faintly, wistful. "Tower Bridge, in London. I was on a work trip, walking across it at sunrise, and I couldn't shake the feeling that it was meant for me. A bridge between who I was and who I had to become. The towers reminded me of my boys. I wanted to carry those reminders with me. So, I put it here." Her voice faltered, her eyes lifting to mine. "Something permanent. Something no one could take."

My thumb brushed the bridge, soft. "Beautiful," I rasped. And then my eyes drifted back up to the black marks half circling her throat. The ones she hadn't spoken for.

She followed my gaze, and for a long moment, silence pressed between us. Finally, her hand rose, fingertips ghosting over the lines inked across the scar beneath.

"These," she whispered, "cover what someone tried to take from me, a long time ago. I refused to let him have the last word. So, I turned it into mine."

The words sank into me, heavy and unshakable. I didn't say anything, didn't really trust myself to. I just let my fingers trace it a little longer.

She hesitated, then her mouth curved with the faintest smirk. "There's one more."

She pushed herself up onto the pool's edge, water streaming down her skin. With deliberate slowness, she hooked her fingers under the waistband of her panties and tugged just enough to bare the ink sitting low under pelvis — right above the soft folds where fabric began.

A kiss. An inked pair of lips across the most private part of her. My chest tightened, pulse spiking hard enough I felt it in my damn throat. The placement alone was enough to undo me. She could have chosen anywhere for that one, but she put it there — claiming it, declaring it.

"This one," she said, voice husky, daring, "is just mine. A

reminder of desire. Of the parts of myself I don't owe to anyone."

Holy. Fucking. Shit.

She was practically bared to me, right there in the public pool. Smooth, shaven and fucking beautiful. Her hip bones sharp, her lower abs veined like a map that led one way only...*lick me.*

I dragged my gaze back to her eyes, but the intimacy of it...her showing me this, something so sexual, so vulnerable — hung between us like a lit fuse. I had to touch her. I *had* to.

"May I?" My voice came out broken, my hand hovering.

Her lips parted, steady eyes betraying just the faintest flicker of nerves. Then she tugged the waistband a fraction lower in silent permission. "Yeah," she whispered.

I raised my hand, steady despite the riot in my chest, and traced the ink. Just the lips. Just the line. Damn...it was fire. My thumb dragged over it, pulling her skin taut, rough and gentle all at once...just enough to make her folds catch against her clit.

Her breath hitched, thighs snapping tight. My eyes locked with hers. *"Beautiful,"* I rasped, fingertips trailing up over her stomach, across her sides. *"Every inch of you."*

Every nerve in me was burning. I wanted my mouth everywhere...on every inch she'd give me. I lifted her wrist, pressed my lips to the ink there. One kiss. Then another. My breath got heavier with each one, her pulse hammering under my mouth.

When I eased her waistband lower again, she shivered. Eyes fluttered shut, thighs clamping like she could hold me there forever. I kissed the ink...soft first. Then harder. Then my tongue traced the curve of her mound, lower, until I hit where ink met the top of her slit.

The sound that ripped out of her... shit. It gutted me.

Her hips rolled forward, needy and desperate. I pressed my palm flat against her stomach, holding her down. Holding myself down. Because fuck—I could already taste her.

Fuck, this is too far.

It's not enough...I need to taste her.

Don't do this. It's too soon.

I can't fucking stop.

Five goddamn years since I touched anyone. Since I even let myself look at anyone like this. Sarah was the last. Always Sarah. And *now*...now I've got Sevynn gasping my name, her hands in my hair, begging without words for more.

One inch lower and I'm gone.

I'll devour her.

I'll lose myself.

I can't.

I want to.

God, I want to.

Her fingers fisted tighter in my hair, holding me there, like she already knew the war tearing me apart. Like she wasn't giving me the chance to run.

My head dipped, tongue tracing her again, right at the top of her slit. I let it slide a little deeper, slow, savoring...until her hips bucked up, sudden and desperate. The barest taste of her arousal hit my mouth, and the sharp graze of my tongue found her clit as she moved.

"Oh. Oh *god*, London." She gasped.

Fuck. I was done.

No. Stop. Breathe.

I pressed my palm harder to her stomach, forcing myself still. My chest heaved, my forehead dropping against her thigh as curses ripped out under my breath.

It took every damn thread of my willpower, but I pulled her panty line back into place as I sucked in air like I'd just broken the surface after drowning.

And still...I couldn't stay away. My nose brushed the heat of her, a stolen touch, a punishment. I pressed a line of kisses along the inside of her thighs, one after another.

My hand slid up, fisting her thigh against the side of my head. Holding her close. Pretending I was letting her go when all I was doing was *clinging*.

Get control.

I dragged my mouth higher, abandoning the battlefield between her legs before I lost it completely. My lips mapped her stomach instead, worshiping the tattoos inked into her skin. Each kiss lower, each mark claimed, her muscles twitching beneath me as if my mouth had sparked pure electricity under her skin.

By the time I reached the stark lines at her neck, she was already trembling. Her head tipped back, lips parted, baring her throat to me like surrender. My mouth followed, sealing against the ink there, then higher, kissing up to her pulse drumming under my lips, wild, frantic—matching mine beat for beat.

And God help me, I wasn't sure which of us was shaking harder.

"Do you feel what you do to me, sweetheart?" I rasped, voice shredded, barely my own. "I could stay here for hours. Just tasting you. Just watching you fall apart for me."

I yanked her closer, grinding my hardness right where she needed it. Her answer wasn't words—it was a guttural moan, torn straight from her chest, her thighs locking around my waist. Her hips lifted again, needy, chasing every bit of friction.

I dragged her into me again and again, and fuck...it looked like she could come from that alone. Her stomach tightened, her abs pulling hard, every sound spilling out of her high and broken.

"Fuck, Sevynn. Goddamn, baby…you could come like this, couldn't you?"

I pulled back just enough to bring my mouth to the ink on her stomach, small bites tracing the center line of her abs. She jolted, body arching off the steps. My hands clamped down on her hips, holding her steady. Because if I didn't anchor her— or myself—I was gone.

I reached up, gently wrapping my fingers around her throat, my forehead pressing to hers. One more breath—

ragged, uneven—before I would finally claim her mouth. I was a split second away from crashing into it when the sound hit.

Voices. Laughter. The squeak of flip-flops and the slap of wet towels hitting plastic chairs.

A group spilled into the pool area, loud and oblivious, arms full of floaties and beach bags. The spell shattered, the world rushed back in like cold water.

We froze. Our breathing was still erratic and desperate. Bodies still straining into each other like stopping hadn't erased a goddamn thing. My hand lingered at her throat a beat too long before I dragged it down, over her chest, over her stomach, greed still gnawing at me.

She pressed her lips tight, eyes wide, chest rising and falling like she'd run ten miles.

"Fuck," I muttered, forcing myself to turn away, yanking at my shorts like that'd hide a thing.

When her eyes caught mine again, it was all still there. The frustration. The hunger. The ache.

We'd pulled back from the edge.

Barely.

5 | SEVYNN

I've never wanted to harm anyone. Not really. I've never daydreamed about yeeting teenagers off the top floor of a hotel before. I'm not a violent woman. I'm pleasant. Demure, even.

But if I had a flamethrower when those kids waltzed into the pool area? They'd be crispy motherfuckers. Marshmallow-roasted, stick-a-fork-in-them, done.

Yes, I'm fully aware it was a public pool. And yes, I was practically begging this man to devour me whole, leaving zero mystery as to what was about to happen. That's not the point here, is it?

The point is: I have *never* felt that kind of edging before. My panties? Done. Ruined. Toast. Drop them in the trash, set them on fire, sweep the ashes into Lake Michigan. This man has a fucking *body*. His hands, his mouth, his tongue...and *those eyes* when he's turned on? Holy shit. If smolder were a weapon, I'd be a chalk outline on the pool deck.

And then the towel thing. Oh my God, the towel thing. He had to *ask* me to get one for him before climbing out of the pool because he was carrying his own oar. When I say big, I mean *biblical.* Like, I see why he designs skyscrapers big. The kind of big that should come with a warning label and its own TSA carry-on restrictions.

We did so much. And not nearly enough. His mouth on my tattoos, his tongue skating right to the line of where I needed him most...and stopping. That little tease, right above my very agreeable pussy? Oh, he knows exactly what he's doing. That smug bastard. I, however, do *not* know what the hell I'm doing. I was one breath, one kiss, one slide of his tongue lower from absolutely coming undone.

And we didn't even *kiss*. And somehow that almost made it worse. Or hotter. Or both? Fuck if I know.

Now here we are...twelve hours in since we met, six old-fashioneds and six shots deep. Barefoot. Still damp from the pool, hair half-dry and curling wild. We're sunk into the hotel lobby couches like college kids dodging curfew, even though we're grown enough to know better. The air between us hums with everything that almost happened. My skin feels branded. My brain won't stop rewinding, over and over, like a song I can't turn off.

Somewhere along the line, our game of twenty questions got sloppy. Neither of us seemed to care. The liquor burned, the laughs came easier, and the space between us on that couch shrank until it might as well not have existed at all.

Here's what I've learned so far in our time together today: his name is London Pierce. He has a twenty-one-year-old daughter. He is not married (thank *every deity across every pantheon that's ever existed*). He's an architect—skyscrapers, no less. Which makes obscene sense, because he looks like a man who builds things just to prove gravity bends for him. And yes, he's a gym fanatic. Again...duh. That body didn't just appear one day like manna from heaven.

I'm sure he told me other things, important things even,

but my brain is shot. One half is gamely trying to log details like a diligent stenographer. The other half is busy engraving the way his dimples cut deep when he smiles, the gravel in his voice when the bourbon kicks in, the way he's somehow made me forget everything that happened at the arcade...something that normally would've had me spiraling for two weeks straight in noise hangovers and shame.

But here I am, tipsy. Draped sideways on a hotel couch with this man. Laughing like my chest doesn't still ache from all the past I've been carrying.

His voice has shifted lower now, rough and lazy, the kind that only comes out after dark and after several drinks. And every time he leans closer, it's like standing too close to a bonfire. Heat licking at my skin, daring me to see how long I can stand it before I combust.

I can't tell if this is flirting, foreplay, or the first chapter of a bad decision I'll replay for the rest of my life. Probably all three.

"Okay," I said, waving my glass slightly. "Question thirteen. Biggest fear?"

London leaned his head back against the couch, eyes half-lidded, the faintest smile tugging at his mouth. "Heights."

I laughed so loudly; it bounced through the empty lobby. "You design skyscrapers and you're afraid of heights?"

"Architect," he corrected, one brow arched like he was grading me. "I *design* them. Doesn't mean I want to dangle off the side of one."

"Still hilarious," I teased, nudging his bare foot with mine.

My pulse jumped at the contact, though I played it off like nothing.

His eyes dropped to where my toes brushed him, then flicked back up, and suddenly the air between us was… thicker. Charged. I pretended not to notice, words tumbling out faster than my heartbeat. "Fourteen. Favorite building you've ever designed?"

He tipped his head back, thinking, his mouth curving like the memory tugged at him. "Hmm. Easy. New York. Biggest design of my career." His voice warmed as he said it, steady but threaded with pride. "The building isn't just tall—it feels alive. The whole lobby opens into this vast atrium, stories of just glass and light. The ceiling is cut so sunlight pours in and moves across the walls like a sundial through the day. At night, it glows from the inside out…the entire structure was built to be a lantern for the city."

His eyes softened, distant. "And right in the center, a fountain—broad, sculpted, it makes people stop. Kids throw coins in it, strangers snap pictures, and without fail, everyone looks up. You can see it hit them, that moment when awe takes over. It wasn't just an add-on. I designed the whole building around that moment—so when people walk in, their eyes are pulled straight to it, and then up. It forces you to look higher, to see the scale of the space."

"The Spire?" I asked carefully, heart already thudding.

"The Nova Spire in Manhattan," he confirmed with a faint smile. "You've seen it?"

"Oh my God, London. Shut up!" I sat bolt upright and smacked his arm. "One of my restaurants is in that building...ground floor. Ironcrest."

His head snapped toward me, eyes sparking. "No fucking way." He leaned closer, grinning wide enough to ruin me. "You're telling me *that's yours*? Sevynn, I eat there every single trip. That's... *yours*?"

I was laughing now, giddy and a little breathless. "Yes! That's mine! Ironcrest is *my* baby. I signed the lease on that corner before the drywall was even up. I nearly bankrupted myself getting it open, but it was worth every sleepless night. And that building, London...holy fuck. I don't know what I pictured when you said you designed buildings, but I wasn't expecting *that*. Every time I walk in, it feels like a cathedral, like the kind of place that makes you want to stand straighter. You did that."

He shook his head like he couldn't believe it, green eyes locked on me with something dangerously close to awe. "How the hell has this not come up the entire damn day?"

I was laughing so hard my sides hurt. "I can't believe this. All day, all the questions, and *that* didn't come up?"

"Sevynn." He said my name like it was brand new in his mouth, rolling it slow, savoring it. His grin softened into something else...something that curled low in my stomach. "I've been there at least a dozen times. Your place is fucking impressive. I've been... in your *world* already."

The laughter faltered on my lips, replaced by that damn flutter in my chest again.

He leaned in, forearms braced on his knees, green eyes catching mine like he could pin me right there. "Huh..." He reaches over, tucking a piece of hair behind my ear. "Your hair was shorter back then. A lot shorter. Auburn, almost copper. But I remember." His mouth twitched, that damn dimple flashing. "You came out to check on the dining room once — short curls, sharp eyes. I thought... she's got a presence. She runs this place. She *owns* this place."

His thumb slowly skimmed over my bottom lip, and it was the single most dangerously seductive thing I'd ever fucking felt. He tipped my chin up, studying my mouth. Heat shot up my throat, my pulse skittering out of control. I tried to cover it, tried for flippant, but the tremor in my voice betrayed me.

"You actually noticed me?"

"Noticed?" His eyes locked on my, then scanned my features. "I couldn't take my eyes off you. You stopped at a few tables, made small talk. You stopped at mine and said —" his voice dropped lower, a perfect echo — "'that's a big-ass steak, you don't win a T-shirt if you don't finish it.'"

I laughed, startled, remembering. "Oh my God. That was *you*? The tomahawk guy?"

"Tomahawk guy," he repeated, grinning slow. "Yeah. I had the steak. Nothing else. And I've never forgotten it. Or you."

The lobby felt too quiet, the bourbon too warm in my veins. My pulse beat against my throat like I'd sprinted the length of the city. And sitting there with him, laughing over a steak and a memory I didn't even realize we shared, it felt less like coincidence and more like inevitability. Like we'd been orbiting the same circle all along, and *finally* collided.

6 | LONDON

The memory hit me so hard; it wasn't just that we'd crossed paths...it was how it happened. About six or seven years ago, one of my New York trips. Sixth time flying in to consult with the building engineers on upgrades for the Spire. Every damn trip, I ate at Ironcrest. Best steakhouse in the city, hands down. I'd dream about it when I wasn't there. Once, I went three nights in a row.

That night was my last in town. I sat down at the bar, already half-dead from meetings, and saw they'd introduced a massive fucking tomahawk steak. No sides, no salad. Just the meat and a cold beer. By the time I was three-quarters through, the meat sweats were real, but there was no chance I was letting an ounce of it go to waste.

And then I saw her.

She'd walked out earlier in the evening, scanned the room like she was taking inventory of every soul in it. Not a server...no apron, no tray. A suit. Auburn curls cropped short and pulled back sharp, almost like a mohawk. She carried this balance...masculine, feminine, both at once—and it was fucking magnetic. Sexy in a way that didn't beg for attention, but demanded it all the same.

I was married to Sarah at the time. Happily. I wasn't

looking for anything. But watching her? That presence... I remember thinking she ran the place. That she owned it.

"How are you enjoying the steak?" She asked when she stopped at my table, checking in on customers.

Fucking beautiful.

"It's a beast," I said, shifting in my chair, "but the best steak I've ever had."

She looked down at my plate, then back up with a smirk sharp enough to gut me. "Take it easy, big guy. You don't win a T-shirt if you finish it."

"Way to ruin a man's dreams, beautiful."

The word slipped before I could catch them. Christ. Was I actually flirting? What the hell was wrong with me?

"Alright then," she teased, lowering her voice. "Leave your forwarding address with my staff and I'll send you a free dinner voucher... *if you finish it*. But—" her eyes flicked to the sweat shining on my brow "—I'm a betting gal. And by the looks of it, big guy... it ain't happening."

The amount of guilt that coursed through me when my cock twitched will haunt me until the day I die.

I cleared my throat, adjusted in my seat like I could somehow hide it. "You're absolutely correct. I can't do it."

She smiled, easy, professional. "I'm glad you enjoyed it, though. Come back and see us sometime...we're always introducing new cuts."

And then she was gone. But the moment stayed burned

into me.

From that night forward, I couldn't bring myself to eat in the dining room again. Anytime I went back to Ironcrest, I ordered to go. It wasn't about temptation...I knew I'd never act on anything. It was about trust. I didn't trust my own body not to betray me again, the way it had that night.

Because here's the truth: I'd never been that guy. The one with the wandering eye, the groping hands, the excuses about marriage being a cage. Sarah was it for me, from the time we left college until the day she died. I didn't just love her. I belonged to her. And people never believed it. They looked at me and saw what they wanted...tall, fit, the jawline, the shoulders. My sister once told me her friends called me "BookTok hot," whatever the hell that means. A man who looked like me was expected to be a cheater. A cliché.

But I wasn't. I could appreciate beauty, but it was just that—something I saw and then let go. It never touched me. Never hit me like a punch in the gut. Not until that night. A steakhouse. A tomahawk I couldn't finish. And a woman with short auburn curls, sharp eyes, and the kind of presence that made the entire room shift around her.

That was all it took. A smile. A smirk about the sweat on my brow. A moment so brief it should've been forgettable. But it wasn't. It branded me. Because for the first time in my entire life, my body betrayed me...reacted to someone who wasn't Sarah. And I carried the guilt of that twitch for years.

Looking at her now, different, older, changed. No auburn curls. No sharp little mohawk. Darker hair, longer. Glasses. Ink crawling over her skin she didn't have back then. But it's her. I'd know her anywhere.

The morning after that trip, I came home bone-tired and restless. Simone was already at school. Sarah was cooking breakfast. I hadn't slept much. I hadn't been able to. The flight left before dawn, and all I could do that night was try to shake her out of me. Sevynn. Though I didn't even know her name then. I tried everything...television, porn, jerking off just to bleed out the tension...but my body kept betraying me.

And then I walked into our house. Into Sarah's arms.

The second I held her, the second I breathed her in, it hit me like a sledgehammer: what the fuck was I thinking? She was everything. My beginning and end. When I finally got her into our bed, buried deep inside her, it was like coming home after being lost at sea. Sarah was it. All I would ever need. All I wanted.

That night in New York became nothing more than a strange flicker. A restless memory shoved so far down it barely registered.

Now, sitting here, I leaned in, forearms braced on my knees, really taking Sevynn in the way I hadn't been able to then. I reached over, tucking a piece of hair behind her ear. "Your hair was shorter back then. A lot shorter. Auburn, almost copper. But I remember." I smiled at the memory. "You came out to check on the dining room a few times. I thought... she's got such a strong presence. She runs this place. She owns this place."

My thumb brushed over her bottom lip almost unconsciously. I remember her mouth. There was this tiny red scar, right under her lip. Not noticeable unless you're standing close. I tipped her chin, and there it was.

It's her...

Heat rushed up her chest. "You actually noticed me?"

"Noticed?" My gaze swept her face. I felt like I was re-mapping what I'd seen then against who she was now. "I couldn't take my eyes off you. You stopped at a few tables, making small talk. You stopped at mine and said—" my voice dropped into a low echo—"'Take it easy, big guy. You don't win a T-shirt if you don't finish it.'"

She laughed, startled, remembering. "Oh, my God. That was you? The tomahawk guy?"

"Tomahawk guy," I repeated, grinning slow. "Yeah. I had the steak. Nothing else. And I've never forgotten it. Or you."

I realized my hand was still lingering on her face, thumb tracing lazy circles at her jaw. Reluctantly, I let it fall, sitting back with a low shake of my head. "We've been circling each other without knowing. That building. That restaurant. And now this."

7 | SEVYNN

He shook his head slowly, like he was still trying to process it, the sheer coincidence—or fate, or whatever the hell this was—finally settling over him like a weight. "We've been circling each other without knowing. That building. That restaurant. And now this."

The words hit me square in the chest. I could feel them sinking in, burrowing under my ribs. For a second, I swear I forgot how to swallow.

So, naturally, I did what I always do when faced with something profound: I panicked and reached for sarcasm. "Wow," I said, nodding solemnly. "You make it sound very You've Got Mail, except with less email and more steak."

His grin cracked, slow and devastating.

My pulse skittered. My humor wasn't fooling anyone, least of all him, so I reached for the bourbon, buying myself a sip to steady the riot in my chest. "Okay, fine. Favorite place you've ever traveled?"

His body shifted again, erasing the distance he'd just created. One arm stretched along the back of the couch behind me, his chest angled toward mine. His voice dropped lower, softer...so intimate it sank straight into my bones.

"Right now. Here."

My pulse jumped, caught between stopping and sprinting. My brain screamed danger. Red flags, fire alarms, the whole emergency drill. But my body? My body leaned in before I could stop it, practically humming under the weight of his gaze.

"Not fair," I managed. My laugh came out breathier than I wanted, like I'd already lost the round. "That wasn't even a real answer."

"Wasn't it?" His mouth and those damn dimples cut in, like he knew exactly what he was doing. He was too close now. Close enough that the scent of him—bourbon, cedar, something darker underneath—slid straight into my lungs and made itself at home.

I swallowed hard, clinging to some last shred of composure. "Okay then. Question fifteen." My voice wobbled. "Biggest turn-on?"

He didn't blink. Didn't even pause. His eyes dragged over me slowly before locking back onto mine with a heat that pinned me in place.

"Right now. Here," he said again. Rougher this time. Certain. Like it wasn't a game anymore.

Well, fuck. My thighs clenched so hard I thought I might snap the cushion in half.

And just like that, twenty questions wasn't twenty questions anymore. It was foreplay disguised as trivia. A slow, brutal striptease of words.

"I think it's your turn now." My laugh came out shaky, so

I drowned it in another sip of bourbon, hiding behind the glass like it could shield me. Smooth move, Sevynn. Nothing screams sexy and mysterious like nearly choking on your drink to avoid eye contact.

London leaned back, stretching his long legs out in front of him like he had all the time in the world. His gaze was steady, thoughtful. "Alright. Question thirteen."

I braced.

"Biggest regret?"

My stomach did a little flip. Of course he would skip past favorite colors and dream vacations and dive straight for the jugular. I could've lied. Said something cute, like "eating Taco Bell before a road trip." But the bourbon had stripped away my filter.

"Not leaving sooner," I admitted, softer than I meant to.

He didn't press. Just nodded once, like he understood more than I wanted him to.

"Question fourteen," he said, lips twitching at the corners. "First crush."

I groaned and covered my face with my hands. "Leonardo DiCaprio. Titanic Leo, specifically. I taped his face to my ceiling and nearly set my room on fire with all the candles I lit to 'romance' him."

London laughed, deep and warm, the kind of sound that rolled through my ribs and settled indecently low. "That's commitment."

"Yeah, well." I shrugged, sipping my drink. "He never

wrote back to my fan letters, so... clearly his loss."

"Question fifteen." His eyes glittered as he leaned closer, too close. "Guilty pleasure."

I raised my glass again, deliberately avoiding his gaze. "Right now. Here."

The rumble that came out of his chest vibrated straight through the couch and bee-lined itself right to my vagina. My thighs clenched instinctively.

"Fuck," he whispered, so quiet it was more for himself than me. His eyes dragged down my face, over my mouth, then back up. "Sixteen." His voice dropped, low and rough, curling down my spine. "Biggest turn-on."

The air between us crackled.

I tipped my glass back, taking an exaggeratedly long sip, like I was buying myself time. The whiskey burned, but I didn't break eye contact. Not this time. When I lowered the glass, I licked a stray drop from my lip and let a smile tug at the corner of my mouth.

"Right here. Now," I said, making it sound almost like a joke—except the heat rolling through me gave me away.

The space between us vibrated. His breathing went jagged, pulled in like he was trying to leash something feral.

He licked his lips, eyes catching on my mouth before dragging back up.

I cocked a brow, deliberately light even as my pulse thundered. "What's next, counselor? Or are you out of questions?"

His mouth curved, sharp and dangerous, though his voice came out rough enough to scrape over my skin. "Seventeen. Biggest fantasy."

You. Every inch of you. The thought hit me so hard it stole my breath. "To need a safe word."

For a second, he froze. His mouth literally fell open, his jaw tight as though every muscle locked at once. His fists curled on his knees, tendons straining. Then, like he'd remembered himself too late, he dragged in a breath, tipped his glass back, and swallowed hard. His hand swept over the back of his neck, slow and shaky, as if he needed the grounding before he came apart.

The air between us went molten. He tipped his head back against the couch, eyes shut, fists still clenched like he was holding back a storm. He didn't say anything. Not for a long, thrumming few seconds that felt like forever.

I swallowed hard, my pulse pounding so loud I swore it echoed in the empty lobby. "I've never... said that out loud before." My voice cracked, too raw. "Hell, I've never even admitted it to myself properly. But that's it. That's my fantasy. Not a huge thing."

Silence stretched, thick and merciless. I almost backpedaled, almost laughed it off, but then his eyes opened...and the way he looked at me told me I hadn't just confessed a fantasy. I'd lit a fuse.

He sat forward, elbows braced to his knees, green eyes pinning me where I sat. The dimples were gone. What was left was sharp. Serious. Predatory.
"Eighteen."

My stomach flipped. "Oh God. We're still going, okay."

He nodded once, voice low enough to curl like smoke down my spine. "Did you like my tongue on your body, Sevynn?"

Air vanished from my lungs. Heat slammed through every nerve, every inch of me raw and trembling under his gaze. "Yes." The word escaped in a whisper, unguarded, before my brain could stop it.

His jaw flexed, satisfaction cutting sharp through his expression. He leaned back a fraction, but his eyes never left mine. "Good. I like the way you taste. The way you sound when you moan my name. The way you shake when you're right there on the edge."

My thighs pressed together, desperate, useless against the fire curling low in my stomach. He was unraveling me with nothing but words.

Then he leaned in—measured, like a man who knew exactly what he was doing to my already over-caffeinated, over-liquored nervous system. The couch dipped under his weight. His palm slid to the back of my neck. Warm. Solid. Anchoring.

And then he kissed me.

Fucking finally. My ovaries practically threw confetti and screamed, *I love this for us!*

His lips were soft at first—testing, almost tentative, like he thought I might pull away.

Spoiler: I did no such fucking thing.

I tilted in, closing the distance fully, lips parting. When my tongue brushed his, he groaned into my mouth...low, rough, the kind of sound that detonates right in your stomach.

Game. Over.

His arm slid around my back, hauling me closer, mouth slanting over mine. I melted...right there in fuzzy slippers on a hotel couch.

And *holy hell*, this man could kiss. His tongue wasn't rushed or sloppy; it was slow, controlled, maddening. Every stroke against mine was like he'd been practicing just for me, like he knew exactly where to press, how to tease, how to make me chase him.

He tasted like bourbon and sin, and when his tongue slid deeper, coaxing instead of demanding, my whole body went liquid. My fists knotted in his shirt, desperate, because he was kissing me like it was an art form, like his mouth was some finely tuned instrument and I was the lucky idiot he'd decided to play.

Then he groaned. Low, rough, sex-on-a-stick kind of sound, and it detonated straight in my stomach. My thighs clenched, my pulse did gymnastics, and I almost whimpered right into his mouth.

And in that exact second, I realized—this wasn't just a kiss. This was him showing me what he could do with nothing but his mouth. Which, frankly, felt like both a promise and a threat.

And the best part? The worst part? I didn't care that we were in the middle of the lobby. Let them stare. Let them gossip. For once, I wasn't the ex-wife, the mom, the fixer. I was just a woman being kissed stupid by a man who tasted like bourbon and bad decisions.

When his hand skimmed under my shirt, nails dragging up my ribs before cupping my breast, I thought I'd combust. The kiss broke on a gasp, and for one wild second I thought he'd lost control—until his hand slipped away. Not a jerk. Not panic. Just... restraint.

"Fuck," he muttered, forehead still pressed to mine. His breath hitched, chest heaving like he was holding himself back by sheer will. "I'm sorry."

The word didn't feel like rejection. It felt like discipline, like a man white-knuckling it when his body was begging him to ruin me right there on the lobby couch.

"Let me walk you to your room." His voice was shredded, low, careful. His thumb stroked the back of my neck, anchoring me even as he steadied himself. "That's all. I'm not asking to come in. I'm not that guy. Scout's honor."

I believed him. He didn't look like a man trying to hustle me upstairs. He looked like a man in a war with his own conscience.

Which, of course, made me want him even more. Because nothing is hotter than a guy with self-restraint when every muscle in his body is screaming to lose it.

I swallowed, trying to catch my breath, trying to remember how to be a functioning adult and not just a puddle in fuzzy slippers. "You don't strike me as a Boy Scout," I managed, my voice half-laugh, half-shaky.

His mouth curved, dimples flashing in the low lobby light. "Trust me, sweetheart. I'm not. That's exactly why I should stop here."

He guided me toward the elevators without another word, his palm warm and steady at the small of my back. Gentlemanly. Protective. Dangerous as hell.

I was a little light on my feet, though I couldn't tell if it was the tequila, the six old fashioneds, or the kiss that was still buzzing through my bloodstream. Probably all three.

When the elevator doors slid shut, I leaned forward and tapped 15 on the glowing pad.

Behind me, he chuckled, low and amused.

I glanced back. "What?"

"Fifteen," he said, that half-grin tugging at his mouth again. "I'm on fifteen too."

I blinked at him, then snorted. "Of course you are. Because that's exactly the kind of plot twist the universe thinks is funny."

His dimple deepened. "Maybe the universe knows what it's doing."

I crossed my arms, trying to look unimpressed when really my knees felt like Jell-O. "Or maybe the universe just wants me to regret this in the morning."

He tilted his head, eyes locked on mine as the elevator hummed higher. "Do you?"

My mouth went dry. And God help me, the answer that came to mind wasn't yes.

So I smirked instead. "I've got to keep *some* mystery about me, Mr. Bridges."

That earned me a groan and a laugh in the same breath. "Ha. So original. London Bridges. Haven't heard that since the third grade." His eyes darkened just enough to make my stomach flip. "I should spank your sexy little ass for that."

The word spank hit me square in the thighs. My breath caught, my brain scrambled, and before I could come up with a clever comeback, the elevator chimed and the doors slid open.

Neither of us moved.

His gaze stayed locked on mine, heavy, waiting. Testing.

"Scout's honor?" I whispered, because apparently bourbon had murdered my filter and left my mouth running on autopilot.

He didn't move. Didn't blink. Just stared at me like he was trying to decide if I was temptation or trouble...or maybe both. The elevator doors began to slide shut again, sealing us in, and that's when he finally reacted.

His arm shot out, palm stopping the doors with an easy strength. He closed his eyes for the briefest second, jaw tightening like he was physically reining himself in.

When he looked at me again, his voice was steady, low. "Let's get you to your room."

Not urgent. Not cold. Just careful. Which somehow made it worse. Because my body didn't want careful. My body wanted him.

I nodded, pretending my heart wasn't trying to crack my

ribcage open as I followed him down the quiet hallway. His hand stayed at the small of my back, warm, steady, solid. And honestly, even if nothing else happened today, that hand alone was enough to do me in.

When I reached my door, I stopped and jabbed a thumb at it like a nervous teenager. "I'm here. Fifteen eighteen."

"I'm there," he said, pointing just across the hall. "Fifteen twenty-one."

Of course he was. Of course fate—or whiskey, or whatever cosmic trickster was running this night...had put him just steps away.

He took a step back, giving me space I didn't actually want. "It was a much nicer day than I originally planned, Sevynn. Thank you."

My throat went tight. Who thanks someone after kissing them stupid in a hotel lobby? Who thanks someone after making them feel alive again?

"Yeah," I said, fumbling with my keycard and a half-smile I hoped looked cooler than I felt. "You, uh... made old-fashioneds and rhinestones a surprisingly good combo."

His smiled again at that, and then he walked over to his room, leaving me in front of my room door with shaking hands, a racing pulse, and the sudden, terrifying thought that I wanted to see him again.

I slid the keycard into the lock, the little green light blinking as I pushed the door open. But something tugged at me...some invisible string pulling me back.

I turned, just for a glance.

London was across the hall, his hand braced flat against his own door, head bowed low between his shoulders. Like a man holding back a tidal wave.

For a heartbeat, I just watched him. That broad back, those tattooed forearms straining as if he could wrestle down whatever war he was fighting.

And then my restraint snapped.

I let my door fall shut and crossed the hall, each step faster than the last. He lifted his head when he heard me, green eyes sparking when he realized I wasn't stopping.

We collided...mouths, hands, heat. His kiss was rougher now, hungry, his palm sliding up to cradle the back of my head while the other dragged me flush against his chest. My fingers fisted in his shirt, desperate, pulling him closer, closer.

He fumbled for the lock behind him, the frantic click sounding just as wild as we felt, and then the door swung open.

We stumbled inside, lips still locked, hands everywhere, the door slamming shut behind us like the universe had just rubber-stamped our bad decisions.

The blur between the slam of that door and my back hitting the mattress was pure chaos—fabric tearing, mouths colliding, gasps that turned into laughter and then back into gasps again. One second I was tugging at his shirt like a starving woman and the next, I was naked, trembling, completely exposed under the weight of his stare.

London loomed over me, fist wrapped tight around his cock, staring down like a man half-starved. I wish I could tell you it was romantic. That the moonlight caught him at the perfect angle, turned him into something sculpted and untouchable. But this was fucking *filthy*, and he was built like every smutty fantasy you're not supposed to admit out loud.

"Fuck, sweetheart," he rasped, his voice shredded with want. His eyes raked over me like he was memorizing every inch, claiming me without even touching me. "You are... breathtaking."

And then his hands were back on me. Rough palms skating over my ribs, cupping my breasts, pinning me like he didn't trust me not to disappear. He kissed me hard, deep, groaning when my nails dug into his shoulders. The sound vibrated straight through me, lighting up every nerve ending like a downed power line.

When his mouth dragged down my throat, teeth scraping over my pulse, my whole body bowed off the bed. He caught me easily, his grip firm at my hips, anchoring me like he could keep me tethered with strength alone.

"Tell me you want this," he demanded against my skin, hot breath ragged and uneven.

I laughed, shaky, wrecked, and so far past pretending. "Do I look like I don't?"

He growled—an actual growl—and hauled me up so effortlessly, tossing me deeper into the bed. I landed with a bounce, hair spilling wild, while he loomed at the edge—every line of him screaming restraint he was about two seconds away from losing.

8 | LONDON

There wasn't an ounce of guilt in me. I thought there might be—hell, I almost expected it. Maybe tomorrow, when the bourbon haze burns off, and the silence comes back, I'll feel it. But not now. Not with her.

Right now, this beautiful, infuriating, intoxicating woman was spread beneath me, trembling, soaked, every inch of her begging me not to hold back. After five years, my body wasn't just alive...it was on fucking fire.

Instinct took the wheel before I even knew I'd let go. Every ounce of discipline, every careful thought, shoved to the backseat. Control slid into place like it had been waiting for her, itching to reclaim what I hadn't touched in years.

I braced my hand against the mattress, my other palm gripping her hip, anchoring her as I hovered over her. My voice came out low, rough, almost a growl. "Tell me you want this."

She laughed...soft, breathless, her body trembling under mine. Her eyes flashed up to meet me, bold even as her lips quivered.

"Do I look like I don't?"

Yeah. That answer. That look. It stripped the last thread of restraint clean out of me.

This was reckless. Irresponsible. She was a complete stranger. We hadn't talked about rules, about condoms, about anything that mattered for this moment. But then she was in my bed, her whole body trembling, and I didn't fucking hesitate.

Something animal took over. My brain shut off, and pure, raw instinct roared through my veins. I draped her leg over my shoulder, peppering kisses inside her thighs, then gliding my finger over her slit.

I'm done for.

"Oh, God."

"You're so fucking wet, sweetheart." I bring my finger to my mouth, taste her, and the first hit is lethal. A drug. Addictive. I'll never get enough.

I spread her open with trembling hands, and whatever was left of my discipline shattered. My mouth crashed into her pussy, desperate, greedy, devouring like she was the only thing keeping me alive. She was wet and soft and so fucking perfect I thought I'd lose my mind.

"London—oh fuck—" she cried, her hips jerking, grinding against my face like she was starving too, chasing every flick of my tongue.

I drove deeper, thrusting my tongue inside her, my hands roaming up to seize her breasts. I pinched, rolled, teased her nipples until she arched so hard she nearly broke against me. Her fingers tangled in my hair, anchoring me there like she'd fall apart completely if I stopped.

I splay one palm against her stomach, feeling it contract, pressing her down as my teeth tug her clit.

Her cry rips through the room, raw and primal. "Oh… God." Her arms flail, searching, reaching, grabbing for anything to hold her together—and it's the most gorgeous fucking thing I've ever seen.

I pressed her harder into the bed, my mouth relentless. Tongue circling, teeth grazing, lips pulling—every flick designed to push her closer.

Her thighs clamped around my head, trembling, holding me there like I was the only oxygen she had left. Her nails scraped my scalp, her whole body taut and quaking.

I caught her clit between my teeth, gave a sharp tug, then flattened my tongue over her swollen flesh. A beat later, I raked the hard plane of my chin, rough with beard, through her slick folds—the scrape a brutal counterpoint to the heat of my tongue. Back and forth.

"London—fuck—I'm—" Her voice broke, high, desperate.

"Come for me, sweetheart," I hissed against her, the vibration making her jolt. "Give it to me. Right now."

Tongue, then beard. Tongue, then beard. The rhythm wrecked her, split her open, until she shattered, screaming my name.

Her body went rigid first, back arcing clean off the bed, a cry ripping free before she broke completely. Then came the flood—her thighs shaking, her stomach clenching, her hips grinding against my mouth like she couldn't stop, like her body belonged to me now. She convulsed around my tongue, wave after wave tearing through her while I held her down, swallowing every sound, every tremor, like I could carve this moment into me forever.

I didn't let up, not until her body finally sagged, boneless, whimpering, her fingers still tangled in my hair but no strength left in them.

I pressed one last kiss to her, soft, reverent, a seal on what I'd just wrecked.

"Mine," I whispered against her skin, tasting the words as much as I said them.

Her body was still trembling beneath me, thighs quaking where I held them open. I shifted forward, dragging my cock along her slick folds, every pulse of it aching, desperate. Her breath hitched, nails sinking into my shoulders like she couldn't hold herself steady.

"London—" she whispered, voice shattered, still riding the aftershocks.

"Shh." My mouth brushed hers, coaxing, claiming. "I've got you, sweetheart. We're not done. Not yet."

Then her lips parted, wrapping around my chin, her tongue tasting herself off my skin.

"Motherfucker..." The curse ripped out of me as my cock jerked, straining, ready to sink into her and never stop.

I lined myself up and pushed in slow — agonizingly slow — stretching her around me, inch by inch, until I could feel every clench, every shiver.

"God," she moaned through gritted teeth, her back arching

as I pressed deeper. A broken sound shuddered free, and I caught it in a kiss, swallowing her cry like it belonged to me.

"That's it," I murmured against her mouth, kissing the corner of her lips, her cheek, her temple. "Take me. Every inch. Such a good fucking girl."

Her arms locked around my neck, dragging me closer, and I drove the last of the way in, bottoming out until I was buried to the hilt. I stayed there, pulsing inside her, letting her body adjust, letting her feel every goddamn inch of me before I moved.

When I finally did, it wasn't rushed. It was steady, measured...long strokes that had her gasping, clutching at me like she'd come apart if I let her go.

"You feel so good," I whispered into her ear, my teeth grazing her skin, my hand cradling her face to keep her eyes on mine. "So fucking perfect around my cock."

Her lips trembled, her body tightening around me, and I slowed, keeping her right there, trapped on the edge.

"Not yet," I coaxed, my thumb drawing slow circles over her hip as I held her down. "Breathe for me. Stay with me. I'll take you there, sweetheart...I promise. But you come when I tell you."

She was so wet I could hear it every time I thrust, slick heat clenching around me like her body was begging for more. Every gasp, every twitch was a war in my head not to lose it...not to flip her over, fuck her raw, spit in her mouth, yank her hair and call her my fucking cumdoll. Damn, the depraved part of me was clawing at the leash. But I couldn't scare her off.

She whimpered, hips straining to meet mine, but I pinned her down, forcing her to take the rhythm I gave her. Her nails dragged down my back, sharp, desperate, and I smiled against her throat. It had been so long since I'd wanted to tear into flesh like this, to leave marks just to prove I'd been there. Holding back felt like breaking bones.

Her body shook under me, every sound she made more ragged than the last, and I kissed her softly — patient, tender — while I drove harder, deeper, grinding until her pleas turned into incoherent whimpers.

"Yes, sweetheart, cry out if you need to, but you don't fucking come until I say so." My hand slid up, wrapping around her throat—firm, not choking, just enough to remind her who owned her body in this moment. "Eyes on me, baby."

Her lashes fluttered, tears clinging at the corners, but she obeyed, gaze locking with mine. And fuck, that obedience lit something primal in me.

"You want to come, don't you?" I rasped, thrusting harder, sharper now, my hips driving her into the mattress.

"Yes," she gasped, voice cracking.

"Say it. Tell me how bad you need it."

"So bad — please, London —"

I tightened my grip on her throat, just a notch. "Beg prettier than that, sweetheart. You want my permission? You earn it."

Her body writhed under me, caught between surrender and defiance, and God it was beautiful. I leaned closer, my forehead pressing hard to hers, every thrust bruising, brutal now.

"You're mine. You come when I say. Say it."

Her lips trembled, her breath stuttering as I held her there, right on the knife's edge.

"I'm yours," she cried, broken. "All yours."

I kissed her, rough and claiming, before I pulled back enough to rasp against her lips, "Good girl. Now fucking come for me."

I caged her in with my arms, driving into her faster, harder, her cries echoing through room.

"Eyes on me," I snapped, gripping her chin when she tried to close them, forcing her gaze back to mine. "I want you looking at me when I take you. Every second."

Her thighs were spread wide around me, but I wanted more...I wanted to own every inch of her surrender. I hooked behind her knees and slammed them into the mattress, pinning her down as I pounded into her. The sound was obscene...wet, slick, brutal.

"Say *red* if it's too much," I rasped, voice rough in her ear. "Because I can't, sweetheart. You'll have to stop me."

I pulled back enough to catch her eyes, forcing her to see me, to give me permission. Her mouth opened in a silent cry, chest heaving. For a heartbeat I thought she might break...but then she nodded. Nodded hard.

That was all I needed. "Good girl," I snarled, hips snapping, relentless.

Her hands shot up, clawing at the headboard, knuckles white as she held on like her life depended on it. And I drove her harder, deeper, burying her into the bed until every cry tore out of her throat raw.

I felt it—the tight pull of her clenching around me, the quake building in her stomach. Her body was seconds from breaking. I bore down harder, giving her no reprieve, fucking her like I could fuck her straight through the mattress.

"London—oh God—" she sobbed, her back arched, every muscle drawn tight as a bowstring.

And when her body seized, when I felt that gush rising inside her, I pulled out and slapped her pussy hard. Twice.

"Oh, FUCK!" she screamed, her voice shattering.

The scream broke into a sob as she gushed, hot release pouring over me, soaking the sheets. My cock throbbed at the sight, at the feel of her coming undone so violently, and I had to grit my teeth.

She convulsed, trembling, waves still crashing while I stroked myself hard above her, watching her drown in it.

"Fuck, Sevynn." My chest heaving as I forced her thighs wider, keeping her open, watching her spasm through every aftershock. "Look at the mess you made, sweetheart. Goddamn... you're perfect."

Her orgasm rippled through her in relentless waves, brutal and merciless, until her body finally sagged, muscles twitching against me. I hovered back over her, and the second I did, her arms wrapped around my neck like she'd never let me go.

I slid back inside, slow but deep, and started moving again—relentless but measured, dragging out every last tremor, making her take it, making her feel me owning her even in the aftermath.

"That's my girl," I rasped, kissing her temple, her jaw, her gasping mouth. Softer now. Worshipful, even as I was still buried to the hilt. "All fucking mine."

Her chest heaved against mine, words stumbling out in fragments. "You...thanks...I don't—"

I brushed damp hair from her face, kissing her swollen lips with a rough laugh still buzzing with adrenaline. "You're not making any sense, baby."

Her nails carved down my back like she wanted to brand me there, her lips trembling, her voice fractured. "Can't think...can't breathe...you—"

I swallowed her words with a kiss, slower this time, even as my hips drove shallow, punishing thrusts that made her whimper. "You don't have to think," I breathed against her mouth. "That's mine now. You just feel. And you're going to give me one more."

Her head shook, tears clinging to her lashes, but her body betrayed her—tightening, trembling, already coiling for another fall.

"Yes, you can," I rasped, hooking her legs over my shoulders, gripping her thighs so hard I knew I'd leave bruises. "One more for me, Sevynn. Be my good girl."

I slammed into her, piston-deep, merciless, every thrust punishing. Her cry burst through the room, raw and feral, her back bowing off the bed as she shattered around me. Her body convulsed, violent tremors wracking her, clamping down on me so tight it dragged a roar from my chest.

That was it. The dam broke. Five years of silence. Five years of restraint. Five years of pretending I didn't need—didn't want—this. All of it tore out of me at once, spilling into her with a force I couldn't stop if I tried.

I drove into her harder, deeper, reckless now, forehead pressed to hers as I lost myself. The sound ripped out of me, harsh and broken, as I emptied into her, my body shaking with it, every pulse tearing through me like it might split me open.

I held her through it, burying myself to the hilt, her body gripping mine like she'd never let me go. Her moans blurred with mine, her sweat-slick skin sliding against me as we came apart together.

When the quake finally eased, I collapsed onto my forearms, my face buried in the crook of her neck. Her pulse thundered against my lips. Her chest heaved beneath mine, frantic, desperate, alive. My own heart was still sprinting like I'd run a marathon with no finish line.

Then, I kissed her like a man starved, desperate, gasping against her mouth.

"I think I love you," I blurted in a breathy chuckle.

Her eyes widened, her lips trembling before she broke into the kind of laugh that shook us both. Breathless, disbelieving. "You better," she managed between gasps, her forehead leaning forward against mine. "Because I cannot imagine it getting any better than this."

That set me off too—laughing, groaning, kissing her again, the insanity of it all crashing down on us in waves. Two wrecked, half-drunk idiots tangled together, already too far gone to care.

For a moment, we just lay there, tangled and shaking, the air thick with the weight of what we'd just done. And what it meant. Her hand drifted up my spine. Light. Soothing. A quiet touch that made my throat tighten.

I hadn't expected her. I hadn't expected *any* of this. But right now? Wrapped around each other, hearts still racing? I didn't want to be anywhere else.

She was tucked against me, skin still warm and flushed, her leg slung over mine like we'd done this a hundred times before. Like her body knew where to go even if her mind hadn't caught up yet.

Then, her voice—soft, a little hoarse—broke the silence. "I really didn't know sex could be like that."

I stilled, my fingers pausing where they'd been tracing slow, lazy circles on her hip. She said it so quietly I almost thought I imagined it—like a secret she wasn't sure she meant to share.

"What's that, sweetheart?" I asked, aiming for casual, calm. Like I hadn't just had my entire nervous system rewired by this woman.

Her face burrowed deeper into the crook of my arm. "I've never... come like that before. Soaking the bed like that. If I'm being honest, London? It's kind of embarrassing, and I'll deny it if you ever bring it up again."

That made me grin wide, completely involuntary. Goddamn, she was something else. "Is that right?"

She groaned and pinched my side, half-hearted but adorable. "Shut up."

"Don't be embarrassed," I murmured, kissing the crown of her hair. I reached down, tilting her chin just enough to see her face. Still pink, still flushed, still fucking beautiful. "I've never experienced anything like that either. It was a first for me, too. And I loved every second of it."

She gave a little shrug, eyes darting away. "It's just... I didn't think I was capable of that. Of letting go like that. I don't usually—"

"You just needed the right man," I cut in before I could stop myself.

Her brow lifted with the kind of arch that could bring a man to his knees. And the corner of her mouth? Smirking like she knew exactly what kind of power she had and didn't plan to use it responsibly.

"Cocky," she said, voice lazy and laced with challenge.

"Confident," I corrected, stone-faced, even as I felt a grin threatening at the edges.

She narrowed her eyes at me, playful and sharp. Dangerous. "Okay, *Mr. Bridges*," she teased, dragging it out like a weapon. "Don't let it go to your head."

"Hmmm. Interesting," I muttered, chuckling as I eased myself up, shifting until I was on my knees beside her, watching her like prey.

Her eyes sparkled. "What's interesting?"

"That you're testing whether I'd keep my word about spanking that sexy little ass."

She barely had time to process the words before I moved.

Smooth, practiced, primal.

In one motion, I pulled her over my lap—her soft frame folding perfectly against me like it was always meant to be there. I gripped her hip with one hand and slid the other between her thighs, fingers slipping through soaked heat.

"Jesus, sweetheart," I groaned, dipping two fingers deep inside her, curling just right until she gasped.

Then I brought my palm down across her ass. A sharp crack echoed through the room, and she jolted forward with a ragged moan that punched the breath from my lungs.

"Oh, fuck," she cried, voice raw and needy and *fucking divine*.

"There she is," I whispered, voice low and dangerous in her ear.

I hit her again, watching the way her skin flushed under my hand. She clenched around my fingers, her body grinding down into my palm like she didn't know how to stop.

She was completely undone. Hair falling in her face, lips parted, body trembling with every sensation I gave her. And still, she arched back for more.

I kept my voice low, but firm. "You gonna keep testing me, Sevynn?"

She moaned something incoherent, something desperate, and my cock throbbed with the need to take her all over again. But I wanted her undone. Shattered. I wanted her to *remember me* every time she touched herself after this.

Her ass was glowing, heat radiating under my palm, but I

wasn't done. I pulled my fingers out slow, dragging slick along the crease of her thigh before plunging them back in — deeper this time, firmer. Her whole body arched like a bow, mouth open in a silent scream.

"Three more," I whispered against her ear. "Think you can take it, sweetheart?"

She nodded frantically, cheek pressed to the mattress, hair falling over her eyes. I couldn't see her face, but I could feel her — every breath, every tremble. She was unraveling and begging for more with every twitch of her hips.

Crack.

This one landed sharper, and she cried out in a sound that broke halfway between pain and pleasure, tumbling into a moan that rattled straight through me. It fed something so fucking primal, something I hadn't been able to let out of its cage in years. It wasn't choice anymore. It was need.

My fingers twisted inside her, driving deeper until I found that perfect spot and punished it again and again. Her body bowed, breath tearing ragged from her throat, her chest heaving like she couldn't catch air.

"Such a greedy little cunt you have, sweetheart. That's one," I said, biting down the growl in my throat. "Count them down."

Her lips trembled, her voice a broken gasp. "One…one."

Crack.

I curled harder, faster, dragging the sound from her chest until her head flew back, her thighs trembling around my wrist.

"Two," she sobbed, hips bucking against me.

"Good girl."

She was *flooding* against my fingers. The sheer devastating beauty of her, taking my punishment, nearly unmade me. My hips thrust up into her side, desperate to feel some friction against my cock.

"Almost there baby, don't come until I tell you. What color, sweetheart?"

"Green." She moaned, breath shallow, sweat beading down her spine.

"Good. Fucking. Girl."

Her body bows over my lap, chest pressed to the bed, ass arched high, thighs trembling around me. My fingers stay buried in her, pace brutal, twisting, curling against that spot deep inside of her. Her ass bouncing with thrust.

Her hands clawed at the sheets, searching for something to hold onto. "London, please—please—"

Once I know she's on the edge of coming, my other hand cracks down across her ass one last time, the sound sharp in the room.

"Come. Right fucking now." I gritted out, continuing the thrust and curl of my fingers.

"Yes—oh fuck, oh fuck!"

I had to bite down a roar. My cock jerks against her hip, leaking precum as her pussy convulses around me, pulsing hard as she gushes over my hand, soaking my wrist, my lap, the sheets beneath us. She screams my name, her body jerking with each wave of release, and I drag her through it, fingers fucking her mercilessly, spanking her again until she's thrashing in overstimulation, gasping for breath.

"Good girl," I pant, my forehead pressed to her spine as she rides it out, my cock grinding into her hip in sharp, helpless thrusts. "

She whimpered something into the sheets, and I didn't need her to repeat it. I already knew. She was mine now. Even if it was just for today.

The rest of the night was a blur of skin, sweat, and sex.

So. Much. Sex.

We explored each other like we had lifetimes to make up for—tongues, hands, mouths chasing every gasp and every moan like they were breath. I took her to the edge again and again until she couldn't say my name without trembling. And when it was her turn—when she dropped to her knees and sucked me like her soul depended on it—I damn near lost my mind. She licked me clean, swallowed every drop, and looked up at me like she already owned me.

By the time we finally collapsed onto the mattress, it was well past 5 a.m. We were soaked in each other, bruised in the best ways, and absolutely spent.

I don't know when she fell asleep. One minute she was curled against me, warm and soft and tucked beneath my arm like she belonged there, and the next...gone. Not gone *gone*, just... out cold, breathing slow and deep. Her lashes fluttered in her sleep, and this ridiculously adorable little snore pushed past her lips every few breaths.

I couldn't stop staring at her.

And God help me, I wasn't thinking about regrets. I wasn't wondering what came next or how the hell we got here.

I just let myself *feel* it...the weight of her against me, the silence between us that felt comfortable instead of awkward, the smell of sex and skin lingering in the air.

And then I drifted off too, just a man in a strange hotel bed, tangled up with a woman I wasn't ready to let go of.

— — — — — — —

"Fuck. Fuck."

The sound pierced through the haze like a gunshot, dragging me out of the best sleep I'd had in years...and straight into a hangover from hell.

I groaned, rolling over with a wince, my skull pounding like Mount Rushmore was trying to crack open from the inside. My mouth tasted like regret and bourbon. "Sevynn?"

She didn't answer, not really. Just kept moving—jerky and frantic, like a woman trying to outrun something. Herself, maybe. Or worse—me.

"Sorry," she mumbled, voice low. "I didn't mean to wake you."

I forced my eyes open and squinted through the morning light, only to see her shuffling around the room like she was trying to disappear. She was hopping on one foot, trying to find her other slipper. Her bra dangled from one hand, her bag clutched to her chest with her panties and shirt. She looked like she was escaping a crime scene.

"Hey," I said, sitting up fast and instantly regretting it. Pain knifed through my temple. "You okay? You don't have to leave."

Still no eye contact. Not even a glance. Just silence. Stiff shoulders. A quiet I didn't know how to read—but it was loud as hell.

"Hey," I repeated, standing and stumbling a little as I got to my feet. "Talk to me. What's going on?"

She held her arms around herself like armor. Slippers on, clothes twisted and half-tucked, panic painted across her face. Her eyes flicked to the floor—then I saw it.

My wedding ring.

The gold band I'd shoved into my pocket the day before now sat glittering under the edge of the chair. Like a fucking landmine I forgot to disarm.

Shit.

"This was a mistake," she whispered, every word like a blow to my ribs. "I don't know what I was thinking."

"No," I breathed, stepping toward her, heart thudding harder than my headache. "No, it wasn't. Sweetheart, please. Not to me. It wasn't."

She shook her head, biting her lip hard like she was holding everything in. She wouldn't look at me. Wouldn't meet my eyes. That's when I panicked.

"Don't call me that," she snapped, her voice breaking. "I... I have to go."

"No. Wait." I moved fast—too fast—cutting her off before she could reach the door. I planted myself in front of it like that could stop her from leaving. Like I had any right to.

"Please," I said, grabbing her gently by the elbows. "Just—just tell me what I did. Let me fix it. Don't walk out like this. Not without talking to me."

"You lied to me!" she exploded, finally looking me in the eyes—and I wished she hadn't. Not with that look. Betrayal, heartbreak, disgust.

She jabbed a finger toward the ring on the floor. "You said you weren't married, and your *goddamn wedding ring* is right there. Fuck London, do you know what that makes me? I am *not* a homewrecker. I will never be *that* woman. And you—" her voice cracked, rage shaking in her chest—"you turned me into the thing I hate *most* in this world."

"Sevynn, I swear to you—"

"I don't want to hear it." She jerked herself out of my grip and threw the door open with trembling hands. "I don't have anything else to fucking say to you."

And then she was gone. The door slammed shut behind her. And for the first time in five fucking years, I felt truly alone.

9 | SEVYNN

"What the fuck was I thinking, Jones?" I groaned, pinching the bridge of my nose as I nursed the hangover cure he shoved in front of me—tomato juice with pickle brine. Disgusting. Effective. The official love language of my lifelong bestie-slash-bad-influence.

"You weren't thinking. At least not with your head," Jones fired back, sprawled in his spa chair like he was posing for a GQ spread instead of waiting on a pedicure. A towel draped over his shoulders, mimosa in hand, the very picture of smug judgment. "You were thinking with your lady balls."

"Jones!" I smacked his arm, nearly baptizing us both in pickle juice. The nail tech kneading my calves glanced up, startled, and I winced. "Sorry," I whispered, mortified. She just smiled politely and went back to working the hangover—and the shame—out of my legs.

Edward-McKenzie Jones—though God forbid you ever use his first name—is my executive chef and one of my best friends. We've been running restaurants together for ten years now, which means he's been my professional and personal sounding board for just as long. The man is a walking contradiction: sculpted body, porcelain skin, shoulder-length waves that deserve their own Pantene commercial, and gray eyes that can cut through your soul—or roll with such disdain you feel physically slapped.

He's also six foot two, built like a Marvel audition, and a *flaming whore* (his words, not mine). Bisexual, gloriously so. Which is the only reason I haven't launched myself across a tequila-soaked table at him at least once. Because objectively? He's fucking delicious. Think Ezra Miller in the shoulder-length hair, five o'clock shadow era. Got it? Lickable, right? I admitted as much once after three margaritas and a freshly signed divorce decree. He still brings it up at every opportunity. But neither of us needs that type of complication in a friendship or work relationship.

"Don't apologize for my truth bombs," Jones said, tipping back his mimosa like he was poolside in Ibiza instead of a hotel salon. "Seriously, Sev—you were due for a good dicking down. If anything, I'm proud. Inspired, even. I should make a TikTok about you: 'Divorced mom of two rediscovers her vagina and thrives.' Hashtag inspo. Hashtag MILF renaissance."

"Jones!" I hissed, burying my face in my hands.

He only grinned wider, wicked as ever, licking his lips shamelessly at the very attractive nail tech working on his feet. "Mmm. If only we could all be so lucky, girl. If London Bridges came tumbling down on me, I'd be shopping for engagement rings by brunch."

"Please never say that again," I groaned.

"Fine." He shrugged, utterly unbothered. "But admit it...you're glowing."

I let my head fall back against the chair, sighing like a dying Victorian heroine. "I'm dying, Jones. Dying. And he's married.

And a liar. A stupid, gorgeous liar."

"And glowing," he repeated, smirk smug enough to earn its own zip code. "Don't forget the glowing."

"Ugh. You're impossible. I regret inviting you." I tipped back the hangover cure and grimaced, the briny tomato concoction making my stomach flip all over again.

Jones gasped dramatically, hand clutching his chest like I'd stabbed him. "Regret? Honey, without me you'd be a puddle of mascara and shame-spiral tears by now. You're welcome."

I glared, but the corner of my mouth betrayed me, twitching.

He leaned in, voice pitched low like a secret. "Besides, who's gonna stop you from starting a fight with the DJ when he plays the wrong version of your song?"

I narrowed my eyes. "One time. That happened *one time*."

His grin was infuriating. "Uh-huh. And who was it that had to drag you off the dance floor before you strangled him with his own headphones?"

I groaned, covering my face. "You're never letting that go."

"Not a chance," he said, smug. "That's why you need me. Damage control."

I groaned, sinking lower into the pedicure chair. "Insufferable."

"And glowing," he added, raising his mimosa in a toast. His smirk turned sly. "Bridges, baby. They suit you."

"Okay, my love. I'll be back in a couple of hours to pick you up

for dinner."

Jones and I froze mid-sip. That voice was impossible to mistake. Jaxon's movie-star drawl, smooth as butter, rehearsed like every line he'd ever spoken was meant for an audience.

I didn't have to look to know. But I did anyway—because I'm a masochist, apparently.

There he was, standing at the counter with Jessica on his arm. She was all glossy hair, glowing skin, and a smile so wide it had to be powered by smug.

Jones caught my eye over the rim of his mimosa, eyebrows shooting up. Our silent conversation went something like: *Of all the nail salons in Chicago...* But we are all at the same hotel, so maybe I should have been the one to think better of coming to this one.

Jessica giggled, pressing a hand against Jaxon's chest like she was in a romcom no one asked to watch. "I'm nervous about tonight," she said, her voice pitched high enough to make my nail tech wince. "It's the first time I'll be around your family. And her."

Her.

Like I was Voldemort. Or a rattlesnake she had to step over in her designer sandals.

Jones nearly choked on his drink, coughing into his towel. *"Her?"* he mouthed at me, eyes gleaming with the kind of feral joy only best friends get when the drama goes nuclear.

"Shut up," I hissed at him, pinching his thigh under the towel so hard he yelped loud enough to make my nail tech snort.

And then Jaxon's voice carried across the room again. Confident. Carefree. Like he wasn't dropping bombs in the middle of a damn spa.

"Nothing to be worried about," he soothed, his tone dripping with movie-star reassurance. "Tonight and the rest of the week will be fine. And we'll tell her and the kids once all the wedding stuff settles down."

My stomach dropped. My throat went tight.

Jones's eyes bulged, his mimosa glass frozen halfway to his mouth. *Tell her and the kids?* His look screamed.

Jaxon leaned down, pressing a kiss to Jessica's temple like they were the leads in some Hallmark knockoff. "I can't wait to tell the world you're about to become my wife."

And then—God—he rested his hand on her stomach. Tender. Public. Final.

I couldn't breathe. My chest was hollow, my pulse hammering in my ears like it was trying to escape. This wasn't just my ex-husband flaunting my twenty-two-year-old replacement. This was him *cementing* it. Building a new family right there in front of me, announcing it like I was already a relic.

I knew she was pregnant. That wasn't news. The tabloids had made sure of that weeks ago. But hearing him say it out loud—watching him touch her belly like it was the crown jewel of his life, like she was his clean slate? That was a different kind of torture.

It's one thing to know. Another thing entirely to have it shoved in your face—his voice dripping with promise, his hand spread possessively over her stomach. His new beginning.

And me? I was background noise. Past tense. The woman who raised his kids and got written out of the story.

Yeah, it fucking sucked. Not because I wanted him back — but because it never feels good to be discarded by someone who once held your whole life in their hands.

Jones slid his hand over mine, squeezing so hard it hurt. His eyes never left me, sharp and protective and absolutely ready to launch into battle.

"Don't you dare cry," he whispered, low enough for only me to hear. "Not here. Not in front of *her.*"

Too late. My eyes burned. And Jessica…pregnant, glowing, smug Jessica…was turning toward the pedicure chairs, headed straight for us. And then, there it was…*eye contact.*

"Sev!" she said, startled, stopping mid-step like she'd just seen a ghost. "Hi."

"It's *Sevynn,*" Jones cut in before I could open my mouth. He enunciated every syllable like he was teaching kindergarten phonics. "*Sev. Ynn.* Can you say Sevynn?"

"Jones…" I hissed, swatting his arm, though my lips twitched against my will. "Hi, Jessica. How are you?"

"Good. Good." She beamed, her teeth practically glinting under the salon lights. "The morning sickness is finally letting up now that I'm out of the first trimester." She placed a glowing little palm over her stomach like she was presenting the Holy Grail.

My jaw locked. My pulse pounded.

It's a felony. It's a felony. It's a felony, I chanted silently, because the urge to slap that hand right off her belly was alive and thriving.

Jones leaned toward me, voice a low whisper only I could hear. "Girl, I'll hold her down if you do it."

I choked on a laugh and turned it into a cough, shaking my head like I was clearing my throat instead of trying not to commit assault.

"Yeah, I heard," I said, because apparently my manners hadn't completely disintegrated. My smile felt brittle, sharp. "Congratulations. That's... big news."

Jessica's grin widened, oblivious. "Thank you! Jaxon's so excited. We can't wait for you and the boys to meet the baby. It's going to be such a special time for all of us."

Special. Sure. If by special she meant me slowly rotting from the inside out while she lived my life in real time.

Jones leaned forward in his chair, flashing Jessica a smile so sugary it could rot teeth. "We are so... so happy for you, Josie, is it? Anyway—just *thrilled*. Babies, booties, and blessings." He waved a hand like he was sprinkling confetti, then tilted his head toward me with a wicked grin.

"But *girlfriend* here and I were just discussing the man who absolutely ravaged her *special* vagina for hours last night until she was limping."

"What? Why?!" I hissed, nearly kicking over my hangover cure. My nail tech froze mid-buff, eyes wide, but pretending to focus like this was just background noise.

Jones wasn't done. Oh no, the man was on a roll. He leaned back, sipped his mimosa with exaggerated calm, and added, "So, we better get back to it—girl talk and whatnot. You enjoy your mani-pedi, *Justine*."

"Jessica," she corrected stiffly, cheeks blotching pink.

"Riiiiight," Jones said sweetly, winking at her. "So sorry about that."

I buried my face in my towel. *It's a felony. It's a felony.*

Jessica's mouth opened like she had a comeback loaded, but nothing came out. Just a little huff, her chin tipping up as she turned on her heel and clacked her way toward the polish wall. A few seconds later, she slid into the chair two stations down, phone already in hand, pretending the last thirty seconds hadn't scorched her soul.

The whole salon buzzed back to life around us, but my body was still vibrating.

"Jones," I groaned, covering my face with my hands. "You did not just do that."

"Oh, I absolutely did," he purred, taking another slow sip of his mimosa. "And you're welcome."

"I'm mortified."

"And glowing," he added, smug as ever.

And damn it... he wasn't wrong. My cheeks were burning, my pulse was still racing, and for the first time since I'd seen Jaxon and Jessica together, I didn't feel like I was drowning.

I wouldn't admit it out loud—not if you paid me—but for

just a flicker of a moment, it felt good.

Really, fucking good.

My phone buzzed in my lap. I glanced down, still smiling in spite of myself over Jones' performance, only to feel my stomach do a full Olympic dive.

Derrick: *You still coming to lunch with me, Marley, and Dad?*

Dad.

Not *Jaxon and Jessica,* thank God. Just my boys and their father. But still — the thought of sitting across a table from Jaxon, with our kids between us like some broken bridge, made my chest ache. I haven't been in the same room with Jaxon since we signed our divorce papers.

I stared at the screen a beat too long, chewing my bottom lip.

Jones clocked my expression instantly. He leaned over, lowering his sunglasses (because of course he wore sunglasses inside a nail salon). "What now?"

I tilted the phone so he could see.

"Lunch," he read aloud in a whisper, then whistled low. "Ooooh. With the boys and Daddy Dearest. No Jessica?"

"No Jessica," I said, relief and dread twisting together.

He leaned back in his chair, smirking. "So basically a cage match with emotional consequences. Don't worry, I'll light a candle for you."

I elbowed him, but my chest still felt tight.

Because no matter how badly I wanted to avoid it, these were the moments that mattered. Derrick and Marley deserved a mom who could sit at the same table as their father without combusting.

I typed back a quick *Yes. Be there soon,* and hit send before I could change my mind.

"I'll change and head that way once we're done. Thanks again for letting me crash in your room."

Jones didn't even look up from his mimosa. "As long as you don't come climbing into my bed with your horny, heterosexual vagina after margaritas again, we're golden, baby."

Like clockwork...

10 | SEVYNN

"Hey, Mom. Where's your personal bodyguard?"

Derrick's voice carried across the lobby before I even spotted him, that familiar mix of teasing and affection rolled into one.

He was the first out of his seat, all six-foot-something of him crushing me in a bear hug that nearly cracked my ribs. "God, Derrick," I wheezed, laughing into his shoulder, "are you trying to finish me off before the wedding?"

"Just making sure you still eat more than kale and tequila shots," he fired back, grinning as he finally released me.

Before I could catch a breath, Marley was right behind him, gangly limbs and broad shoulders swooping me up like he was still twelve. His arms slung around me, chin digging into the top of my head. "Missed you, Ma."

I squeezed him tighter, heart clenching. "Missed you too, baby."

"You smell like mimosas," Marley muttered into my hair, smirking when he pulled back. "Been hanging with Jones again?"

"Of course she has," Derrick cut in, shaking his head with

mock exasperation. "I'm shocked he isn't right here beside her with a towel turban and a martini."

Marley snorted. "No thanks. He flirts with me every time he comes around. I'm afraid for my ass."

"Marley Joseph Moore!" I gasped, swatting his arm while Derrick doubled over laughing.

"What?!" Marley threw his hands up, grinning despite himself. "The man looks at me like I'm dessert. It's terrifying."

"Terrifying?" Derrick barked, wiping a tear from his eye. "More like humbling. Jones only flirts with people he thinks are pretty, bro. Take the compliment."

Marley groaned, dragging a hand down his face. "This is my life, now. My family thinks it's hilarious to auction me off to Mom's hot best friend."

"Ahh, so you *do* think he's hot?" I smirked, leaning in just to twist the knife. "Did you hear that, Derrick?"

"Oh, I heard it loud and clear." Derrick grinned wickedly. "Should I text Jones now? Let him know you've been daydreaming?"

"Don't you dare," Marley snapped, pointing at both of us like we were feral children. His ears were red now, which only made it better. "And besides—I've seen him kiss Mom on the lips. Eww."

I bit my lip to keep from laughing, but failed miserably. "Relax, baby. No one's auctioning you off. Our kisses are harmless. You don't need to worry about that."

"I'm straight, *Mother*. A small little detail you both seem to be forgetting."

Derrick and I exchanged a quick, knowing glance while Marley went back to his bread, cheeks blazing, ears crimson, doing a piss-poor job of hiding it.

I let out a quiet sigh of relief that Jaxon wasn't here. Not yet, at least.

"You got this, Mom," Derrick said knowingly, reaching across the table to squeeze my hand. His eyes were steady, his voice low but firm. "*Seriously*. You got this."

God, how did I get so lucky with them?

Neither Derrick nor Marley had wanted to invite Jaxon to the wedding. Neither had been quick to offer forgiveness. And honestly? I couldn't blame them. It's not like I've forgiven him either. I don't think that's something a person ever really does. What we have is more of a truce. A mutual acknowledgment that our boys still need us—even if they're technically grown, parenting doesn't just end the second they turn eighteen.

To look at Derrick, you wouldn't guess he's only twenty-three. Six-foot-two, broad shouldered, with a full dirty-blonde beard and shoulder-length hair that might as well be his crown and glory. He's not just older in appearance—he's wise, steady and sure of himself.

At eighteen, he took his inheritance and bought a house. Renovated it. Flipped it. Turned it into a small fortune. And he didn't stop there—he's spun it into a legitimate business, all while knocking out his college degree in record time. That's Derrick. He's always known what he wanted, and he's never been afraid to chase it.

So, no, it doesn't shock me that he's marrying young. Do I wish he'd wait, give himself a few more years, really make sure Simmy is the right girl for him? Absolutely. But if there's one thing I've learned, it's that Derrick's not the type you can steer off course. He's the type you support and pray for, even when you're not sure he's ready.

Marley, on the other hand...

Marley is twenty-three now, trailing just ten months behind his brother—and let's just say "level-headed" isn't exactly in his repertoire. He's changed his major four times, given me two pregnancy scares that shaved ten years off my life, and somehow manages to run out of gas on a weekly basis.

His inheritance? Gone before he even hit nineteen.

We'd been determined not to interfere when it came to their money—figured it was theirs to learn from. Hindsight being 20/20, I wish I'd built a few more guardrails. Just in case.

Marley is chaos in human form. Beautiful, frustrating, lovable chaos. He's just as tall and broad as his brother, though where Derrick wears his height like armor, Marley wears his like a threat. Both of them stand well over six feet, which still leaves me wondering where the hell it came from—Jaxon barely scrapes five-nine, and me? I top out at five-four on a good day, in boots.

Marley wears his heart on his sleeve—reckless, unapologetic. A flirt, a shameless womanizer most days, though I've always feared that side of him was a shield. Derrick and I have long suspected Marley wasn't being fully transparent about his sexuality. That suspicion was solidified the night of prom, when we walked in on him feverishly kissing Andrew Forus behind the house… while his date, Leslie, waited inside.

We never said a word. Not to him, not to anyone. He never knew we saw. And we sure as hell never told Jaxon. God forbid—that man would keel over at the thought of his sons being anything other than ladies' men.

Marley tries not to check out attractive men, and for the most part he hides it well. Unless, of course, you're his mother. Or his brother.

But when he falls—into something, or someone—he dives headfirst. No half-measures. And I love that about him. That reckless willingness to hand over his whole self, even if it means crashing and burning.

And here they were now—my boys—flanking me at the table. One calm, steady flame; the other a wildfire threatening to burn the place down. Reminding me without saying a word that no matter what else had been ripped apart in my life, this was still mine. They were still mine.

"Are you getting cold feet yet, Ricky?" Marley asked, his words muffled as he tore into the bread basket like he hadn't eaten in weeks. He slathered what seemed like a half stick of butter onto a single roll, then shoved it in his mouth before Derrick could even answer. "Not too late to come to your senses, man." He mumbled through chewing.

Derrick's jaw ticked, but he kept his cool—he always does. He folded his napkin neatly over his lap, like the responsible adult he's been since he was fifteen, and gave his brother a look that landed somewhere between *amused* and *stop talking before I kill you.*

"Not a chance," Derrick said evenly, reaching for his water instead of rising to the bait. "Simmy's the best thing that's ever happened to me."

Marley groaned dramatically, rolling his eyes. "That's exactly what people say right before they end up on *Divorce Court*."

"Marley," I cut in, giving him the patented *Mom Voice* I hadn't had to use in years. "Let your brother breathe."

Derrick just shook his head, smirking into his glass. "I'm good, Mom. Don't worry. He's just jealous."

Marley's head snapped up, eyes wide like Derrick had just accused him of murder. "Dude. *Jealous?*" He slapped his hand against the table for emphasis, nearly sending the butter dish flying. "Have you *seen* the women at Tulane? Google it, bitch. I got all the pu—" His eyes flicked to me, and for once his brain caught up with his mouth. "—*women*. I got all the *women* I need within a ten-mile radius."

I pressed my napkin to my mouth to hide my laugh. "Smooth save."

Derrick rolled his eyes. "You're an idiot."

"And yet," Marley said with a wink, reaching for another roll, "I'm a happy idiot."

"My boyyyyyyysssssssss."

That voice. Too loud. Too familiar. My stomach sank.

"Fucking hell, I hoped he just forgot," Derrick muttered, his composure cracking as he slammed his napkin onto the table and stood. A flash of the boy who still carried the weight of betrayal under all that maturity.

"Be nice," I whispered under my breath, even though I knew I was asking for the impossible.

"Hey, Dad. Glad you could make it." Derrick's tone was clipped, too sharp around the edges, but he corrected himself just enough as he stepped forward. The hug that followed was stiff, all male-coded shoulder claps and unspoken tension.

"Hey, Dad." Marley didn't bother standing, didn't even glance up from the bread basket. His voice was flat, heavy with disinterest as he kept tearing into another roll.

"Hey Derrick, hey Mar."

Jaxon's eyes flicked between them, his smile tugging just a little tighter as he tried to play it casual. Then his gaze landed on me.

He rubbed a hand across my back in a way that felt both too familiar and too foreign, then leaned down to press a kiss against my cheek. The kind of greeting that would look normal to anyone else, but to me? It was a minefield.

"Hey, Sev," he murmured, low and smooth. "Good to see you."

I forced a polite smile, every muscle in my face aching with the effort. "You too."

But the truth sat in my chest like a stone: no, it wasn't.

"Four-day wedding, huh, big guy?" Jaxon said as he patted Derrick's shoulder on his way past, sliding into the chair beside him like he belonged there. "Me and your mom did a shotgun wedding at the courthouse, and we were happy as ever."

My jaw clenched so hard I thought I might chip a molar. *Happy as ever.* Right. Tell that to the hotel balcony and the twenty-two-year-old clinging to his arm.

Derrick's mouth tightened, but he didn't bite. He just adjusted his napkin, polite to a fault, the tension rolling off him in waves.

Marley, on the other hand, let out a scoff that turned into a half-snort. He tore another roll in half, slathered it with butter, and shoved it into his mouth like this was his own personal stage. He raised his hand to flag down the server, barely sparing Jaxon a glance. "Can I have a beer, please?"

Derrick pinched the bridge of his nose. I pressed my fingers into my temples. And Jaxon? He just laughed, loud and easy, like we were all playing our parts in his sitcom.

We all did our best impression of a normal family, making small talk about work and busy schedules while pretending the air wasn't thick enough to cut with a steak knife.

I ordered a salad—mostly because my stomach couldn't handle much more than lettuce and regret. Derrick and Marley both went for the biggest burgers on the menu. If there's one thing my boys will always agree on, it's that ground beef is a food group. Honestly, if you gave them a football field full of burgers, they'd treat it like a personal challenge.

Jaxon, of course, ordered the steak. Medium rare. Always medium rare. Because in his world, *"men eat medium rare steaks."* He'd told the boys that so many times it might as well have been carved into the damn family crest. He called it raising men; I called it performative masculinity.

When the food arrived, I could've cried from relief. At least chewing gave us an excuse not to keep scraping together polite conversation from the scraps of our fractured history. I pushed my fork through the lettuce, nodding along as the boys devoured their plates like they hadn't eaten in days.

The truth was, this lunch wasn't about catching up. It was a formality—a necessary evil to soften the edges before the wedding madness really began. Derrick had been the one to suggest it. His logic: if we had to invite their father, maybe it was better to deal with him here, in broad daylight over burgers, rather than our first collision happening tonight at the welcome dinner with all the extended family watching.

One hundred and fifty people. Family. Friends. In-laws. All smiling, sipping wine, waiting for the bride and groom to make their entrance.

And me, across the room from my ex-husband and his glowing fiancée.

My stomach turned, and it wasn't because of the salad.

Jaxon was the first to clear his plate, setting his fork down with a satisfied sigh. While the rest of us were still working through burgers and salad, he pulled out his phone and lit up the screen, scrolling with his thumb.

"Alright," he said, tone casual but with that hint of command he always carried. "Tonight's the welcome dinner, but I don't see the rest of the events in here. I broke my old phone last month, so I lost everything. Give me the rundown so I can add it to this one, Derrick."

Derrick's shoulders stiffened, and for the first time all lunch, his composure wavered. He dabbed at his mouth with his napkin, buying himself a beat before responding.

"I already emailed you the full itinerary when we sent it out to the rest of the family," Derrick said evenly, though his jaw was tight. "You should have it."

"I didn't see it," Jaxon pressed, tapping at his screen. "Come on, big guy, just rattle it off. I'll put it in now."

I glanced at Derrick, who was sitting straighter now, spine like a steel rod. He didn't look at me, didn't look at his father—he just lifted his water glass with intentional calm, like if he held it any tighter it might shatter.

Derrick set his glass down with care, then leaned back in his chair, the picture of restraint. "Fine. Tonight is the welcome dinner," he began, his tone flat and efficient, like he was reading off a work agenda. "Tomorrow we've got the family games in the morning—think sack races, trivia, the kind of icebreakers Simmy's family is obsessed with—followed by the bachelor / bachelorette parties tomorrow night. No parents allowed, sorry. Friday morning is recovery for everyone. We'll all be hungover; that night is the rehearsal and the rehearsal dinner. Saturday is the ceremony, plus the reception that's supposed to go until midnight. Sunday morning is the farewell brunch and the gift opening."

He ticked them off on his fingers, precise and clipped, never once glancing at his father. "That's the whole weekend. Four days. You're caught up."

Jaxon nodded, thumbs flying as he tapped the events into his phone. "Got it. Appreciate it."

Across the table, Marley let out a snort. "Yeah, welcome to *Weddingpalooza 2025.* Don't forget the matching T-shirts and family Olympics."

I shot him a look, but Derrick's mouth twitched at the corner, just barely. He smoothed it away before Jaxon could notice, taking another sip of his water like this was business, not personal.

But I knew better.

This wasn't just logistics. This was Derrick holding the line. Marley lobbing grenades. And Jaxon pretending everything was fine while my boys made it clear he was no longer in charge of a damn thing.

"Hey, Sev, could we step to the bar and chat real quick?" Jaxon asked casually, like he was asking for the salt. He took another sip of his water, then pushed back from the table, already rising to his feet.

"That's not a good idea, Dad."

Derrick stood too, tall and steady, his six-foot-two frame casting a shadow over Jaxon's five-nine. It wasn't just height— it was presence. Authority. A son protecting what was left of his mother's peace.

"It's fine, love."

I placed a hand on Derrick's arm, squeezing gently before squaring my shoulders and standing. My pulse was a drumbeat in my ears, but my chin stayed high. "It's fine," I repeated. "I've got it."

I led the way toward the bar, each step deliberate. I refused—absolutely refused—to walk at his heels ever again.

When we reached the empty stretch of bar top, Jaxon

pulled out a chair for me like muscle memory. The gesture used to come with tenderness; now it felt like theater. I kept my expression neutral, sliding into the seat, allowing it because composure was a weapon too.

He sat beside me, turning slightly so his body angled toward mine. His eyes searched my face with the kind of familiarity I didn't want him to still have.

"How you doing, Sev?" he asked softly, like we hadn't been living on opposite sides of a scandal. Like the answer wasn't obvious.

I folded my hands on the bar, spine straight, forcing myself to meet his gaze.

"Depends on how honest you want me to be."

"Well, I just want to make sure we're okay," Jaxon said, lowering his voice like we were co-conspirators instead of exes. "We've got a lot of eyes on us this week, and..." He paused, smoothing a hand over his jaw in that practiced, camera-ready way. "I've got a role I'm up for."

There it is. The real reason. Not peace. Not the boys. Not *me.* His career. His image. The eternal lighthouse guiding every one of his decisions.

He cleared his throat, leaning in just slightly. "Lou saw you last night in the lobby, Sev, making out with some guy."

My stomach dropped, but I kept my face still, fists clenched. Of course. The man who'd publicly humiliated me with a pregnant twenty-two-year-old had the audacity to clutch pearls over me kissing someone in a hotel lobby.

I smiled—sweet, sharp. "Did your brother also see you on

that hotel balcony with your makeup artist, or was that more of a private screening?"

His jaw ticked. "That's not the same, Sev."

"No, you're right." I leaned in, just enough to force his eyes to mine. "Because mine didn't make headlines. And we're divorced. Which means I can fuck whomever I please."

His composure wavered—just a flicker, but I caught it. His eyes darted back to mine, questions simmering there, unasked.

"I just don't want this week to become... messy," he said finally. "For the boys. For me. The press is already circling, and if someone saw you—"

I cut him off with a laugh, quiet but jagged, like glass underfoot. "There it is. Not worried about me. Not worried about Derrick or Marley. Worried about you. Always you."

His jaw tightened. He lifted a hand, palm out like he could stop my words before they cut deeper. "That's not fair, Sevynn. I'm just saying—if someone saw—"

I leaned in, close enough for him to see the rage burning under my smile. "Are you going to tuck your fiancée away tonight? Hide her in the kitchen while you make nice for the cameras? Or do these rules only apply to me?"

His eyes flickered, the mask slipping for a heartbeat, and it was all I needed to see. I pressed harder, my voice dropping, laced with venom. "You don't get to drag a twenty-two-year-old pregnant sidepiece into my son's wedding and then tell me how not to embarrass you, Jax. You lost that right a long time ago."

He exhaled sharply, leaning in. "Jessica said Jones was

bragging about some man you slept with last night. Just... be careful, if it's true."

"It's true," I said simply, holding his gaze. "Anything else?"

His mouth twitched, surprise flashing across his face. "Oh. Okay. That's... surprising." He had the audacity to look pained about it.

I let out a humorless laugh. "I'm sure it is surprising to you. Anything else? Or are we done here?"

I slid off the barstool, my spine straight, my heels clicking against the floor like a drumbeat of finality. "See you and your fiancée tonight, Jaxon. Should be an *interesting* evening."

His jaw dropped, his polished composure slipping just enough for me to catch it before I turned away. Good. Let him choke on it.

I walked back to the table, my pulse thundering in my ears. My boys both looked up, eyes sharp and watchful, reading me the way only they could.

"Bye, boys," I said lightly, forcing a smile that didn't come close to my eyes. I leaned down, kissing the crown of Derrick's head, then Marley's. "I love you. See you later."

And quieter, my lips brushing each of their ears in turn: "I'm fine. Promise."

A lie.

Because the second I straightened and walked toward the exit, my chest felt like it was splintering in two. And no amount of poise could hold me together forever.

11 | LONDON

"You look…" My throat closed up, words sticking somewhere between my chest and my mouth. I shook my head, tried again. "Wow, honey. Just… wow."

Her face lit up, all soft blush and bright eyes, and I swore my knees went weak. "Simone, baby, you are a sight. Your mom would be in full-blown tears right now if she could see you."

And she would have been. Sarah would've been standing here with her hand over her mouth, mascara already running, clutching tissues she'd never actually use because she'd always end up sobbing into her sleeve.

Instead, it was just me. My very adult, very grown-ass daughter standing in front of me in her first wedding outfit of the week.

This man—my future son-in-law—was spoiling the hell out of her. And I couldn't say I hated it. Couldn't say I didn't appreciate the way her eyes sparkled, the way she carried herself like she was walking a little taller because of how loved she felt.

Her blonde curls tumbled down her back, makeup soft and simple, letting her natural beauty take center stage. She looked every inch the bride already, even if it was only the first event.

I didn't quite care for the damn plunge in the front of the dress. Deep, low, too much. I'd begged her three times already to put a camisole under it, just something, anything, to keep the neckline from taunting every man with a pulse.

"No one will notice, Dad," she'd said.

Bullshit. Everyone would notice.

But I bit my tongue, because as much as the overprotective father in me wanted to throw a blazer over her shoulders, I couldn't deny the truth staring me in the face.

She was a beautiful fucking bride if I'd ever seen one.

"You knooooowwwwww."

Oh, here we go.

Simone's voice took on that singsong tone I knew too well—the same one she used at sixteen when she tried to convince me her curfew should be midnight instead of ten.

"My boss brought his sister, Meghan, as his plus one," she went on, brushing her hands over my jacket like she was tidying me up for inspection. Her blonde curls bounced as she leaned back to assess me, then leaned in again to fuss with the lapel.

"She'll be here all week," Simone said, eyes glinting like she was setting me up for a checkmate. "She's super pretty. And single. Did I mention she's single?"

I groaned, tipping my head back toward the ceiling. "Simone..."

"What?" she shot back, all innocence except for the mischievous grin betraying her. "You're handsome. Kinda nerdy, sure, but in that tall-dark-and-broody way women eat up. You clean up nice. Don't give me that look."

My head snapped down, scandalized. "Nerdy?!"

She just smirked, sipping her drink like she was the parent here. "Relax, Dad. It's a compliment. Nerdy is hot now. Haven't you heard?"

It was easier to let her chatter about some mythical single woman than admit what the thought stirred in me. That I hadn't been on a date in years. That I still wore my wedding ring until last night. That Sarah's absence was stitched into my bones so tightly I wasn't sure there was room for anyone else.

But Simone didn't see the weight. She just saw her dad. Alone. And maybe she thought she was fixing me.

"Meghan's... nice," she added, her voice softer now, as though she sensed the edge in my silence. "Just... think about it, okay?"

I forced a smile, tugging gently on one of her curls. "We'll see, baby girl. Let's get you married first before we start plotting my love life."

She rolled her eyes but didn't push it further.

Thank God.

My mind immediately went to Sevynn.

I'd tried knocking on her door this morning, calling her room. Nothing. The front desk told me she'd moved to a different room, no forwarding info. Just like that, she was a ghost.

And maybe she wanted it that way.

But I hadn't been able to get her off my mind all damn day. The look in her eyes when she saw the ring on the floor—it gutted me. Not anger. Not even disgust. Hurt. Like I'd confirmed the very worst thing she already believed about men. About me.

I wanted to tell her the truth. God, I wanted to. But the words caught in my throat every time, heavy and jagged like glass.

She'd asked me point-blank if I was married. And I'd said no.

It was the truth. I wasn't married. Hadn't been for five years. But it still felt like a lie, because I hadn't told her the rest. That my wife was gone. That cancer had taken Sarah from me in a slow, brutal way I still woke up sweating from. That I'd been wearing that ring because letting go of it felt like letting go of her.

I wanted to tell Sevynn all of it right then. But I didn't. Because the second I opened that door, everything would turn into pity. Into hushed voices, sympathetic looks, me being the widower again instead of just a man.

And for one night—for just one fucking night—I wanted to be numb. To forget that hollow side of me, the one carved out by loss. To just enjoy her laugh. Her sass. That spark in her eyes that made me feel alive again. To just enjoy *her*.

"You ready, old man?" Simone's voice pulled me back to the present, light and teasing, her smile too bright to ignore.

"Hey now," I grumbled, squaring my shoulders as I adjusted my jacket. "Watch it. I still gotta walk you down that aisle, remember?"

She giggled, soft and unguarded, and for a heartbeat I was looking at her as if time had folded in on itself. My baby girl again—five years old, hair flying everywhere as she tore through the living room, cheeks fat and rosy, laugh filling every corner of our house.

The memory hit like a punch to the gut. I cleared my throat, forcing it down, swallowing the emotion that threatened to crack me wide open. She didn't need my grief right now. She needed her dad.

"All set, baby girl," I said, voice steadying as I straightened my tie. I extended my arm for her to take. "Lead the way."

And when her small hand slipped into the crook of my elbow, the weight of it anchored me. My daughter. My pride. My reason.

Even if my heart was already somewhere else.

— — — — — — — — — — — — —

"Holy shit, Simone. This place is massive. Who are all these fucking people?"

"Dad." She hissed the word through clenched teeth, nudging me hard with her shoulder as her eyes flicked around the grand ballroom. "You're cursing too much again."

I smirked. "Again? I didn't know there was a quota."

She rolled her eyes, tugging at the skirt of her dress as though adjusting it would keep her nerves in check. "It's all friends and family, Dad. Some people from Ricky's job, some from mine. Just... be nice. Please. And no interrogating him."

"You mean the boy who didn't ask me for my daughter's hand? Who I haven't even met in person? Who you're marrying in less than two months after knowing for less than a year? That guy?"

Simone stopped dead, arm snapping out of mine like I'd shocked her. She planted her fists on her hips, blue eyes blazing. "Don't start."

I held both hands up in mock surrender. "I kid. I kid." My grin softened as I leaned closer, lowering my voice so only she could hear. "I'll behave. Scout's honor and all that."

She narrowed her eyes, unconvinced. "Yeah, I've heard that only a million times before."

I chuckled, shaking my head. "And yet, here we are. Me in a suit. You, looking like the goddamn cover of a bridal magazine. Clearly, I'm capable of miracles."

Her lips twitched, but she fought the smile. "Don't make me regret bringing you, old man."

I looped her arm through mine again, squeezing just enough for her to feel it. "Never gonna happen, baby girl."

But the second Simone spotted Ricky across the ballroom, she ripped away from me like a shot. Half power-walk, half jog, curls bouncing as she closed the distance.

I had about two seconds to process before he was scooping her up, one arm slung around her waist while the other casually held a flute of champagne. Massive. Confident. Comfortable enough to show everyone in the room she was his.

Her arms wrapped around his neck, and then they were kissing—unapologetic, in the center of the crowd, like they were the only two people alive.

God. I wasn't sure I was going to make it through this week.

I felt it before I saw it—the subtle shift in the air, the way her voice lifted as she tugged him closer. "Come, meet my dad."

And then his eyes found mine. So it begins.

What gutted me at the moment wasn't just him. It was Simone. The way she clung to his arm like it was her anchor. The way she tilted her face up toward him, smiling wide, like he was the safest place in the whole world. Just like she used to do with me when she was little. When I was the one she believed could fix anything.

I stuffed the ache down hard, buried it under the armor I'd built years ago, and forced my lips into a smile. For her. Always for her.

"Dad," Simone said, glowing as she tugged the mountain of a man closer. "This is Ricky. Ricky, this is my dad, London."

The kid set his champagne down on a passing tray and extended his hand without hesitation. His grip was firm, steady, his eyes locked on mine with the kind of confidence that made my chest tighten.

"Mr. Pierce," he said, voice calm but sure. "It's good to

finally meet you in person, sir."

Sir. Jesus, I was officially the old man in the room.

"Ricky," I returned, squeezing back just as firmly. "Heard plenty about you."

"Hopefully good things," he said with the faintest smile, though I could tell he already knew better.

Simone elbowed me before I could answer, all but hissing, "Dad."

I cleared my throat, plastering on a smile. "She's said you've got drive; I'll give you that. Business degree, flipping houses. Ambitious."

He didn't flinch. Just nodded once. "I work hard. And I love your daughter."

Simone practically vibrated with pride, squeezing his arm as though to punctuate the point.

"Well," Ricky said after a beat, glancing toward the cluster of people gathered near the stage, "why don't I introduce you to my family? They've been dying to meet you both."

"Oh, joy," I muttered under my breath, but Simone caught it and gave me a look sharp enough to slice steel.

I straightened my jacket, forcing another smile as Ricky led us across the room. Because like it or not, this was the beginning.

Nerves started licking up my spine, the kind that made it impossible to stand still. My hands went restless — straightening my jacket, smoothing the front of my shirt, fiddling with the crease of my pants like the right angle of fabric could save me. I even glanced down at my shoes, checking for scuffs I knew weren't there.

"Guys," Ricky's voice rang out, clear and steady, "this is Simmy and her dad, London."

I forced my hands still, pulled my shoulders back. When my mind finally caught up and I lifted my gaze—

I saw her.

Sevynn.

Her eyes locked on mine, just for a second, and the air punched clean out of my lungs. She flicked her gaze between me and Simone, confusion sparking, anger shadowing, a hundred questions written in the space of a heartbeat.

The room kept moving—laughter, glasses clinking, the swell of conversation—but all of it blurred. My pulse roared in my ears. The only thing clear and sharp was her.

Ricky gestured as he finished the introductions. "This is my mom, Sev. This is her ex-husband, Jaxon, our close family friend, Jones and my brother, Marley."

Her name sat heavy in the air between us, her presence undeniable, her stare pinning me to the spot.

The woman who wrecked me in the best and worst ways yesterday, now sitting here as the mother of the groom, the man marrying my daughter.

Fuck.

12 | SEVYNN

What the fuck do you mean, Dad? Like Daddy? Like Daughter's Daddy? Simmy? Simone?

I'm spiraling. It's hot. It's wrong. It's so wrong. Ohhhh fuck. Oh fuck, oh fuck.

"Nice to meet you both," Marley said, standing and offering his hand.

"You're as beautiful as Derrick described, Simmy," Jaxon added smoothly, then turned to London like he wasn't detonating a bomb. "Nice to meet you, London. I'm Jaxon, Derrick's *father*, and this is my girlfriend, Jessica."

Girlfriend. Jessica. Of course. Kill me now.

"Mom," Derrick whispered, his voice tight, as he leaned down to my ear. "Are you okay?"

"Me?!" *I'm yelling.* "Me?" *Better. Sort of.* "I'm fine. Super fine."

I scrambled to my feet, knocking my napkin to the floor, and reached across the table to Simmy. "So nice to meet you, Simmy. Nice to meet you, Lon—Lon—"

"London," he supplied, voice low and steady, eyes locked on mine with the same horror itching under my skin.

Jones' eyes snapped up from across the table, wide as saucers, silently screaming the obvious at me: *Yes, London Bridges, Jones. I fucking know!*

"Right. Yes. London." My laugh cracked in half. I backed away so fast my chair screeched against the floor. "I'm so sorry, I'm just going to run to the ladies' room and panic—PEE. Fuck. I mean powder my nose."

I clapped my hand over my mouth, heat flooding my face. "Excuse me."

And then I bolted, praying for the ground to split open and drag me under before I had to go sit next to the man whose cock I'd had in my mouth less than twenty-four hours ago. And everywhere else. And I do mean everywhere.

"I could use the little girls' room, also," Jones announced grandly, trailing me step-for-step as we sped down the hallway. He shoved us both into the nearest family restroom and locked the door with a dramatic click.

"Bitch."

"Oh my God, Jones. Oh, my *GOD*." I clutched the sink like it might save me from drowning, my reflection already blotchy and wide-eyed.

He fanned himself with his hand. "That man is *fuckable fine*, Sev. I mean lick-me-up-and-down, risk-it-all fine. And now we know he's not just fine—he's *daddy* fine."

"Jones!" I shrieked, covering my face with my hands.

"What?" He shrugged like he was reading a brunch menu. "If London Bridges wants to fall down on me, I'll bring the nursery rhymes."

I groaned into my palms. "The universe fucking hates me. That's the only explanation. How else could this have happened?"

Jones leaned his hip against the sink, arching one perfectly groomed brow. "Well, honey, maybe because you decided to audition for *Cougar Town* the literal night before meeting your son's future in-laws?"

"Stop talking."

He snorted, looping his arm through mine and squeezing. "Relax. Nobody knows except you, me, and your vagina. Which, by the way, deserves a standing ovation for last night's performance."

"Jones!"

"What?!" He grinned, unbothered, tugging me upright. "You should be thanking me. If I weren't here, you'd be crying into the complimentary hand towels."

I dropped my head against his shoulder, groaning. "I'm never leaving this bathroom." I whined.

"Oh, you're leaving," he said, smug. "You're going to reapply your lipstick, lift your tits, and march back out there like you didn't just deep-throat your future in-law's dad. Scout's honor."

I slapped his chest, mortified. "Why are you this way?"

"Because I'm fabulous and you'd be dead without me," he sing-songed, digging in his pocket for a compact.

And, God help me, he wasn't wrong.

"Wait here."

Before I could argue, Jones flung the door open, slipped into the hallway, and was back in under thirty seconds like some kind of Queer James Bond. The door clicked shut behind him, and he was holding a silver tray stacked with four champagne flutes.

"Jones," I gasped, eyes wide. "Did you just—"

"Steal these? Absolutely." He set the tray dramatically on the counter, like a magician unveiling his trick. "Three for you, one for me. Drink up, bitch. Tonight just got interesting."

I blinked at the glasses, then at him. "Are you trying to get me drunk or arrested?"

"Both," he said without hesitation, handing me two flutes at once. "But mostly drunk. Because, honey, you cannot panic-sweat your way through meeting your son's fiancée while looking like you just walked out of a sex scandal."

"I *did* just walk out of a sex scandal!" I whisper-yelled, clutching both glasses like they were grenades.

"Semantics," Jones said, already sipping his own champagne like the civilized half of this duo. "Now, bottoms up. By the time we get back out there, you'll be glowing so hard no one will question why London Bridges is staring at you like he wants a second helping of your Sevynn layer dip."

"Jones!"

"What? I'm rooting for you!"

I groaned, knocking back one flute in three gulps. "I hate you."

"You love me," Jones corrected, passing me the third flute. "And you're welcome."

I tipped all three glasses back like they were shots of tequila, my throat burning, my head buzzing instantly. By the time I set the empties on the counter, Jones had already unpacked what he proudly called his *panic bag*—a Mary Poppins-level arsenal of makeup, blotting papers, perfume, and God knows what else.

"Why do you even have this?" I asked, eyes squinting as he dabbed concealer under them.

"Because, bitch," he said, snapping his compact shut with a flourish, "I knew something was gonna go down. I just didn't know what or when. And now look at you—*crisis chic.*"

By the time he was done, I looked flawless. Like a woman who had her life together. Even if my eyes screamed, *I'm drunk* and my insides screamed *I'm spiraling.*

We made our way back to the table, my heels clicking too loud in my ears, Jones strutting beside me like a bodyguard who also knew how to contour.

My boys' eyes bounced nervously between me and him. Derrick was the first to move, rising from his chair to pull me into a hug, his tall frame bending over mine.

"You okay, Mom?" he whispered, voice low enough that no one else could hear.

"Yes, baby. I'm okay." The lie slipped out too smoothly, practiced.

I slid back into my seat, Jones dropping into his across from me with a wink and a smug little nod, like he'd just landed the plane after both engines blew.

"I'm sorry for running out like that, everyone," I said, clearing my throat, trying to soften the sharp edges of champagne still coating my voice. "Lunch isn't agreeing with me. Luckily, Jones brought some antacids."

Jones clinked his water glass like a toast. "You're welcome again."

I forced a smile, turning toward Simmy. "But seriously — Simmy, you look absolutely breathtaking."

Her eyes softened, her cheeks pinking under the compliment, and for one blessed second, the storm at the table calmed.

"Sevynn."

London said my name like it was something decadent on his tongue, slow and thick, and it hit me low in my stomach. His voice had this deep, growly quality that made my thighs clench under the table before my brain could even scold me.

"That's a beautiful name, by the way."

Stop talking. *Stop talking.*

"Your boys were just giving me their backstories," he went on, eyes steady on mine. "You've got some pretty impressive kids there."

I swallowed hard, forcing myself to glance down at my napkin before I said something wildly inappropriate. "Thanks," I managed, my voice steadier than I felt. "They are the very best of me, that's for sure."

Instinctively, I reached out to either side—my hands brushing Derrick's sleeve on my right, Marley's on my left. They sat like perched protectors, silent but alert, like they could sense the shift in me.

And that's when Jaxon decided to chime in.

"Well, of course they're impressive," Jaxon said smoothly, leaning back in his chair with that self-satisfied grin I used to mistake for charm. "Look who their father is."

The table went quiet for a beat too long, the kind of silence that wasn't silence at all—it was a taut wire about to snap. You could practically taste the tension in the air.

I forced my lips into a smile, nails digging crescent moons into my palms beneath the tablecloth. Because if London's voice made me clench, Jaxon's arrogance made me want to vomit.

"Well, I'd argue that I get my business mind from Mom," Derrick said evenly, his tone as calm as if he were reading off a grocery list. "And Marley gets his reckless abandon and disregard for the emotional well-being of others from you, Dad."

My head snapped toward him so fast I swore something in my neck popped. Derrick didn't even flinch. He just lifted his glass, sipping his drink like he hadn't just thrown Jaxon *and* his brother under the same barreling bus and set it on fire.

"Damn," Marley muttered around a mouthful of bread, raising his glass in mock salute. "Thanks, Ricky."

Jaxon's jaw tightened, the smug curve of his mouth faltering for the briefest moment. But he chuckled anyway, a hollow, practiced sound that didn't reach his eyes.

And me? I wanted to hug Derrick and ground him for life in the same breath.

"Simmy, is your mother able to make it tonight? I'm looking forward to meeting the rest of your family." I point a razer edged eye at London, reminding myself that even though his beautiful eyes keep gazing over at me that he's a selfish fucking liar that turned me into Jessica of all fucking people.

Derrick squeezed my hand underneath the table as Simmy cleared her throat. London's eyes fell to his napkin, and I could swear I saw them welling up with tears. Yeah, fucking choke on it, you bastard.

"My mom, uhh...she passed away five years ago. This weekend, actually, will be the anniversary of her death."

Oh. My. God. Earth swallow me now.

"Derrick suggested that we get married on that date so she'd be with us in spirit in a way, you know? Turn that day into something special, instead of always dreading it when it rolls around." She reached over and grabbed London's hand. "That's why it seems fast; I couldn't say no to that."

Tears spilled down both of their faces—hers soft and steady, his raw and unguarded—as London cupped Simone's face in his hands and kissed her cheeks.

Then he stood, reaching for Derrick's hand. Derrick took it without hesitation, and London pulled him to his feet and into a tight embrace.

The whole table seemed to go still, the clink of cutlery, the hum of voices around us fading under the weight of their grief and love, bound together.

And me... I sat frozen, heat rising in my throat, realizing with a sick twist in my stomach that I had gotten London all wrong.

13 | *LONDON*

As I made my way to the front of the ballroom, my palms were slick, my chest tight. My nerves were at an all-time high. I didn't do public speaking. Put me in a room with a handful of engineers and construction guys, and I could talk shop all night. Blueprints, steel, concrete—that was my language. But this? A ballroom full of faces, crystal chandeliers, and my daughter glowing in white? Holy hell. This was different. This was making me sweat.

The alcohol didn't help. Neither did the relentless glances from Sevynn, her eyes catching mine like magnets every damn time I tried to look away.

I cleared my throat as I stepped up to the mic, adjusting it down an inch, though really I just needed the extra second to breathe. My heart hammered so hard I wondered if it was echoing through the speakers.

"Here goes fucking nothing," I muttered into the mic—forgetting it was on. The crowd broke into laughter, and my ears went hot.

I gripped the podium tighter, grounding myself. "Uh... I'll be honest with you all. I'm not a speech guy. Never have been. My daughter knows that. So if I stumble, if I say the wrong thing—just know this: what I mean will always be bigger than what I manage to say."

I looked at Simone, and my throat closed instantly. God, she was radiant. Curls caught the light. Hand wrapped around Ricky's like she'd been holding it her whole life.

"She's uhh... Simone is my baby girl," I said, the word baby cracking right out of me. "The first time I held her, I knew my life wasn't mine anymore—it was hers. I promised I'd love her enough for two. That she'd never go without, never question her worth, never feel unloved. And I know I failed sometimes. God knows I did. But looking at her tonight, strong and brilliant and so damn loved—I think maybe I didn't fail as much as I thought."

Tears blurred my vision. I laughed, shaking my head. "Told myself I'd man up and not cry. Guess I lied."

I wiped quickly at my eyes, sniffed, and pressed on. "And Ricky—son—" I looked straight at him, steady. "You've got the most important job in the world now. Loving her. Protecting her. Making her laugh. Don't bother trying to be perfect—you'll screw up, same as the rest of us. But don't you ever let her close her eyes at night without knowing she's your whole damn world. If you can do that, you'll be fine."

I swallowed hard, the lump thick in my throat.

"When my wife, Sarah—Simone's mother—passed away five years ago... it was just me and her. Before she went, Sarah told me, there would come a day I'd stand here without her, giving this speech." My voice wavered, but I forced the words through. "She asked me to tell you this, babygirl: You are the sun, the moon, the stars, my love. You are the winter, the spring, the fall, my love. Whenever you are sad, my love, remember that Mommy will always be there."

By then the tears were free falling, and I didn't care. My chest was torn wide open.

"She is with you tonight, and always, my love."

I lifted my glass, my hand unsteady, but my voice finally even.

"To Simone and Ricky. May your love be bigger than the fear. Braver than the storms. And stronger than anything that tries to take it down."

The room erupted in applause as I stepped back from the mic, but all I heard was my own ragged breathing.

Simone practically launched herself at me as I stepped down from the podium, her arms flung tight around my neck. Her cheeks were wet and rosy, pressed against mine, and I felt her whole body shake with the force of her emotions.

"I love you so damn much, Dad."

I laughed through the tightness in my throat, squeezing her just as fiercely. "Language, young lady."

She pulled back just enough to roll her eyes at me, tears clinging to her lashes. "And you're not a speech guy. Yeah, yeah. Sure, Dad."

"Whatever," I muttered, though my voice cracked with pride. I set her gently back on her feet, smoothing one of her curls like I'd done since she was five.

Her smile broke me in two.

I cleared my throat, trying to steady myself. "I'm gonna hit the little boy's room, be right back. Save me a dance."

She nodded, already pulled back to Ricky's side, glowing like she belonged nowhere else.

The tears started falling again as soon as I turned the corner, unstoppable. I swiped at them with the back of my hand, but it was no use. I didn't know what I expected out of this week, but it sure as hell wasn't to feel gutted before the first night was even over.

It was like I had to give her up every damn minute. Remind myself that she wasn't mine to protect anymore. That she wasn't the little girl with curls and scraped knees. She was an adult, stepping into her own life, her own marriage. And my job now—my only job—was to let her go.

I was still trying to swallow the bitter, acidic truth when my hand reached for the restroom door. But before my fingers could make contact, the heavy door swung inward.

And there she was.

Sevynn.

She was dabbing at the corners of her eyes with her fingertips, a futile attempt to mask the raw, telling redness. But when her gaze landed on me, her hand froze mid-air, hovering like a wounded bird.

"Sevynn," I breathed, my voice shredded by the morning's revelations and the ghost of last night's whiskey.

Her lips parted in a soft, startled expression. I watched as her spine straightened, her shoulders drawing back as if donning an invisible suit of armor. "London."

The sound of my name on her lips—that familiar, intimate syllable now laced with a new, devastating formality—nearly undid me. It was a gut punch, stealing the air from my lungs.

For a single, suspended moment, neither of us moved. Just two strangers with tear-streaked faces and a history too new and fragile to name, trapped in a hallway thick with the weight of everything left unsaid.

It felt like minutes passed, though it couldn't have been more than a few frantic heartbeats, before she cleared her throat. Her voice was steadier than her haunted eyes. "Sorry," she murmured, shifting her weight to step aside and grant me passage. A polite, final dismissal. "It's all yours."

And with that single, resigned breath, I understood. We both did. An unspoken agreement settled between us, heavy and absolute. Whatever had happened last night—whatever reckless, passionate thing we'd been to each other—it ended the moment we learned who we truly were.

I nodded, a sharp, jerky motion, swallowing hard as the cold, leaden weight of disappointment lodged itself permanently in my chest.

As we moved to pass each other in the narrow space, the back of my hand brushed against hers. Just a graze. A whisper of skin on skin. Barely a contact at all.

But her breath hitched, a sharp, audible catch in her throat. Mine stuttered in response.

The electricity was still there—undeniable, unrelenting. It had survived the alcohol, the morning-after fallout, the seismic crash of truth. It was the one real thing in this nightmare.

I couldn't let it end like this.

In one fluid motion, my fingers closed around her wrist. I gently pulled her back into the dim, quiet room, kicking the door shut behind us with a final, echoing thud.

The lock clicked into place.

Pinned against the door, her eyes were wide, a storm of confusion and want. I didn't give her time to speak. I crashed my mouth into hers. My arm wrapped around her waist, hauling her body flush against mine, and I could feel the frantic hammering of her heart against my own.

She gasped into my mouth, a sound I swallowed whole. My free hand found the hem of her dress, gathering the fabric and pushing it up her thighs. I slid my palm over the delicate lace of her panties, feeling the damp heat already seeping through. A groan ripped from my throat. Fuck.

"I need to feel you," I rasped against her lips, my voice thick with a need that felt like madness. "I'm addicted to you. I haven't been able to think of anything else. Not since last night. Not since the moment I first tasted you."

I hooked my fingers into the waistband of her panties and slid them aside. Then I plunged two fingers deep into her slick, welcoming heat.

She softly cried out, her head falling back against the door with a soft thump. Her body arched at my touch, every nerve ending screaming its approval. She was so wet, so ready, clenching around me as I thrust my fingers deep, curling them to find that spot I knew would make her unravel.

I swallowed her moans with my kiss, dragging every

sound from her like it belonged to me. It wasn't language anymore, not words — just a raw, reckless rhythm.

Then I set her on her feet, not to let her go, but to move her where I wanted her. I spun her gently but firmly, pressing her palms to the cool porcelain of the sink. "There," I murmured against her ear, my hand guiding her until she braced. "Just like that. Eyes up."

Her gaze caught mine in the mirror, wide and trembling. A storm of want and resistance. I slowly slid her dress higher, baring her inch by inch. She shivered under my touch, but didn't look away.

"Good girl." My hands mapped her hips, her waist, the curve of her back as I pressed close, grinding my heat against hers.

She gasped, her breath fogging the mirror.

"Watch yourself," I growled, eyes locked on hers in the reflection. "Watch what you do to me."

Her knuckles whitened against the sink, her lips parting on a moan as I slid inside of her. My hand shot forward, gripping the porcelain, fighting for control I was seconds away from losing.

"London—" her whisper broke, trembling on my name.

"Say it again," I demanded, my thrust harder this time, sharp enough to draw a cry from her throat.

"London," she moaned, head tipping back, eyelids fluttering shut.

"No," I rasped, my voice jagged. I cupped her chin, forcing

her to meet her own reflection, to meet my gaze in it. "Eyes open. Let me see you give in."

Her lashes lifted, icy and wild, and the sight tore a groan from my chest. I sank deeper, fingers bruising into her hip, grinding forward until every inch of me was buried in her slick, desperate heat.

"Fuck, you feel..." I couldn't finish, the words catching as I pulled back, then drove into her again, harder. Her necklace rattled against the sink, her breasts bouncing with every slam of my hips.

Her voice fractured into breathy pleas, half words, half broken sounds. "Don't stop—oh God, don't stop."

"I couldn't if I tried," I whispered against her ear, thrusts sharp and relentless. "You're mine right now. Every sound, every inch—you're mine."

I turned her, lifting her effortlessly onto the sink, her legs wrapping tight around my waist. Sliding back into her, I swallowed her cry with my mouth, kissing her hard, devouring her.

She whispered against my lips, trembling, "London... I'm—"

"Do it." My thumb circled her nipple through the thin fabric of her top, my hand gripping her ass to drive her down onto me. "Come for me, sweetheart. Right here. Right now."

Her body seized, back arching, cry shattering into my kiss. The sight and sound broke me open; I slammed deep, groaning raw into her mouth as the coil in my core snapped hard.

"Fuck—Sevynn..." My forehead pressed to hers, our heavy

breathing tangled as the room filled with the aftermath—ragged, desperate, alive.

The silence after was deafening. Just broken breaths, the faint buzz of the ballroom beyond the door, and the hard fact of what we'd just done.

Her body still trembled against mine, legs loose around my waist, lips parted like she'd forgotten how to breathe. My forehead pressed to hers, and for one second I wanted nothing more than to freeze time, keep us here, keep her mine.

But reality bled back in—our kids, the party, the dozens of people only a few feet away.

I brushed her hair back, voice rough and low. "I'm going to dream about this all night... you walking out there, glowing, with my cum still warm inside you."

Her sharp inhale cut through me, her nails flexing against my shoulders. "London..."

I kissed her again, softer this time. Not claiming, not devouring. Just... lingering. A gentleness that felt dangerous in its own way.

When I pulled back, her eyes searched mine, wide and conflicted. "We can't—"

"I know, sweetheart." I thumbed her swollen lower lip, shaking my head. "I'll go out first. Give it a minute, then follow. No one will know."

I kissed her forehead once before forcing myself to step back, to tuck myself away, to square my shoulders like I hadn't just come apart inside her in a hotel bathroom.

Then I unlocked the door, jaw tight, opened it—

And froze.

"Well, no wonder you were taking forever," the man smirked, slowly stepping into the room. "Here I thought I needed to come in and check on my bestie—but my bestie was already *coming*."

Sevynn groaned, rushing over and shoving at his chest. "Jones! Shut up." She tried to steer him back, but he bent low, scooping her into a bear hug. The door clicked shut behind him, sealing the three of us in.

"You look ravished," he purred, spinning her once, his voice deep and theatrical. "Glowing. Positively radiant. Who do I have to thank for this? Or should I say—who do I have to kill?"

My jaw locked. Every muscle in me went tight, my body coiling before I could stop it. His hand slid down her back like he was staking a claim, and it burned like a brand across my nerves. He was handsome—too handsome. Sharp jaw, broad shoulders, wavy hair that belonged in some cologne ad. And he was all over her.

Then his hand grazed down as grabbed her ass. Tight.

"Hmmm. Goddamn. This dress, baby, fuck," he teased, squeezing like it was his right.

"Put me down, you idiot!" Sevynn laughed, swatting at him, but he only tightened his grip, burying his face dramatically in her neck.

"Not until you tell me who you've been sneaking off to do filthy things with in hotel bathrooms," he crooned in a weirdly seductive growl that actually made the hairs on my neck rise. His gray eyes cut to me, sharp and smug, like he already knew.

My fists clenched. My pulse hammered so hard it drowned everything else out. I was one second away from ripping him off her.

"Jones!" Sevynn shoved at him again, finally wriggling free. She planted both palms on his chest, glaring up at him. "For fuck's sake. Behave."

He only grinned, brushing an invisible speck of lint off his designer shirt. "What? I'm just saying—he better have a jawline worth drooling over and credit that won't bounce a check, or I'm not impressed."

"God," Sevynn muttered, dragging a hand down her face before finally stepping between us, cheeks flushed. "London, this is Edward-McKenzie Jones—Jones, for short. He's my executive chef. And unfortunately, also my best friend."

Jones gasped like she'd just insulted royalty. "Unfortunately? Excuse you. I'm the best thing to happen to you since wireless vibrators."

"Why are you this way?" Sevynn hissed, shoving at his arm. "Why are you doing this to me right now? Have I done something to hurt you in a past life?"

Jones ignored her entirely, zeroing in on me with sharp gray eyes that made me feel like I was under a microscope. He crossed his arms over his broad chest and smirked—an expression that belonged on a Broadway villain right before they broke into song.

"So this... is... *him*," he said, drawing out every syllable like he was narrating the opening scene of a soap opera. "Mr. Bridges. The mystery man. The one with the dimples... and the skyscraper thighs."

My brows shot up. Sevynn groaned like she wanted the ground to open up and swallow her whole.

Then Jones leaned in, conspiratorial, cupping his hand around his mouth in the world's least subtle whisper. "And the monster cock that had her limping all day long."

"Oh, my God!" Sevynn shrieked, shoving him so hard he almost stumbled.

He just grinned wider, utterly unrepentant. "Oh please, sweetheart, you know I live for the details. I thought you were exaggerating. Turns out..." His gaze flicked to me again, lingering, "...you were severely underselling."

My brows twitched, but I stayed quiet. Who the fuck is this guy? I couldn't tell if I hated him... or respected the hell out of him.

Jones tilted his head, feigning sympathy as he rested his chin on his hand like a gossip columnist. "So tell me, London Baby—how exactly were you two planning to get out of this little kerfuffle? Hmm? Bathroom quickie, then what? Walk out separately and hope no one notices her glowing like she just swallowed the sun?"

"I'm so close to a felony right now," Sevynn whispered, eyes locked on the side of his head like she was manifesting laser vision.

I bit back a smirk. He didn't budge. "Jones to the rescue, babes. Always. Don't worry, I'll run interference. But you—"

he jabbed a finger toward me, his smirk sharp—"you're awfully quiet there, London Baby. You okay?"

I forced a breath through my nose, jaw tight. My pulse was still hammering, my instincts coiled, but I shoved a hand out across the space between us, anyway. "Sorry. No. Yes. I'm fine." My voice came out rough, clipped. "Nice to meet you."

For a beat, Jones just looked at my hand like I'd offered him a dead fish. Then, slow as hell, he slipped his into mine, squeezing just a hair too firm, smirk never wavering. "Mmm. Likewise."

Jones gave Sevynn a once-over like he was running stage directions. "Alright, here's the plan. You act drunk—real sloppy—and we'll help you out of the bathroom. Oscar-level cover. Nobody questions it."

Sevynn gaped at him. "No! I'm not pretending to be drunk."

"Baby doll, you already look drunk. Swollen lips, flushed cheeks, fresh fucked bed head. Own it."

She shoved his arm. "Absolutely not."

I'd had enough. My patience was already frayed, my pulse still hammering from what just happened. "Forget it. I'll go first. You two wait a beat, then follow."

I squared my shoulders, forced myself to look like a man who hadn't just had his mouth all over her body, and pulled the door open—

—and walked straight into a stranger standing there, hand halfway up to knock.

Fuck.

"She's drunk; we're helping!" The words shot out of me, loud, desperate, before my brain could catch up.

The guy blinked. Just stood there, eyes darting from me to the door like he'd walked in on an orgy.

I dropped my head, jaw tight.

Smooth, Pierce. Really nailed that one.

I brushed past him fast. My ears were burning, my stomach in knots.

Behind me, I heard Jones' laugh detonate—loud, unrestrained, absolutely losing his shit. "She's drunk, we're helping?" he howled. "Oh, London Baby, *you* are a treasure. I swear to God, I'm stitching that on a pillow!"

I didn't look back. Couldn't. My fists were clenched so tight my knuckles cracked, and all I could think was how badly I wanted a wall to punch—or another taste of her to drown in.

14 | SEVYNN

"So, we Pierces make a big deal out of icebreakers," Simmy announced, standing tall at the microphone like she was running the world's most chaotic TED Talk. Behind her, the hotel courtyard had been transformed into a battlefield of pure wedding-week chaos: rows of burlap sacks lined like soldiers, orange cones marking sprint lanes, balloons bobbing in buckets of water, even a tug-of-war rope coiled on the grass. Field Day: Wedding Edition. God help us all.

She lifted the bucket in front of her. It was stuffed full of folded slips of paper. She shook it with a flourish. "Today is especially important," she went on, voice bright and commanding, "because—as my Dad has relentlessly pointed out—we are, in fact, getting married pretty damn quick."

"Language!" London's voice boomed across the courtyard, deep and paternal, as if he were presiding over a courtroom instead of a sack race.

"Shush, Dad!" Simmy shot back, finger stabbing in his direction. The crowd erupted in laughter, the kind that loosened shoulders and made everyone lean in closer.

I bit the inside of my cheek to keep from grinning, though it was useless. God, she was radiant—fire and sparkle, completely unshaken.

And London? He was all blacked out. Black henley, black athletic shorts, socks and sneakers. Like a dark shadow dropped into the middle of sunshine and balloons. The shirt clung to him, hugging every line of his chest and arms, and I'd spent the better part of the last hour actively trying not to look. Not to let my gaze snag on the way his forearms flexed when he crossed them, or how the fabric stretched across his back when he leaned down to talk to someone.

Trying not to remember how those same arms had held me. How that same voice had told me to breathe.

It was ridiculous—standing in a courtyard full of laughter and family and potato sacks, and I was coming undone because the man in black across the lawn wouldn't stop existing.

"Here's the rules," Simmy announced, shaking the bucket like it held the secrets of the universe. "Pick a name, and that's your partner for the first activity... sack races!"

The courtyard rippled with reactions—half the crowd groaning, the other half laughing like kids already lining up for detention.

"Oh, honey, I can't do this one," Jessica drawled from her seat, one manicured hand resting dramatically on her barely-there bump as she leaned into Jaxon's chest. "The baby."

Jones, planted loyally at my side, leaned in with a smirk sharp enough to cut glass. "Oh, princess, sucks to be *you*." His shoulder bumped mine, and I had to bite the inside of my cheek to stop from spitting laughter right onto my mimosa.

And then—chaos.

"You and me, Mama. You and me!" Derrick barreled into my side and scooped me up like I was a rag doll instead of his fully grown mother. My squeal was instant, setting off another round of howling from the crowd.

"Put me down, you mammoth!" I shrieked, smacking at his shoulder while my legs kicked in the air. "You have to pull my name first!"

"Oh, I will," he boomed, spinning me once for good measure, grinning like a ten-year-old hopped up on Mountain Dew. "I've got a sixth sense about these things."

Laughter roared around us, and I could feel every single pair of eyes watching—family, friends, strangers all tangled in this wedding-week circus—but Derrick was unstoppable. My cheeks burned, but I couldn't help it. His joy was contagious.

"Ever the competitor," I muttered when he finally set me down, breathless, my head spinning. He just shot me that wild, boyish grin—the one I'd swear he stole straight from my own face—and for a moment, the chaos melted.

One by one, names were pulled from the bucket. Pairs formed, laughter and groans mixing until the courtyard sounded less like a wedding weekend and more like a summer camp free-for-all.

And there was Simmy—radiant, bossy, completely in her element, it seemed. She glided through the chaos with her clipboard like she was directing Broadway instead of a sack race, teasing one cousin for cheating, encouraging a little girl to take the bigger sack, redirecting anyone slow to line up. Every ounce of her father's charisma, and I bet every ounce of Sarah's warmth. God, she was beautiful. Spirited. Magnetic.

Marley tugged a slip from the bucket, unfolded it, and grinned so wide I could see it from halfway across the lawn. His partner was a girl about his age—short pixie cut, delicate features with edges sharp enough to slice. The way he flushed—deep, red ears, stupid grin—I could practically hear the love story forming in his head. That boy.

Meanwhile, Derrick was vibrating like he'd downed five espressos, bouncing on his toes, eyes locked on that bucket like it held the keys to the kingdom. I had to clap a hand over my mouth, but the sound that escaped me was a full-blown giggle. Girlish. Unrestrained. Because I knew that look.

We were sack-race champions. Every summer at Camp Pendleton—year after year, without fail—he and I had obliterated the competition. Marley had cried foul after our fourth straight win, swearing it was cheating, which, okay, it absolutely was. But neither Derrick nor I cared. We were unstoppable.

When his name finally got called, Derrick unfolded his slip slowly, milking the moment for every ounce of drama. Then he dropped to his knees, arms raised to the sky like he'd just won Olympic gold.

"Mamaaaaaaaa!" he bellowed, voice booming across the crowd.

And me—thirty-eight years old, mother of two, allegedly a responsible adult—squealed like a kid, clapped my hands, and sprinted toward the line of burlap sacks.

We high-fived so hard my palm stung, both of us doubled over laughing, grinning like idiots.

From behind us, Jaxon and Marley groaned in unison.

Of course. London and Simmy ended up together. Rigged. Had to be.

"You ready, baby?" Derrick scooped Simmy up, spinning her once before setting her down with a kiss to her cheek. "This loss is going to be brutal for you. Hope you can forgive me."

"Ohhh... Dad. Did you hear this guy?" Simmy smirked as she jogged back to her lane, high-fiving London.

"Oh, I heard him," London said, his smirk wicked—cutting straight through me like it had a target. "Should we take it easy on them?"

Shit.

"Not a chance, London Bridges," I fired back, my smirk bolder than the pulse stampeding through me. "Do your worst."

"Hell yeah, go Mom!" Marley shouted, pumping his fist like he was at WrestleMania.

Playing with fire there, Sev.

Simmy squealed, clapping her hands and bouncing like a cheerleader. "I love her! London Bridges!" She darted across the line, high-fived me, then yanked me into a hug before I could brace for it. "My mom used to call him that to piss him off all the time."

The whole crowd laughed, but my chest tightened. London's grin faltered—barely, but I caught it.

One of the event coordinators jogged to the front, clipboard in hand, raising his voice over the noise. "Alright, folks, sack racers to the line!"

The lanes stretched ahead of us, cones bright against the grass, a finish line that might as well have been the Olympic trials. Derrick and I climbed into our sack, both of us laughing before the damn thing even started. He gave me a wink—the same cocky, twelve-year-old grin I'd seen a thousand times—and I knew. We were about to dominate.

London and Simmy lined up in the next lane. She was bouncing in her sack like a kid on a sugar high, curls flying, eyes alight. London stood steady at her side, all controlled muscle and competitive tension, jaw set, eyes locked forward. And when he bent to adjust the burlap around his thighs—Jesus. My brain supplied a dozen wildly inappropriate thoughts before I could even blink.

Two lanes over, Jaxon looked like he was about to star in a Nike ad. He'd been paired with one of Derrick's groomsmen, a tall, awkward kid who clearly had zero experience in sack-based athletics. They were already bickering about footing while Jaxon puffed his chest.

The coordinator raised his hand. "Racers ready?"

Derrick bounced once beside me, gripping the edge of the sack tight. "Mom, you better keep up."

"Keep up?" I snapped my head toward him, feigning outrage. "Young man, I taught you how to win these things."

"Three!" the coordinator called. I crouched low, heart pounding in my ears.

"Two!" London glanced sideways—just once—but it was enough. Heat shot through me, sharp as the cannon's fuse.

"One!" The confetti cannon exploded, and we were off.

Derrick and I launched forward in perfect sync, years of camp practice sparking muscle memory like a switch. One jump. Two. Three. We shot ahead, laughter bubbling out of me as the crowd roared.

Simmy shrieked beside us, already veering into London's lane. "Dad, you're too slow!"

"I'm not slow; you're reckless!" London barked back, grinning even as his long legs powered them forward, every stride like a freight train.

Behind us came the inevitable: "Higher, kid, higher!" Jaxon bellowed at his poor groomsman partner right before the guy ate grass. Both of them toppled into a tangle of limbs and burlap, Jaxon popping back up like a diva rising from the ashes, brushing grass off his shirt with disgust. The crowd lost it—laughter, whistles, clapping.

"Focus!" Derrick snapped, his grip tightening around mine. "We've got this!"

"Oh, we've *got this*," I wheezed, sweat slicking my palms. My thighs burned, but I matched him hop for hop, every jump pulling us closer.

London and Simmy surged up on our flank, his stride controlled and lethal, hers chaotic but fast as hell. For one electric second, our shoulders almost collided—burlap scraping burlap, breath catching breath.

"Take it easy, Bridges," I shot, smirking through gasps.

"Not a chance," he spat back, grin feral, eyes on fire.

The crowd was on its feet now, names flying, claps echoing. Derrick whooped as we cleared the final cone, dragging me into one last push. We launched across the finish line in a blur of burlap and limbs—Simmy and London right on our heels.

The confetti gun boomed again, raining down scraps of paper like victory fireworks.

"Fuck yeah!" Derrick bellowed, hauling me upright and spinning me senseless. My laugh ripped out, wild and breathless, my stomach cramping from joy.

London and Simmy stumbled across the finish seconds later. Simmy bent over with her hands on her knees, breathless but triumphant. Jaxon and his poor partner dragged themselves in dead last, Jaxon muttering curses under his breath while the crowd doubled over in laughter.

Derrick planted me back on my feet, still grinning ear to ear, before yanking our joined hands into the air like champions. Then he was off, running to Simmy and sweeping her straight into his arms.

She tried for indignation, lips pouted, but it cracked almost immediately as laughter spilled out. "Fine, fine—you guys were great." And then, in front of everyone, she tilted her face down and kissed him deep, softening like he was the only thing in the world.

I turned away, pressing a hand to my chest as I caught my breath. My cheeks ached from smiling, my heart full in a way that nearly unmoored me. For a blissful moment, all I felt was joy.

Until I glanced at London.

His gaze lingered. Just a beat too long.

And there it was again—the fire I kept pretending wasn't there. The one that hadn't burned out, no matter how badly I wanted it to. It smoldered in his eyes, sharp and hungry, burning me alive all over again.

"Good job, Bridges," I said, forcing a lightness into my voice. "Second place isn't bad. It's not *first*—but it's not bad."

He closed the distance between us slowly, every step measured, and the air around me heated. My thighs clenched. That look in his eyes... it was the same one from that night. Dangerous. Consuming.

"Guess you don't remember what happens when you call me that," he said, voice dropping to a rumble that went straight to my nipples.

Fuck.

His gaze dipped lower, and the proof of his reaction was impossible to ignore—thick, straining, unapologetic.

My mouth curved, reckless. Taunting. "Why else do you think I said it?"

His hands flexed out at his sides, restraint fraying at the edges. He was one second away from snapping—one second away from pulling me into that heat—

And then I was lifted clean off my feet.

"Sev, baby! Just like old times." Jaxon's voice was bright, too loud, cutting through the moment like a knife. His arms locked around me, his lips brushing my neck as he spun me in a dizzying circle.

For a brief, nauseating second, the scent of his cologne

dragged me back ten years, to summers when we'd dominated sack races together, when I'd thought that his arms, his kiss, his charm…was forever.

But forever had expired, and now it just felt suffocating.

I caught London's face over Jaxon's shoulder—his expression unreadable. He dragged a hand through his hair, jaw tight, before turning and walking away without a word.

The ache that ripped through me nearly buckled my knees.

"Put me down, Jaxon." My voice was flat, stripped bare of humor.

"Sorry, just got swept up." He set me back on my feet gently, his voice softened like it excused the act. He turned immediately to Derrick as he and Simmy approached, patting his shoulder. "Good job, son."

Before I could exhale, Simmy was in front of me, her cheeks flushed, her smile bright. "Mrs. Moore, you did great. That was amazing." She wrapped her arms around me in the tightest damn hug, all warmth and sincerity.

I froze for half a second, then melted into it. I'd always wanted a daughter. Always imagined what it would be like to have one in the mix of my boys, someone to braid hair with, swap dresses with, cry over silly movies with. And here she was—pressing herself into my arms like she'd been mine all along.

"Call me Sev, please," I murmured, squeezing her just as tightly. I really need to get around to changing my name back. "And ditto, kiddo. You and your dad almost had us there for a sec."

Her body went stiff in my embrace, the smile faltering in the space of a breath. But she didn't let go.

"My mom used to say that too," she whispered, so softly it was almost lost under the crowd's chatter.

My chest caved in, the words striking like a dart straight through the cracks. And all at once, I felt it—the shadow of Sarah hovering, the grief, the love, the absence, all tied into this girl holding onto me like maybe I could fill even a fraction of that void.

15 | LONDON

"Oh, Jax. We totally got this one!" Jessica squealed from across the courtyard, bouncing on her toes like she'd just won a game show.

Sevynn and I traded a look—equal parts disgust and resignation. Same thought, same timing. God help me, I almost smiled.

She shook her head, lips twitching. "You first or me?"

I'd pulled her name from the bucket. Blindfold Maze. Whoever designed this insanity deserved a medal or a lawsuit—I hadn't decided which. One partner blindfolded, the other guiding them through a maze of cones, ropes, and random inflatable flamingos. Chaos. Which meant Sevynn and me, tethered together again. Close enough that I could feel her heat, hear her breath. Close enough that the pulse I'd been trying to ignore since last night thundered back to life like it never left.

"I'll always let you get there first," I murmured, leaning down so only she could hear.

Her breath caught. The flush hit her cheeks instantly, blooming red across that flawless skin. She tried to cover it with a sharp inhale, but her eyes betrayed her —wide, flicking up to mine before darting away like she couldn't stand to look too long.

And God help me, I wanted to drag her face back to me. Wanted her looking. Always looking.

From across the lawn, Jaxon's voice cut through, smug as hell. "Better not trip, Sev. Don't think London could carry you through that thing like I could."

My jaw flexed so hard it ached. I didn't take my eyes off her, though. Not for a second.

Because she was blushing, because she was mine in ways he couldn't touch, and because if I focused on Jaxon one second longer, I'd bury him in those goddamn inflatable flamingos.

"Everyone ready?" the coordinator bellowed, clipboard raised like he was commanding troops instead of drunk wedding guests. "Let's start in three... two... one!"

The lawn erupted. A cacophony of voices—shouting, laughing, panicked directions—crashed over us like a wave. People were already careening into cones, partners screaming "LEFT!" and "NO, YOUR OTHER LEFT!" The kind of chaos that could swallow someone whole.

Sevynn's shoulders shot up instantly, tightening around her ears. Even with the noise-cancellers in place, it was too much. Blindfolded and raw to every sound, I saw it in the small tells; the hard set of her jaw, the flex of her hands at her sides, the way her whole body braced as if for impact.

I closed the distance in a breath, chest flush to her back, my mouth at her ear. "Don't listen to the noise, baby. Listen to me.

I'm right here. Lock in with me. Are you okay with doing this? If not, we stop right here."

Her breath stuttered out, shaky, but she gave the smallest nod. Brave. Always so goddamn brave.

"Good girl," I whispered, low enough that only she could hear. My hand locked behind my back to not break the rules and touch her. "Step forward. One at a time. Just you and me."

She moved—hesitant at first, but with each step syncing closer to the rhythm of my voice. "There you go. Perfect. Straight ahead. Now right—small turn. Beautiful."

The rest of the lawn may as well have vanished. It was just her and me, her blindfolded, trusting, and me guiding her like she was the only person who mattered. Because she was.

"Left turn. Just a little. That's it. Now straight ahead. You're doing beautiful."

With every step she took, blindfolded and sure, something in me pulled tighter. The trust she was giving me—here, in the middle of a wedding circus, with her ex ten feet away—it was fucking undoing me.

"Right, now. Careful... yes. Perfect. Keep going, Sevynn." My voice had gone hoarse, rougher with every command. She followed every single one like a good fucking girl.

By the halfway point, she was breathing hard—not panic, but focus. Her lips parted, blindfold tugged across her face, and she whispered, "I can only hear you."

Yeah... I nearly lost it right there.

I steadied my voice, even as my pulse thundered. "That's

all you need, baby. Just me. Straight ahead now. Finish line's close."

And together, step by step, she crossed it. Blindfolded. Unflinching. Mine.

The confetti cannon boomed, raining strips of color across the field as the coordinator shouted our win.

Sevynn tore the blindfold off, blinking fast in the sunlight. Before she could say a word, I lifted my hand, and she slapped it with a grin that nearly gutted me. But I didn't let go. I clasped our fingers together for just a second longer than the moment allowed, tightening just enough that she'd feel it.

I leaned in, voice low, for her and only her. "Good girl. So fucking proud of you."

Her eyes widened, her breath catching like I'd kissed her instead of whispered it, and I had to force myself to let her hand go before I did something reckless in front of the entire crowd.

It was like the world turned off the mute button and off to the side, Jaxon's voice cracked across the chaos like a bad joke. "I mean my left, Jessica! MY left!" She was shrieking back at him, pointing like he'd just tanked their chance at Olympic gold. Other pairs were tripping over cones, arguing, collapsing into heaps of laughter or frustration, absolute chaos everywhere.

But not us. We'd cut clean through it. Because she listened only to me. And damn if that wasn't the sweetest fucking victory I'd ever tasted.

Next up was Piggyback Gauntlet—because apparently

sack races and blindfold mazes weren't humiliating enough for one afternoon—and Jaxon practically fist-pumped when he pulled Sevynn's name. Of course, he did. He lit up like the world was suddenly right again, and I wanted to wipe that smug grin clean off his face.

It was the last event of the day, and by now everyone was spread out, chatting, laughing, cross-pollinating between families like it was summer camp. Which would've been fine if I weren't running on fumes. My thighs burned from all the running and racing, my voice was hoarse from yelling and cheering, and now... piggybacks. Fucking hell.

And who do I pull? Meghan. Yeah—*that* Meghan. The one Simone's been sneakily dangling in front of me like bait.

Now, I'll be honest: the woman is a fucking smokeshow. Red hair glinting in the sun, a laugh that turns heads, and legs for days. Any sane man would be thanking the universe. But me? Nothing. No spark. No pull. Not even a flicker. Because across the field, Sevynn was brushing her curls back, adjusting the straps of her top, and climbing onto Jaxon's back with that reluctant, eye-roll grin—and my entire bloodstream turned to fire.

Meghan gave me a playful little wink, looping her arms over my shoulders. "Ready to win, partner?"

I forced a smile, nodding. "Ready." But the truth? My eyes weren't on her.

They were locked on Sevynn. And on the man carrying her like he still had any fucking right.

The whistle blew, and we were off.

Meghan tightened her arms around my shoulders as I surged forward, legs pumping, but I barely registered her weight. She was light as air. The real weight was two lanes over.

Jaxon.

Of course he looked like he was auditioning for a Nike commercial—shirt clinging, biceps flexing as he gripped Sevynn's thighs like he owned them. Too tight. Too high. His palms spread across skin that should've been mine to hold, and I had to force my jaw not to lock until it cracked.

The gauntlet stretched out ahead—cones, ropes, and inflatable obstacles set up like some twisted carnival course. I vaulted the first hurdle easy, but Jaxon took it as his personal soapbox.

"Come on, baby, hang on!" he hollered, his grin feral as he leapt the barrier with Sevynn bouncing against his back. "Still got it! Twenty years later, I've still got it!"

I wanted to plant him face-first into the grass.

"Breathe, Jax, it's a wedding game, not the goddamn Olympics," Sevynn laughed, clutching tighter to him. Fuck me—she *laughed*. Not polite, not forced. A real laugh, spilling out as he nearly tripped on the second cone, arms flailing like an idiot. She threw her head back, curls flying, lips parted—and it gutted me.

"Pick it up, London!" Meghan squealed in my ear as I cleared another hurdle, bouncing against me like she had no clue she was just cargo in a much bigger war.

Jaxon was still running his mouth two lanes over. "You see

this? You see this, baby? You're light as a feather. Doesn't even slow me down. Just like old times, huh, Sev?"

My grip on Meghan's legs flexed hard enough she yelped. I didn't hear her. Didn't hear anything but him. Him and her. The laugh that still rang in my ears, the way his hands slid to adjust his grip.

Halfway through, a wall of inflatable flamingos waited, wobbling in the wind. I barreled through, head down, driving Meghan over like it was nothing. Jaxon stumbled in the middle of them, Sevynn squealing as one nearly took them both down. He spun it into a show, strutting out the other side like he'd meant it.

"Still smooth, baby," he crowed. "Still smooth!"

What all would I need? A large plastic bag, a shovel, duct tape, rope. Maybe a fucking alibi.

I drove harder, thighs burning, lungs raw, each obstacle another reason to win. Not for Meghan. Not for the goddamn game. For Sevynn. To prove I could outpace him, out-carry him, outlast him.

The finish line loomed, the crowd roaring, feet pounding. I dug in, legs burning, Meghan clinging like she was actually invested. But one lane over, Jaxon surged—showboating bastard—veering ahead in the last stretch.

They crossed first.

He damn near launched Sevynn off his back, spinning her in his arms like they were prom king and queen all over again. And then—before I could even process—he bent and pressed a kiss to her mouth.

Right there. In front of everyone. It wasn't a peck; I saw his tongue trace her bottom lip.

The crowd whooped. Cheered. Thought it was part of the game.

But I saw her. I saw the way her whole body froze in his arms, her hands pushing at his chest a second too late, her face flushed crimson—not with joy, not with pride, but with shock. With embarrassment. With anger.

"Jax!" Jessica's shrill voice cut through the noise, sharp as glass. She was on her feet, face twisted with fury. "Are you fucking kidding me?!"

He set Sevynn down, hands raised in some mock defense. "It was just a celebration peck! Jesus, calm down, Jess!" He jogged after her as she stormed toward the hotel, calling over the din, "Don't make this a thing!"

The crowd laughed nervously, some clapping, some whispering. The moment fractured—half comedy, half scandal.

And Sevynn?

She stood there, cheeks blazing, shoulders pulled tight like she wanted to fold herself inside out. She drew in a deep, steadying breath, then walked—stiffly and quietly—over to the benches at the edge of the courtyard. She sat down, spine straight, head tipped back as if the sky could swallow her whole.

Beside me, Meghan said something—probably a joke, maybe a compliment, I couldn't even hear it. My ears were ringing. My chest was in a vise. My pulse was a hammer in my throat.

Because all I could see was Jaxon's hands on her. Jaxon's mouth stealing space that wasn't his. Jaxon taking what was not, and never would be again, his to claim.

My hand was already in my pocket, phone unlocked before I could think better of it. My thumbs flew across the screen.

London: *Breathe, baby. You're okay.*

I watched her check her phone; her lips parted, just barely. Her chest rose, slower this time. And even if no one else noticed, I did. I'd pulled her back from the brink before—and I'd do it a thousand times if I had to.

6 | LONDON

"Put me down!" Simone squealed, legs kicking as my brothers jostled her up and down like she was still five years old instead of a bride-to-be.

"Simmy Simmy coco puff, Simmy Simmy koko bop, Simmy Simmy bop!" they sang in ridiculous unison, bouncing her until her hair flew everywhere.

"Dad!" she shrieked, laughing so hard her voice cracked. "Get your people!"

"Sorry, babygirl, can't hear you," I called back, grinning like an idiot.

My family had finally started trickling in today for day two of wedding madness. Not everyone could swing the full run of events—not when it meant four or five days minimum, plus travel, hotel, time off work. That was a big ask. But my brothers? They showed up first, naturally. And now here they were, tormenting my daughter like they'd been waiting years for the chance.

I'm the oldest by a stretch. Then came Joe—fourteen years later. Yep. Fourteen. Just when my parents thought they were done, surprise! After Joe came Marcus, then Sloane, my baby sister, the last of us, born when I was already out of college.

She just turned eighteen.

So yeah, my siblings span nearly a quarter-century. Big families are funny that way. Sometimes it feels like I grew up twice—once as a kid, once as the built-in uncle before I'd even had kids of my own. By the time Sloane came along, people mistook me for her dad more than once.

"Alright, alright, enough!" I finally stepped in as Simone's squeals turned breathless, her face red from laughing and kicking at her uncles. "You're gonna break her before the wedding."

The brothers reluctantly set her down, both of them grinning like wolves, still chanting their stupid little song under their breath as Simone smoothed her hair and tried to catch her breath.

But then she froze.

I followed her gaze, and my own chest tightened.

"Grandma? Grandpa?" Her voice cracked, soft and disbelieving.

And there they were. My parents.

Dad stood taller than I remembered, still broad-shouldered though age had slowed him, his once-black hair now silver at the temples. Mom was on his arm, petite as ever, tears already streaking her cheeks.

They'd flown in from Germany the night before— retirement had carried them across the ocean years ago, and though we talked often, the miles were heavy. We hadn't seen them or Sloane in years, not since before Sarah... before everything.

"Baby girl," Mom whispered, and that was all it took.

Simone broke. She bolted across the room and crashed into her grandmother's arms, sobbing openly as Mom cradled her face, murmuring in rapid-fire Spanish the way she always did when she was emotional. Dad wrapped his arms around them both, his own eyes brimming, his big hand rubbing circles over Simone's back.

I stood frozen, my throat tight, watching the three of them fold into each other like no time had passed, like nothing had changed. But everything had.

Simone pulled back just enough to cup Mom's face in her hands. "I can't believe you're here."

Mom kissed her cheeks, her forehead, every place she could reach. "Of course we're here. Nothing could keep us from your wedding day, Mija."

"Don't take all my hugs, dammit!"

The voice came booming across the room, loud and unapologetic, followed by the unmistakable *clunk, clunk* of rolling suitcases against the tile.

Sloane.

My baby sister, eighteen and already too big for the world to contain, came barreling through the doors. Her wild curls were half-tamed under a bucket hat, earbuds dangling from her neck, and her oversized hoodie was swallowed up by the duffel strapped across her chest.

She let her bags crash to the floor with zero care, arms wide as she stormed straight into the huddle of Simone, Mom, and Dad. "Move over, people, I want in!"

Simone squealed again, this time breaking into laughter as Sloane wedged herself into the hug pile with all the subtlety of a bulldozer.

"God, I missed you!" Sloane declared, squeezing Simone so hard she lifted her an inch off the ground. "You look so... *old*. Like, adult old. It's *weird*."

"Gee, thanks," Simone said, swatting at her, but her face was glowing, cheeks still wet with tears.

Mom threw her hands up. "First my granddaughter, now my baby—*ay Dios mío*, my arms are going to fall off with all these hugs."

"Don't lie," Sloane teased, planting a noisy kiss on Mom's cheek. "You live for it."

Dad chuckled, shaking his head. "Some things never change."

The room was still vibrating with laughter—Sloane clinging to Simone, Mom fussing over her hair, Dad booming his approval like the proud patriarch he was.

And then their eyes shifted.

First Mom's. Then Dad's.

And suddenly, it wasn't about Simone anymore.

It was about me.

"London," Mom breathed, her voice breaking on my name.

That single word cracked something open in me. I'd been bracing for this, trying to act like I wasn't, but now that it was here—seeing her face, lined deeper than the last time, streaked with tears I hadn't been there to catch—God, it nearly drove me to my knees.

She cupped my face in both hands before I could stop her, her palms warm and familiar. "Mi hijo. Look at you." Her thumbs brushed away tears I didn't even realize had fallen. "Still so handsome, my little boy."

My throat closed. I tried to laugh it off, tried to be that stoic grown man I always forced myself to be, but the sound that came out was jagged, broken.

And then Dad stepped in, his hand gripping the back of my neck, pulling me into him like I was still twenty instead of forty-two. His chest hit mine, solid and safe. Against everything I've taught myself over the years, this time I let myself lean into it.

"You did good, son," he said quietly, his voice rumbling deep. "You raised her right. Your mom and I—we're proud. Damn proud."

That was it. That was all it took. The dam split wide open.

I choked out a sound, ugly and raw, and buried my face in Dad's shoulder. My arms clutched around both of them, Mom's hands still cradling my face, Dad's grip tight on the back of my neck. My body shook, years of holding it together bleeding out all at once.

I wasn't the architect. I wasn't the single father. I wasn't the man who had to be strong for Simone.

I was just their boy, and I let myself break.

"Oh my God, Lon. When did you become such a damn softy?"

Marcus' voice sliced through the moment like a badly timed cymbal crash. He flopped onto the nearest couch, long legs sprawling, and dropped his feet on the coffee table.

I pulled back from Mom and Dad, swiping my sleeve across my face, trying to mask the mess of tears. My chest was still heaving, my throat raw, but Marcus just smirked like he'd caught me red-handed.

"Seriously, man. You crying over hugs now?" He grabbed a handful of peanuts from the side bowl and tossed one into his mouth, chewing loud enough to make Mom swat at him.

"Marcus," Dad barked, half warning, half amused.

"What? I'm just saying." He leaned forward, elbows on his knees. "This the same guy who used to body-check me into the pool and call me a wuss if I even sniffled? Look at you, bro. Forty-two and soft as a marshmallow."

"Mijo." Mom's voice cut sharp through the room.

He held his hands up in mock surrender but grinned, anyway. "Relax, I'm proud of him. He finally pulled the stick outta his ass."

I shook my head, laughing once, hoarse and shaky, even as my eyes burned. "Same shit as always," I muttered.

"Damn right," he said, leaning back, perfectly smug.

But Mom reached for my hand again, squeezing it tight, and Dad rested his palm on my shoulder. And even with Marcus' ribbing, the weight of their presence anchored me in a way I hadn't felt in years.

Eventually the noise shifted—the girls spilled off to

Simone's room in a flurry of chatter and excitement, arms full of garment bags and makeup kits. They were buzzing about the wedding dress, about hair and shoes and a hundred details that I'd never understand but knew mattered to them.

That left the rest of us — the guys.

We cracked open beers, the hiss of the caps giving way to that first cold swallow. The laughter dulled into something quieter, more grounded, the kind of silence that wasn't awkward, just... lived-in. The hum of family.

I sank back into the couch, bottle in hand, and let myself breathe it in. I hadn't had all my family around me in so many years. Not since before Mom and Dad moved to Germany. Not since before Sarah. Hell, maybe not since I was a kid.

It felt surreal. Like I'd stumbled into someone else's life — one where the weight wasn't all on my shoulders, where I wasn't holding everything together alone. My brothers bickered in the corner over who got the good chair, Dad stretched his legs out with a sigh, and for once, the air didn't feel heavy.

17 | SEVYNN

"Bitch, you are *drunk*, drunk." Jones' voice came out muffled, like he was talking into a pillow.

I glanced over and nearly snorted — because he *was* talking into a pillow. He had stolen one of the poolside loungers, stretched out like Cleopatra, face buried in the cushion dramatically.

I giggled, dangling my feet in the water, the cool ripple soothing against my warm skin. "I am not. I'm tipsy at best."

"Mhm. If you say so." He didn't even lift his head, just flopped a hand in my direction like a dying Victorian heroine.

"The kiddies are out to play for the night," I declared, spreading my arms wide like I was presenting a stage, "and the adults get to hang back and enjoy a night off from sack races and dirtbag kiss stealing exes, baby."

"Cheers to that," Jones mumbled, finally rolling over and waving his half-empty margarita glass at me. Lime wedge clung stubbornly to the rim like it was hanging on for dear life.

I kicked at the water, sending a little splash across his legs. "God, I needed this. Just... a breather. Some laughter. Something not loaded with family drama and wedding schedules."

"And," he said, sitting up with a flourish, "London Bridges."

"Don't." I pointed at him, warning in my tone.

"Ohhh, don't give me that finger, Sev. That man looked at you today like you were the winning lottery ticket and he had the last dollar in his wallet. Don't you dare play dumb with me."

I groaned, flopping backward onto the hot concrete, staring up at the stars. "Why can't I just have one weekend? One. Without my vagina complicating things."

Jones cackled so loud, it echoed off the pool water. "Because, babe, you were *born* complicated. And your vagina's just keeping on brand."

"True. So true," I admitted, grinning at the sky.

"I'm *get in the bed drunk*, way past *side-of-the-pool drunk*," he announced, staggering to his feet like a Broadway star taking his final bow. He wobbled once, adjusted his shirt, and then pointed at me dramatically. "You coming or staying?"

"I'll stay," I said, lifting my hand like I was swearing in court. "And I promise I won't get in the pool before you say anything."

"Damn straight." He narrowed his eyes at me. "I'll check on you later, make sure you still have your legs closed."

"Oh, fuck off," I laughed, tossing a splash of water in his direction.

"Well, hell's bells and dickly spells. Speaking of keeping your legs closed..."

I blinked at him, confused, until I followed his gaze. My stomach sank.

Jaxon.

He was cutting across the patio alone, towel slung around his neck, earbuds dangling as he thumbed through his phone. He hadn't spotted us yet. His stride was loose, casual, like this was just another hotel pool and not the scene of my worst-case-scenario.

"You want me to stay, girl?" Jones asked, his tone low now, serious under the sass.

I swallowed hard. My pulse jumped. "No. No need. Get your beauty rest. I can't deal with you being a cranky bitch because you didn't get your ten hours."

Jones arched a brow, like he didn't believe me for a second, but he still leaned down and kissed the top of my head. "Scream once for drama, twice for help."

"Go," I whispered, shoving him lightly.

He sauntered off, hips swaying, throwing Jaxon the dirtiest side-eye as they passed. Jaxon didn't even look up.

And just like that, it was me. Alone. With *him*.

I could tell my head was swimming from the obscene amount of alcohol Jones and I had just put away by the sheer fact that, one: I hadn't left the pool yet, and two: I was... checking Jaxon out.

God help me, the man was a bastard, but he was still built like a fucking model. His shorts hung low on his hips, that deep V carved down his stomach like a reminder of everything

I hated about him—that he could look like that and still be the worst decision I ever made.

He didn't see me at first. He was still glued to his phone, sliding off his shoes with one hand, towel dangling from the other. He tossed both onto the bench, scrolled a few seconds longer, then finally set the phone down.

And when he looked up, he froze.

"Shit. Sev." His brows lifted, his mouth parting like he'd been caught doing something wrong. "Sorry."

I lifted my glass, swirling the last of my drink like it mattered. "No worries. You were in your own little world over there."

He exhaled a sharp little laugh, rubbing the back of his neck. "Guess I was."

The silence stretched, broken only by the ripple of water at my toes.

I shouldn't have been here. He shouldn't have been here. And yet, there we were—two ghosts haunting the same poolside.

"I was just coming to do a few laps," Jaxon said, nodding toward the water like he needed to explain himself. His voice was casual, but his hand kept raking through his hair, like it wouldn't lie flat. "I can give you some space and come back later if you want."

"It's a pretty big pool, Jax." My tone came out light, but there was an edge there, one I didn't bother sanding down.

He shifted on his feet, glancing at the water, then back at

me. For once, he didn't swagger. Didn't smirk. Didn't fill the air with his usual bravado.

And that's when it hit me—he was nervous.

Why the hell was *he* nervous?

This was the man who could charm a camera lens, who'd built a career on his smirk alone. The man who blew up our marriage in full technicolor scandal without so much as blinking. And now here he was, standing by the pool like a teenager about to ask someone to prom.

I took another sip, watching him carefully over the rim of my glass. "Relax. I'm not gonna bite."

He huffed out a laugh, short and awkward. "Yeah... I know."

But the way he kept shifting his weight, the way his eyes skittered off mine, told a different story. Finally, it wasn't me who felt off balance.

"Jaxon?"

His head snapped up, eyes catching mine like he wasn't sure if I was about to throw him out or throw him a line.

"Yeah?"

I swirled the last sip of my drink, letting the silence drag just long enough for him to fidget. Then I smirked.

"Get in the damn pool."

For a second, he just blinked at me, caught between disbelief and something else—something hotter, heavier. Then his mouth curved into that half-grin, the one I used to mistake for irresistible.

"You serious?" he asked, tugging at the waistband of his shorts like he needed confirmation.

"Dead serious," I said, leaning back on my elbows, letting my legs kick gently in the water. "What's the point of all those Calvin Klein abs if you don't use them for a couple laps?"

That got a laugh out of him—low, real, not the polished press junket kind. He toed off his socks, peeled off the athletic shorts he'd had on over his swim trunks, and in one smooth motion dove cleanly into the water with barely a splash.

And damn it, even after everything—after the betrayal, the humiliation, the scorched earth he'd left behind—watching Jaxon cut through that water with the same easy grace he always had... my chest tightened.

Because the bastard was still beautiful. I couldn't tell if I wanted to kiss him or drown him, both equally possible with my current alcohol level.

I watched him glide up and down the length of the pool, lap after lap, the water catching the glow of the lights, breaking around his shoulders like it couldn't contain him either. Every time he came up for air, dragging his hands through his hair, the water dripping down his chest, my thighs clenched tighter against the edge of the concrete.

When it was good with Jaxon, it was *so fucking good*. My alcohol-soaked brain betrayed me, replaying flashes I hadn't asked for: the tight coil of his abs when he thrust, the veins that mapped his hips, the way his body had always known mine too damn well. Painful memories dressed up as temptation, and I hated that they still had the power to make my pulse race.

His laps quickened, almost frantic, like he was burning something out of his system. And when he finally climbed out—on my side of the pool, of course—he was breathless, dripping, and way too fucking close.

Too close to my bare legs, my flushed skin, my unsteady resolve.

I forced my eyes up to his face, ignoring the way water tracked down his chest. My voice came out sharper than I intended.

"Where's Jessica? Out with the girls?"

There it was again—that flicker of nerves. The shift in his jaw, the quick glance away, like the question had snagged something raw.

"She's going home." His voice was low, almost drowned out by the hum of the pool lights. He dragged a hand through his wet hair, exhaling like it cost him. "We got into a fight, and she left. She won't be at the wedding."

I blinked, the alcohol fuzz sharpening in an instant. "Wait—what?"

His eyes finally met mine, and they were darker than the water still dripping from his lashes. He looked... tired. Hollow. Not the movie star grin, not the billboard jawline, just a man stripped bare.

"She's gone, Sev." He shrugged like it was nothing, but the muscles in his shoulders were wound tight, straining. "She went to a different hotel for now, gonna catch a flight home."

The words hit like a slap. And for half a heartbeat, I didn't know if I felt relief, satisfaction, or just plain disbelief. My ex-husband—the man who'd blown up my life for a girl half my age—was suddenly standing in front of me without her.

And I had no idea what the hell to do with that.

"What did you do?" The words slipped out before I could stop them, sharp, instinctive. Because I knew. Of course I knew. With Jaxon, there was always a *what did you do.*

He froze for a beat, shoulders tense, eyes skittering away. "It doesn't matter, Sev."

"Humor me, Jax." My voice was quieter now, steadier than I felt.

His throat worked, Adam's apple bobbing. Then he dragged both hands down his face, exhaling so hard it sounded like it hurt. "I moaned your name," he said finally, each word gravel in his mouth. "When I came with her. Your name, Sev. Not hers. That fucking kiss was on my mind, as innocent as it was. And it just fucking happened."

The air between us snapped like a live wire.

"We fought after that," he continued, almost spitting it out now, like getting rid of poison. "I told her it was over between you and me. That there was nothing between us, not even friendship at this point. Nothing I said mattered, because in that moment—" He broke off, his voice cracking, then steadied it. "In that moment, it was your name on my lips. And I can't fix that."

Silence swallowed the patio. The only sound was the dripping water sliding off him, hitting the concrete between us.

Then he laughed bitterly, running his hand through his hair again, tugging at the ends until his scalp went red. "Happy?"

And goddammit, I wasn't happy. My pulse raced, my chest ached, my skin burned with the truth of it.

Because once again, Jaxon had set fire to everything—and I was the one left standing in the smoke.

I slid down deeper into the pool until I was right in front of him, and my pulse was a goddamn war drum in my chest. I knew I would regret this in the morning. Hell, maybe in the next five minutes. But regret was familiar. What I wanted now was something else. Reclamation.

I wasn't doing this because I wanted him back. I wasn't doing it because of the way he looked at me, or the way he always thought he owned me. No. This was mine. This was me taking back a piece of myself he thought he stole.

His eyes widened when I stepped closer. Then they lit, infernos blazing, his mouth parting like he was about to say something. Before he could, I grabbed the back of his neck, dragged his face down to mine, and kissed him first.

I gasped against him, my hands clutching at his shoulders as my mouth devoured him, desperate and hungry, like I was making up for years in a single kiss. My legs moved, wrapping around his waist, pulling him deeper into me.

He growled into my mouth, low and husky, and grabbed a fistful of my hair, yanking my head back just enough to trail his mouth down my throat. Heat exploded where his lips sucked against my skin, sharp little nips that had my spine arching, offering more.

My nails dug into his shoulders as I locked my legs tighter around him. The hard length of him pressed against me through wet fabric, grinding up into the place I'd been trying to ignore all night. The friction tore a moan right out of him, ragged and needy.

"Fuck, Sev." His desperate voice broke against my neck. "*Fuck.*"

My back hit the cool edge of the pool, tiles biting into my skin—and then his hand was there, shoving my bikini bottom aside like it was nothing. Two fingers plunged deep, hard and unrelenting, and my body reacted immediately, arching off the ledge, a sharp gasp ripping free before I could keep it quiet.

His mouth hovered near my ear, hot and venomous. "Did he touch you like this? When he fucked you?" His thrusts were punishing now, desperate, each one demanding an answer. "Did you moan for him the way you moan for me?"

"No." My breath shook, but my voice cut clean. "I moaned louder."

His growl vibrated against my skin, his pace quickening, frantic. "Did he fuck you like I fuck you?" He spat the words like a challenge, like he needed the sordid details to claw his way back into my head.

I tilted my head, met his eyes with ice. "He fucked me better than you ever have."

"I hate this side of you," he rasped, teeth grazing my throat. "Fuck, I can't get you out of my head."

"This isn't some love connection, Jax." My nails dug into his shoulders, pulling him closer anyway. "Now shut the fuck up and make me come so I can get back to my room."

"Fucking slut."

My hand cracked across his face before I even thought about it. The sting in my palm lit something feral in me, and before he could even react, I crashed my mouth into his—biting, taking, owning.

"Not for you," I hissed against his lips. "Not anymore."

I fisted his hair, yanking his head back just enough to remind him who was in control, my other hand clamping around his wrist to pin him exactly where I wanted him. Then I ground down hard, riding his fingers, every movement calculated, merciless.

"Stay right fucking there," I panted, my voice ragged, command threaded with desperation. "You don't move until I come."

His mouth was everywhere—biting my shoulder, sucking at my throat, devouring me like I was oxygen. The slap of water against the tile kept time with us, his fingers plunging harder, faster, curling in ways that made my body tremble on the edge of release.

I was right there—strung so tight it felt like my skin might split. My body was begging, trembling, teetering on the edge, and then—he curled his fingers just right. Deep. Hard. Ruthless.

The orgasm tore through me like fire catching dry kindling. My hips jerked up, my back snapped against the tiles, and a sound ripped out of me that didn't sound like mine at all. I bit into my palm on one, trying to keep quiet where we were, clutching at the edge of the pool with the other, clawing for something solid while wave after wave crashed through me, dragging me under.

"Goddamn, Sev," he groaned against my throat. "Fucking hell."

But I barely heard him. My body was boneless and buzzing, floating in the wreckage of release. I had never felt so untouchable. So powerful. Knowing I'd taken back something he thought he would always own.

I caught my breath in sharp, deep pulls, then peeled his hand off me finger by finger. He was still panting, still staring at me like he'd just unearthed buried treasure.

I leaned in, pressed the lightest kiss to his cheek — soft enough to confuse, cutting enough to sting. "Thanks, babe."

Then I pulled myself out of the pool, step by slow step, water slicking down my skin, every movement deliberate. I wrapped the towel around my shoulders, bent to slip my sandals on, gathering my bag without so much as a backward glance.

"Wait—what?" His voice cracked behind me, disbelief and desperation bleeding through.

I turned halfway, arching a brow like he was nothing more than an interruption. "What?"

"Do you... do you want to come to my room?" he stammered, trying for smooth but landing squarely in pathetic. "We can...finish what we started."

That pulled a laugh straight from my stomach. "I did finish what I started, Jaxon."

And then I walked away. Not rushed, not flustered—calm, measured, owning every step. Leaving him hard, confused, and furious in the pool, nothing but ripples where I'd been.

The towel clung damp to my skin as I pushed open the pool door, head high, pulse still thundering with the aftershocks of what I'd just claimed back for myself.

And then I froze.

Because waiting on the other side—standing in the low glow of the hallway lights like he'd been carved out of shadow and fury—was London.

His gaze hit me first. Direct. Unforgiving. Those green eyes swept over me once—towel clutched tight, damp hair dripping, steam still rising off my skin—before locking back onto mine like a target acquired.

And just like that, the air left my lungs.

Behind him, a couple of families lingered with towels and floaties, clearly waiting to be let into the pool. London didn't so much as glance their way. His voice cut through the space, steady, commanding:

"Pool's open now, folks. Sorry for the inconvenience."

He stepped aside to let them pass, but his eyes never moved off me. Not once.

Fuck.

Fuck, fuck, fuck.

When the last pair of flip-flops squeaked past and the hallway cleared, his expression changed; anger, hurt, and jealousy rolled into one. It was written all over him, no matter how hard he tried to school his features.

"London…" I whispered, but the name felt too fragile in the air, too small against the storm brewing in his chest.

"Didn't want them getting an eyeful of your… adventures in there," he said, low and unflinching. "Have a good night, Sevynn." He whispered, then turned and walked away towards the elevators.

18 | LONDON

"You have to at least put your feet in; don't be such an old man!" Joe shoved my back as we headed toward the pool.

"He probably can't swim. They didn't have swim lessons in the 1900s," Marcus added with that shit-eating grin of his.

"Fuck you both," I laughed, swatting at them as we walked. "Wait till y'all get gray hair. I'm never letting you live it down."

"You won't be around that long, Lon," Joe shot back. "You've got one foot in the grave already."

We were still pushing and shoving, laughter echoing, when I opened the door to the poolroom.

And then we stopped. Because the laughter wasn't ours anymore. It was moans. Low, breathy, unmistakable.

The guys whispered amongst themselves, snickering under their breath about somebody having sex in the pool. I should've laughed too. Should've turned right around and dragged them back out with me.

But I walked in, because I knew that moan. I dreamed about it last night, woke up fucking my fist because of it.

As soon as I stepped in, the world stopped moving.

Her head was thrown back, mouth parted, face flushed in those telltale splotches I knew by heart. Sevynn.

Her body arched against the edge of the pool while Jaxon's broad back blocked most of her from view—most, but not enough. His arm was moving, hand clearly working her under the water. Her soft moans carried across the tiles, filling the space, filling my ears, shredding every memory I'd been trying to hold onto.

I moved fast, shoving my brothers back toward the door before they could register who it was. My voice came out clipped, hard, not my own. "We'll come back, boys."

They went, awkward and silent now, their whispers bleeding away into the hall.

But I stayed. Because my feet wouldn't fucking move.

I stood there, rooted, a soldier on the wrong battlefield. Guard dog. Gatekeeper. Anything but a man breaking apart inside while the only woman who'd made me feel alive in years was falling apart for someone else.

A family of four rounded the corner with floaties and towels in hand, chattering about pool noodles. My chest heaved once, twice. Then I pulled the mask on tight, because what the fuck else could I do?

"Pool's under quick maintenance, folks," I said evenly, no crack in my tone, no sign of the blood running out of me. "Ten minutes and you'll be good to go."

They nodded, disappointed but oblivious, and I stayed planted right there, back to the door, while behind me her muffled moans kept cutting me open, one by one.

After a beat, I didn't hear the muffled noises anymore. Didn't hear Jaxon's voice or her gasps. Just the pounding in my ears, my pulse raging so loud it drowned out everything else.

And then—movement.

The pool door swung open, and she stepped through.

Sevynn.

Her towel clutched in one hand, her hair damp, clinging in dark waves to her flushed skin. Eyes still glassy, mouth swollen. My mouth. My name. My goddamn undoing.

The sight hit me like a wrecking ball. Fury, jealousy, want—an entire arsenal detonated in my chest all at once.

Behind me, a couple of people and kids still lingered on the benches with floaties and juice boxes, waiting for the all-clear. I turned just enough, forcing my voice into something steady, controlled. "Pool's open now, folks. Sorry for the inconvenience."

They shuffled past, chattering, but I didn't watch them.

Because Sevynn was standing in front of me, frozen mid-step, staring up like I was the last man on earth she wanted to see—and maybe the only one she did.

My gaze raked over her. The towel. The damp skin. The tremor still in her shoulders.

I swallowed hard, my voice dropping, meant only for her. "Didn't want them getting an eyeful of your adventures in there."

The words came out low, rough, laced with a venom I

couldn't disguise. Before I said anything I couldn't take back, I turned to head back to my room.

"London..."

Her voice cracked like it hurt to say it. She followed quickly at my feet. But I couldn't speak.

"It wasn't what it looked like, London." Her words tumbled out, breathless, like if she said them fast enough they might actually be true.

I rounded the corner, then pressed the call button, keeping my eyes on the glowing numbers above the door, jaw grinding. "It's not my business, Sevynn."

"Yes, it is." She moved closer, water still dripping from her hair, her voice sharp with something halfway between anger and pleading. "God, you think I planned this? You think I wanted him—" She faltered, biting the inside of her cheek. "I didn't. I swear I didn't."

I turned my head slowly, every muscle fighting the urge to just reach for her. My thoughts were a riot, hammering in my skull, but my voice came out low, clipped, contained.

"I know what I saw. Which is none of... my. Fucking. Business."

Her throat worked, the hard swallow visible. She took a step closer, almost cornering me against the elevator doors. Her voice cracked, softer, like a confession she didn't want to give.

"What you saw was a moment that didn't mean anything. Not like that, anyway." Her gaze flicked up, raw, pleading. "What you saw was... me taking something back. It wasn't about him."

Her words shouldn't have mattered. We weren't anything. We weren't supposed to be anything.

But the way her eyes held mine—wide, raw, stripped bare—made my chest seize like she'd stolen all the air out of the elevator.

The ding of the doors broke the silence, but neither of us moved.

We just stood there, tethered by something we couldn't name, both of us choking on justifications we didn't believe.

And Christ—I still wanted her.

Every instinct screamed at me to close the space. To drag her in. To drown in her the way I had before. My hands flexed uselessly at my sides, trembling with the urge to touch.

Instead, I forced myself forward. One step. Then another. Into the elevator.

If I kissed her now, if I gave in, we'd both regret it the second the sun came up.

"Go back to your husband, Sevynn." My voice came out low, rough, shredded.

Her lips parted like she wanted to protest, but I didn't give her the chance.

I pressed fifteen and let the doors seal her out. My fists clenched so tight my knuckles ached.

By the time I shoved the keycard into my door, my chest felt like it was splintering open. The little green light blinked, mocking, and then I was inside, breathless, burning, and angry.

My brothers had already made it back and sprawled out in my suite instead of their own. Not that I minded most nights, but right now? I didn't have it in me.

Joe was sprawled across the couch like he paid the rent, Marcus rifling through the minibar like a raccoon with a credit card.

"Y'all couldn't stay in your own rooms?" My voice was sharper than I meant it to be, but I didn't care.

Marcus glanced up, beer already in hand. "What, and miss out on bonding time? Please." He squinted at me, his grin slow and knowing. "You knew that chick?"

My pulse kicked. "No," I said too quickly, stalking toward the bedroom. "Not really. She's Ricky's mom is all."

"'Is all,'" Joe repeated, his tone mocking, like he'd just smelled blood. "Right."

I didn't bite. I couldn't. I shoved the bedroom door shut behind me, leaning against it with a long exhale.

I needed a beat. A minute. A lifetime. Because if my brothers saw even half of what I was feeling right now, they'd know the truth—that I was already in too deep.

I'd made my way to the bed, lying there, staring at nothing for what felt like forever. Time blurred, slipping past in pieces I couldn't hold onto.

A knock at the door broke through, then muffled voices followed, cutting straight across the chaos in my head, pulling me back to the surface whether I was ready or not.

"Lon, somebody's here for you," Joe called, and then I heard the door shut again.

I dragged a hand over my face, half hoping I'd imagined it. But when I stepped back out, there she was.

Sevynn.

Fully dressed now, damp hair pulled back, hands folded tight in her lap as she sat on the couch like she belonged there. My brothers were nowhere in sight—smart enough, for once, to vanish.

Her eyes lifted to mine. "Hi," she said softly, the word barely carrying across the room.

I swallowed, the sound too loud in the silence. "Hey, Sevynn." My voice came out rougher than I intended. "What are you doing here?"

Because fuck, she was the last person I had the strength to face. And the only one I wanted.

"I needed to talk to you," she said, her voice tentative but steady. "About what you saw."

I shook my head, keeping my distance, arms crossed tight across my chest like armor. "Like I said, not my business. Nothing to discuss."

Her brows pulled together, a flicker of fire under all that softness. "Then why are you upset?"

The words hit me square in the chest.

I opened my mouth, closed it again. My throat was raw,

my jaw tight enough to ache.

She was right. I *was* upset. Furious. Gutted. But admitting it out loud meant admitting that less than one week of knowing her had gotten under my skin in ways I couldn't claw back from.

I dragged a hand through my hair and forced a laugh that didn't sound like me. "I'm not upset, Sevynn."

I moved past her without another word, retreating to the kitchenette like I could drown the chaos in my head with something as simple as water. I filled a glass, downed it in three gulps, and still felt dry.

When I set the glass down, Sevynn was still watching me. Eyes steady. Unflinching. Like she was waiting me out.

I gripped the edge of the counter, dropped my head, my breath coming hard. And then it broke out of me, low and rough.

"He cheated on you, Sevynn." The words scraped my throat raw. "His pregnant girlfriend is here, parading around letting the world know that she already replaced you." I shook my head, my hands tightening on the counter until my knuckles went white. "And you deserve so much fucking better than letting those hands ever touch you again."

Silence crashed into the space between us, thick and suffocating.

I lifted my head finally, meeting her eyes. And what I saw there—hurt, fire, confusion—only twisted the knife deeper.

Because all I wanted was to cross the room, to rip away every trace of him from her skin, to prove with my hands and mouth that she wasn't his anymore.

But all I managed was a stuttering, "You deserve better, Sevynn. So much better."

"London..." she breathed, my name trembling out of her like a secret, her body tilting a step closer.

For one dangerous second, I almost let her. Almost closed the space, almost reached for her like I'd been starving my whole damn life.

Instead, I raised a hand—stopping her, stopping myself. "Like I said, Sevynn. It's not my business."

Her brows pinched, lips parting to argue, but I forced my gaze up to hers, steady, brutal. "You're my son-in-law's mother." The words tasted like ash. "It's not my business. It can't...be my business."

I dragged in a sharp breath, the ache in my chest near splitting me in half. "It's best if you get back to your room."

The silence after was deafening, filled with all the things I wouldn't let myself say.

Because the truth was burning in my throat, in my fists, in the pounding of my pulse: it was already my business. She was already my undoing.

But none of that mattered as she silently walked out of the room, letting the door close behind her.

19 | SEVYNN

I unlocked Jones' room with hands that wouldn't stop shaking, tears already blurring my vision before I even got the door open. Between the alcohol buzzing in my veins, the humiliation burning hot in my skin, and the memory of Jaxon's hands on me, London's face—I just wanted to disappear. Crawl into a hole. Erase myself.

Jones was in bed, propped up on pillows, the glow of his phone painting his face in soft blue light. He smirked when the door creaked wider.

"Well...well...well. Look what the—"

He didn't finish his remark. The second his eyes registered my face, the smirk vanished. The phone hit the nightstand with a clatter, forgotten. He was on his feet in an instant, crossing the room in three strides.

Strong arms wrapped around me before I could even fall apart, pulling me clean off the ground. My legs locked around his waist out of instinct, my forehead pressing into the crick of his neck as the sob tore free. He just held me—steady, unshakable, rubbing long, slow circles into my back while I shook.

That was Jones. Loud as hell when the world was calm. Silent, immovable when mine was crumbling. As flamboyant and ridiculous as he loved to be, when people truly needed him—he was this. An anchor.

He'd been my anchor before. The night I was attacked. Not even Jaxon knows what happened—it's just me, Jones, and the police report.

It was opening week for the North Current, and late nights were routine. I didn't think anything of it. A man had been harassing me all night, flirting too aggressively with the waitresses until we had to have him removed. It was nearly 3 a.m. when I finally left, bone-tired and walking alone toward my rental car.

That's when I felt him. His arm, his knife at my throat, sharp enough to break skin as he shoved me against the wall. His hands roamed where he wanted while I begged him not to kill me, begged him to let me go because I had kids who needed me. He cut into my neck twice.

"Now we're linked forever," he hissed, tilting his head to show me the twin marks carved into his own flesh, as if binding me to his madness. Warm blood slid down my skin, soaking through my shirt.

"Fuck you!" I spat, shoving against him, fighting to twist free. My body was strong, but he was taller by at least eight inches, heavier by a hundred pounds, and I was no match for that mass bearing down.

So when he slapped me across the face, it ripped a carnal scream out of me as I hit the ground—a scream that woke Jones, who had nodded off in his car waiting for me to finish. I hadn't even known he was there.

He was out of the car in seconds. Then chaos. Jones ripped him off me, the two of them wrestling for the knife. The blade sank once into Jones' side, but he barely flinched. He just fought harder, slamming the man's head into the concrete until he went limp. Out cold until the EMTs loaded him onto a stretcher.

Both of us carry scars from that night. Him, a near three inch one just under his rib cage, and me two jagged lines buried under the ink that now covers them, refusing to give that night any power over me.

But what I remember most isn't the blood or the flashing red lights. It's Jones—bleeding himself—lifting me in his arms anyway. Holding me. Just like he was holding me now. Even when the EMTs arrived, he never let go. He was still holding me that night, exactly like this. Silent. Steady. Loving.

I told Jaxon it was an accident in the kitchen. And it's been Jones and my secret ever since.

He carried me to the bed without a word, setting me down with the gentleness of someone who knew I was made of glass tonight. Then he climbed in beside me, pulling the covers over both of us, tugging me into the shelter of his chest. His heartbeat thudded steady against my ear as I let the tears run, hot and endless.

No advice. No jokes. No commentary. Just the weight of his hand tracing soft circles on my back, his lips pressing a kiss into my hair, like he was silently promising he wasn't going anywhere.

And for the first time since Jaxon's lips touched mine, I could breathe again.

"I let him touch me tonight, Jones." The confession ripped out of me, jagged, humiliating. My throat burned, my chest caved. "God, I feel so fucking stupid. Pathetic."

His hand never stopped moving—slow, steady circles on my back. The kind of touch that didn't ask for anything, didn't demand I pull it together.

"And London—" The name broke out of me like it hurt. I clutched at his shirt, knuckles white, trembling. "London showed up at the pool while Jaxon was..." My stomach lurched, my voice shredding. "...two fingers inside me."

The shame hollowed me out so fast I could barely breathe. "You should've seen his face. Jones, the look in his eyes—when he saw me after that." My words dissolved into broken sobs, ugly and raw. "I can't even explain it. I don't—God, I can't—"

I buried deeper into him, like maybe if I pressed hard enough I could disappear into his chest and never have to face any of it.

"I really like him," I whispered, the words so small they barely cleared my lips. Then louder, angrier, like I had to convince him—or myself. "London. God, I like him so fucking much. It's insane. Three days. Three. And I feel like I..." My chest heaved, the truth tearing itself free. "...I feel like I love him. How fucked up is that?"

The tears came harder, a flood I couldn't stop. "And now nothing can happen. Nothing. The kids can never know, and when this weekend is over, we'll go back to our lives. And I'll have to live with him being one town over—thirty fucking minutes away—and I can't have him."

A bitter, broken laugh cracked out of me before it curdled into another sob. "And then Jaxon—" His name made my whole body tense, recoil. "He told me he said my name while he was fucking Jessica. And instead of being horrified, instead of being sick—" I clutched at him harder, nails digging. "I felt vindicated. Like somehow that meant something. Like I'd won."

My voice dropped, sharp, frantic. "I slapped him, Jones. You know how long I've wanted to slap that motherfucker? And then I told him London fucked me better, that I moaned louder. I thought I was reclaiming something—taking it back." My voice cracked wide open, dissolving into sobs. "But I just gave him my body. Again."

He didn't move. Didn't even look at me. His eyes stayed fixed on the ceiling, jaw tight, voice flat. "Are you done?"

Every ounce of flair was gone. No Jones jokes or theatrics. Just that deep, measured tone. The kind that left no room for games.

I nodded, small, because I knew that voice. It meant I was about to get read within an inch of my life.

"Good." He rolled me on top of him, bracketing my knees on either side of his waist, pulling me down until my chest pressed against his. His arms locked around me, steady, unyielding. He kissed my temple once—soft, anchoring.

"First of all," he murmured, "I'm going to need better details about Jaxon later, because that was Queen-level shit. You didn't hand him anything—*you took it back*. Old Sev would've never had the lady balls to do that. That man is somewhere right now, hard as a rock, reeling, probably fucking his fist trying to burn you out of his head. And you know what? Good. Let him choke on that shit. I'm fucking proud of you."

His arms tightened, his lips brushing my hairline. "Second of all, you are not pathetic. Don't you ever say that shit in front of me again. You've spent your entire goddamn life catering to that man and his fragile ego, shrinking yourself so he could feel tall. You gave him everything—your time, your body, your dreams. And you're still here. You built empires while he built excuses. So no, baby. You're not pathetic. You're free."

He tipped my chin up, gray eyes sharp, unwavering. "And now? Now *you* own you. Every fucking piece. He doesn't get to dictate your worth anymore. He doesn't get to tell you how not to embarrass him. He'll do well to remember *you're the one he lost*, not the other way around."

"Lastly, London isn't going anywhere, Sev." His voice dropped lower, steady, like he was laying bricks under my feet. "I've never been one to believe in fate or love at first sight—always thought that shit was Hallmark Channel nonsense. But that's my cynicism to deal with, not yours. That man? He's infatuated. He's jealous. He wants you. And when the time's right, you'll figure it out. I promise you that."

He smirked then, brushing his lips against my temple like he couldn't resist breaking the moment. "Some kind of divine shit is at play here. If only they'd come sprinkle some of that rainbow colored pixie dust on *my* life too, you hoggy bitch."

I laughed, wet and messy, tears streaking down my cheeks. "You're such an asshole."

Jones only grinned, cupping my face between his palms, his thumbs brushing away the wetness from my face. "You may have only been divorced officially for six months, but you've been rebuilding this version of yourself for a hell of a lot longer. You're exactly who you're meant to be—and you take *whatever* the fuck you want out of this life. You understand me?"

I nodded as he wiped away the last of my tears.

"There she is."

His fingers closed around my chin, firm but not forceful, guiding me down until our mouths met. The kiss lingered, soft and sure, his lips pressing into mine like he was trying to breathe calm straight into me.

Then came the faintest dip of his tongue along my bottom lip, just enough to make me shiver, to remind me he was there and paying attention, but not enough to turn it into something it wasn't. It was grounding. A tether.

The first time we kissed like this was the night I found out about Jaxon's affairs. I was crashing—alone in the house, the boys off at college, my chest caving in on itself.

Jones was there within minutes. And all I could do was wail. He tried everything to calm me, but I was unraveling fast, tipping into full panic, my breath catching in jagged bursts. He didn't know what else to do, so he kissed me.

It shocked my system, jolted me so hard I was slammed back into my body. He smoothed my tears away, then leaned down and kissed me again. Not a frantic, tear-into-each-other kind of kiss, but the most intimate kiss I'd ever experienced. Deep. Grounding.

When he pulled back, he cupped my face. *"You're okay, okay?"*

I nodded. And that became our grounding point.

Fast forward to six months ago; I'd just signed the divorce papers. Two pitchers of margaritas deep, I called an Uber to his house at two a.m. We'd had keys to each other's homes for years, so I let myself in. I threw myself at him, stripping every stitch of clothing before climbing into his bed.

That was the only time I can truly say there was physical heat between me and Jones. Before then, it had been banter and glitter bombs. But that night, we nearly crossed a major line. In some ways, we did.

We unraveled together—kissing, his fingers inside me, his mouth on my breasts. He made me come with his mouth and hands, and by the time I reached for his cock to take things further, both of us realized tears were streaming down my face.

He grabbed my wrists, holding me still, eyes locking on mine like he was seeing me for the first time since I'd crawled into his bed.

"Sev, you're drunk."

He let my wrists go, pushing up from the bed, dragging a hand through his hair. His voice broke. *"You're fucking drunk, and you just let me... fuck."*

"I'm okay. I want to. I want you."

He shook his head, pained but steady. *"You don't though, darling. And that's okay. I didn't realize what this was. But I'm not that much of a manwhore."*

He went to the kitchen and came back with a glass of water and some pain pills. Pressed them into my hand, watched me drink. The pills were for the morning—God knew I'd need them.

Then he stretched out beside me, pulled me against his chest, his palm rubbing slow circles over my back.

"I'm never going to let you live this down, by the way."

It made me laugh and cry harder all at once, until exhaustion dragged me under—grounded, safe, loved.

And now, here he was, with that same intimacy, that same sweetness he'd always shown me.

"Are you sure you're okay?" he murmured against my mouth, his steel-gray eyes locking onto mine, holding me steady. Like he already knew the answer, but needed to hear it anyway.

"Yes." My voice was steadier this time, even if my chest still trembled. "Thank you, Jones."

This was second nature to us now, this kind of closeness and intimacy. I could straddle him, kiss him, breathe him in, and still walk out of this room with our friendship untouched. We'd been extensions of each other since the first day we met—two people who knew exactly how to remind the other they were safe, wanted, tethered.

But the truth has always hummed there too, quiet and undeniable: if either of us ever chose to cash that chip in, the fuse was already lit six months ago. Though we both know we never would.

"Good." He tugged me down for one more soft, grounding kiss before pulling back with a wicked grin. "Now get the hell off me—you're making me horny, and you've got Jaxon cooties all over you. Go take a shower, you *whore*."

I woke up hungover. Again.

At this point, I really need to reevaluate my life choices this week—or at least start hydrating like a responsible adult.

Jones and I were a tangle of limbs and hair, starfished dramatically across the bed like some avant-garde art installation titled *Two Idiots Who Drank Too Much Tequila*. His leg was hooked over mine, one arm thrown across my chest like he was protecting me from burglars.

The only silver lining? No scheduled daytime activities today. All the "young ones" had scattered off to their respective bachelor and bachelorette parties last night, which meant I was free to marinate in my hangover shame in peace.

…Except peace doesn't exist in this family.

At four in the morning, I was serenaded awake by Marley. Loudly. Badly. I cracked open the door to find him and Derrick clinging to each other like drunk frat boys, howling what I *think* was supposed to be the Chipmunks soundtrack.

The second they saw me, Derrick started hissing and clawing the air like a feral cat. Marley shielded his face with his jacket and shouted, *"She can't see us! We're drunkens—it's bad luck before the wedding!"* before collapsing into hysterics.

The noise? Imagine the laughing-gas scene in *Ice Age*. That's exactly where my brain went as I watched them lose all motor control. The only thing missing was the green haze.

Then they staggered off down the hall, bouncing off the walls like pinballs, still laughing like hyenas.

I just shut the door and said a prayer for the future of humanity because... what the actual fuck? I climbed back into bed and passed right back out.

Hot shower. Strong black coffee from the little bistro downstairs. Maybe some eye drops so I didn't look like a raccoon in family photos. That was the survival plan. Solid. Foolproof. Good as new—or at least, as good as a thirty-eight-year-old pretending she could drink like she was twenty-one and failing spectacularly.

I started to roll out of bed, but Jones' arm came out of nowhere, looping around my waist like a damn octopus and dragging me back against his chest. His breath was hot on the back of my neck, voice low and scratchy with sleep. "No. Stay, Sev."

"No," I groaned, prying at his arm like it was made of steel cable. "Coffee first. I have a hangover from hell."

He sighed into my hair, melodramatic even half-asleep. "I hate you."

"You love me," I shot back automatically.

And then, because I'm an agent of chaos even before caffeine, I flicked him in the balls. Hard enough. He bolted upright like he'd been tasered. "Motherfucker!" he yelped, clutching himself like a wounded soldier.

I flopped back onto the bed, grinning at the ceiling. "Better than coffee."

The weight hit me a second later—Jones launching himself across the mattress like a linebacker. He landed square on top of me, mouth wide open over my boob, and bit down like I was brunch.

"Jones! You son of a bitch!" I shrieked, swatting at his head.

He pulled back just enough to smirk, lips still dangerously close to nipple territory. "Payback is the bitch, not me, honey." Then he sauntered off the bed with the grace of a runway model, hips swaying like he was showing off couture, and disappeared into the bathroom. The door clicked shut, the shower cranking on a second later.

"Oh, you're dead," I muttered to myself, already plotting. My eyes landed on the kitchenette. Ice water. Direct hit over the shower curtain. Perfect.

But before I could execute *Operation Frost Nipples*, a knock rattled the door.

I groaned, dragging myself upright, still rubbing my assaulted boob. I shuffled over, muttering curses under my breath, and yanked the door open—

Jaxon. Of course, Jaxon.

He didn't wait for an invitation. He pushed the door—and me—aside with the same arrogance that used to make me want to scream into pillows. He stormed two steps in, hand raking through his perfectly styled hair, jaw tight enough to crack.

Then he swung back around, eyes blazing. "What the fuck was that last night, Sev?"

"What was *what*?" I asked evenly, one hand still on the doorknob, keeping the door wide open behind me so he knew damn well he wasn't invited to stay.

He gestured wildly, like he couldn't believe I was going to

make him say it. "What was... that fucking *show* you put on at the pool. Some kind of seduction-revenge plot? Is that it?"

His voice dripped accusation, as if he had any right to call me out after parading Jessica and her baby bump through my son's wedding week like a trophy.

"I needed an orgasm, and you were there." I shrugged. "So I took said orgasm. What's not to understand here, Jax?"

For a second, he just stared at me. Mouth open. Eyes narrowed. Like he'd come here armed for a fight and I'd yanked the sword clean out of his hand.

"You can't—" He faltered, raking a hand through his hair so hard it stuck up at odd angles. "You can't just say shit like that, Sev. Like it was nothing."

"It *was* nothing." I tilted my head, crossing my arms, calm as a judge delivering a verdict. "What exactly did you think it was, Jax? You have a pregnant fiancée. I've moved on. So... forgive my confusion."

His mouth opened, some protest forming—but before he could spit it out, the bathroom door swung open.

"Sev!" Jones strolled out, towel slung dangerously low on his hips, water still dripping down his chest. He was holding an empty condom box, eyebrows raised like he'd just discovered a crime scene. "We used the last one. Think they sell them downstairs?"

I almost choked on a laugh, biting the inside of my cheek so hard it hurt.

Jones finally looked up, noticing Jaxon frozen in the middle of the room. He grinned slow, wicked, like a cat who'd just found the cream. "Well hey, Jax. Didn't see you there. What are you doing here?" Then, without missing a beat, he turned back to me. "What's he doing here, baby?"

"He was just leaving," I said smoothly, not even glancing at Jaxon as I let the door close, walking over and plucking the empty box from Jones' hand. I tossed it on the dresser, then looked back at Jones with a smirk I knew would land like a dagger. "If they don't sell them, we'll just Instacart from the grocer's."

Jaxon's face went blood-red. His jaw flexed like he was seconds from grinding his molars into dust. "Wow," he spat. "Of course you're fucking Jones. He's the guy Lou saw you with in the lobby." His gaze darted around the room, landing on the heap of clothes and a flash of lace tossed by the chair. Perfectly innocent—Jones' towel, my dress from last night, underwear—but I could see the story he was writing in his head. "All this fucking time. Jesus, Sev."

"Jax."

Jones' voice was calm, almost too calm, the way he got when he was about to deliver a kill shot. He crossed the room unhurriedly, then slid an arm around my waist from the side, pulling me lightly against him like we'd rehearsed it. His gray eyes never left Jaxon's.

"What matters is Sev's happiness, right? Should it really matter *who* that happiness is with?" He tilted his head, lips quirking, the epitome of polite dagger-work. "You should make your peace with it, and get on back to Jennifer."

"Jessica," Jaxon snapped, color rising higher in his neck.

"Riiiight." Jones didn't even blink. "So sorry about that."

He bent down, fingers brushing my jaw, and kissed me. It was chaste, slow, intimate in a way that wasn't just *provable*, it was *combustible*. You could hear the steam coming from Jaxon's ears. Then, as if he hadn't just tossed a grenade into the room, he murmured, "I'm going to get dressed and we'll get you something to eat, baby. You must be exhausted after last night."

The swat to my ass was loud. Performative. The sound cracked through the silence like a gunshot.

Jones padded back into the bathroom, towel barely clinging to his hips, leaving Jaxon standing there with his fists clenched, breathing hard, fury rolling off him in waves.

"Guess he's not so gay after all, huh? Another fucking lie."

"Bisexual, Jax." My tone was flat as I moved toward the door, motioning for him to follow. "I need to get dressed and head downstairs. We'll see you tonight."

A string of curses hissed under his breath as the door shut behind him.

I exhaled hard, adrenaline still buzzing, then rushed to the bathroom to find Jones and give him the biggest fucking high five. I shoved the door open—and immediately got an eyeful.

"Fuck, sorry!" I yelped, slamming it shut again. My forehead thunked against the wall, heat flooding my face. Holy *shit*.

"Why would you charge in here, Sev?! A man's getting dressed!" he shouted through the door.

"I didn't see anything, I swear!"

"Liar!"

"I didn't!"

The door swung open and he appeared again, towel slung low on his hips. My eyes betrayed me—flicked down for a split second—and like he'd been waiting for it, he pounced.

"I *knew* it! You better not fucking tell a soul, Sevynn."

My face burned hotter than a bonfire. "Tell who?! But— why didn't *you* tell *me*?"

His grin went wicked. "Because, darling, it's not exactly small talk. You don't drop *that* over cocktails. It's more of a… 'let me show you in vivid detail' kind of disclosure. Not, 'hey, nice to meet you, have I mentioned my cock is pierced?'"

"I get that, but it's *me*, Jones." My hands flew up, half-scandalized, half-demanding. "That seems like a huge fucking thing to have done and not tell your *best friend*. Did it hurt? Does it *still* hurt? Does it… feel good?"

His grin went full wolf. "Why, are you curious? Want the demo package? Because I can drop this towel right now and *personally* show you how good it feels, Sev."

"Fine, be a dick." I rolled my eyes so hard it almost hurt. "Let's just get dressed and eat. Thanks for the Oscar-worthy performance back there, by the way."

He groaned like I was the exhausting one here. "Ugh, fine. I got it a year ago. Yes, it hurt. No, it doesn't anymore. And yes—it feels fucking amazing. For *all*… parties involved." He leveled me with a pointed look, then flicked his hand at me like he was swatting a fly. "Now can we drop it? And never mention this again? Or the fact that you've now seen me naked? *Ever?"*

"Okay." I nodded way too fast, throat dry, trying not to picture what I was absolutely picturing. "Sure. Dropped. Gone."

His eyes narrowed, lips twitching like he could already read me. "You're thinking about it now, aren't you?"

"I can't help it!"

20 | LONDON

I don't know what the hell I was thinking. Actually, that's a lie. I do know. *Move the fuck on.* That's what I was thinking.

So I texted Simone, had her send Meghan my way, and now here I am, sitting at brunch across from a woman who is, by every objective standard, beautiful. Smart. Easy to talk to. She laughs at the right places, tosses her hair in a way that would usually work on me. But the whole thing feels... hollow. Boneless. Like chewing food with no flavor.

And I did it to myself.

I'm not an asshole, so I keep the charm turned on. Pleasantries. Flirtation. Smiling like I'm supposed to be here instead of halfway across town replaying last night on a loop. Meghan deserves that much—hell, she deserves better than some man treating her like a distraction. But that's exactly what I made her. A distraction.

The truth is, I acted on impulse. On the sting of seeing Sevynn with Jaxon. Watching him touch her like he still had the right. That was the gut punch. The one that reminded me exactly why I needed to get my shit together. Reminded me that what Sevynn and I had—it was a fling. A reckless, brutal, perfect fling. The kind I hadn't let myself have since before Sarah. And that's all it was supposed to be.

So I told myself Meghan was the next step. She looked the part. She was primped up in a sundress and a hat way too big for her head—inside, no less. Why the hell was she wearing it inside? Anyway. She looked cute enough. Dressier than me, sitting here in shorts, a black henley, and sandals like I'd wandered into brunch by mistake.

She leaned forward, smile sweet and practiced. "What kind of hobbies are you into, London?"

Hobbies. Christ. Like this was a dating profile Q&A.

I took a slow sip of my drink, buying time. "Work's most of it these days. Gym when I can. Reading." My mouth curved, because fuck it, might as well be honest. "Sometimes bourbon tasting, if you want to call that a hobby."

Her laugh was light, tinkling, like she'd been trained for it. It didn't hit anywhere in me. Didn't grab, didn't spark. Not like Sevynn's laugh—that wild, unfiltered thing that made her whole body shake.

I forced a smile, nodding politely. "What about you?"

"Oh, the usual," she said, brushing imaginary crumbs off her lap. "Yoga, brunch with the girls, a little bit of tennis when the weather's nice. Oh, and I've gotten into pottery recently. It's supposed to be grounding."

Grounding. All I could think was: I already had grounding. In the form of a woman sitting on hotel lobby couches barefoot in fuzzy slippers, sipping old-fashioneds like they were oxygen, laughing like she'd forgotten the world was watching.

I took another drink to cover the way my jaw clenched.

Meghan tilted her head, that oversized hat shadowing half

her face as she pouted playfully. "Do you mind if I come sit on your bench with you? You're so far away."

Christ.
It was brunch, not a middle school dance. But I smiled anyway, because I wasn't a dick, and nodded toward the space beside me.

She slid over, crossing her legs, perfume wafting up — sweet, floral, not unpleasant, just... not *her*. Not the faint citrus and bourbon and pool chlorine I couldn't shake out of my head.

Meghan's hand brushed my arm as she settled in, and I kept my shoulders loose, neutral, even though everything in me tightened. I should've been here for this. She was smart, beautiful, put-together, and clearly interested. But the entire time she was talking, all I could think about was Sevynn sitting on a bench twenty feet away yesterday, cheeks still pink from Jaxon's kiss, holding herself together like she hadn't just been gutted in front of everyone. His fingers working her in the pool last night, her arms draped around him, her head thrown back on the edge of coming.

Meghan laughed at something I half-heard, half-missed, then reached up and tugged the ridiculous sunhat off her head, tossing it onto the table with a flourish. Her hair tumbled free around her shoulders, and she shifted closer.

Before I could lean back, her hand smoothed along my thigh. Slow. Intentional.

"You have really sexy thighs, London." Her voice dipped low, flirty, and then — *shit* — she leaned in and brushed her lips against mine. Just the faintest touch. Testing.

My whole body went rigid.

She was beautiful. Young. Every bit the kind of woman a man like me should want to want. And once, maybe, I could've leaned in and let myself fall into it. Convinced myself this was moving on. Convincing myself I wasn't still stuck somewhere I shouldn't be.

But instead of heat, all I felt was the echo of Sevynn's nails dragging down my back. The sound of her moan when I whispered *good girl* against her throat. The taste of her still burned into me.

Her lips brushed mine once, tentative. And instead of pulling back, instead of stopping her, I did the one thing I'd been telling myself I had to do all damn morning.

I leaned in.

My hand slid to her hip, steady, guiding, and I kissed her properly. Slow at first, then harder, trying like hell to make it feel like something. To make *her* feel like something.

Her mouth opened under mine, eager, practiced. She made a soft little sound against my lips, and it should've been enough. Any man in his right mind would've been hard and hungry by now, ready to take this wherever she'd let it go.

But all I could taste was *not her*.

Not Sevynn.

Not the woman who shook apart under my tongue, who looked me dead in the eye when she shattered around me, who made me feel like I'd been waiting five goddamn years for her without even knowing it.

I pushed harder, desperate, trying to drown it out—the ghost of Sevynn's moan, the way her body had fit against mine like it had always been meant to. Meghan kissed me back, perfectly willing, her fingers clutching at my thigh.

But my chest was hollow. My pulse was frantic for the wrong reasons.

This wasn't heat. It was running.

And the only place my mind kept running back to was her.

Meghan pulled back first, her lips swollen, her hand still idly tracing the top of my thigh like she'd just won something. "A good kisser too," she said lightly, grabbing the menu with a satisfied smile, already scanning the brunch options like we hadn't just crossed a line.

I forced a small laugh, low and rough, and reached for my glass. The bourbon burned harder than it should've, but at least it gave me something to do with my hands. Something to distract me from the sinking in my gut.

And that's when I looked up.

Two tables over.

Sevynn.

She wasn't looking at me—neither was Jones, for that matter—but I didn't need her eyes to know she'd seen. Her chest was rising too fast, her knuckles white where they strangled the edges of her menu, like if she let go, she'd fall apart right there in the middle of the goddamn restaurant.

Fuck.

The kiss with Meghan hadn't made me feel a thing, but Sevynn's reaction? That charged through my veins. My pulse slammed in my throat, my chest tightening with something that had nothing to do with the alcohol.

I pushed back my chair; the legs scraping too loud against the tile, heart pounding, knowing I'd just made a decision I couldn't walk back. I needed to see her. Needed to close the distance, lean down, whisper in her ear the same way she'd wanted to explain to me last night.

But before I could take a step, Jones' head snapped up like he'd been waiting for me to move. One sharp shake, then another—his gray eyes cutting directly through me. His mouth formed a clear, firm *no*. Then, just as quick, he dropped his gaze back to the menu, casual, like nothing had happened. Like he hadn't just pinned me to the damn floor without moving a muscle.

My jaw clenched, heat flooding my neck.

"Everything okay?" Meghan asked, her voice light, curious, fingers still grazing my thigh like she owned the right.

I forced myself to sit back down, each movement stiff, guarded. "Yeah," I muttered, lifting my glass again even though it was already empty. "Everything's fine."

But it wasn't. Not even close.

Because two tables away, Sevynn still hadn't lifted her eyes. And the fact that she wouldn't—that she couldn't—was ripping me to pieces.

Halfway through brunch, I nearly choked on my coffee when Jaxon swaggered into the courtyard. Of course, he made a beeline for her table. Of course.

He slid in like it was the most natural thing in the world, flashing that easy grin I'd seen in old modeling shots — the one that probably still sold cologne ads and bad movies.

Sevynn stiffened. Just enough for me to notice.

Then she looked at Jones, gave the tiniest nod, and I watched my one ally in the whole damn circus stand, gather his cup, and walk off without a word.

Leaving her. With *him.*

I stared, my fork hanging in the air like I'd forgotten how to use it.

Meghan was saying something about vacationing in Greece, but the words barely registered. All I could see was Sevynn across the patio, sitting straighter, chin high, her hands fisting in her lap while Jaxon leaned in closer.

Talking to her. Smiling at her. Like he had any fucking right.

And the worst part? She still hadn't looked at me. Not once. Not fucking once.

Jaxon was the kind of arrogant bastard who thought the world bent to him just because he smirked at it. What he lacked in height, he made up for with being the single most irritating presence in any room. And here he was — leaning in, grazing her arm, fingertips brushing hers like he owned some piece of her.

My grip on the fork went white-knuckled. What the hell were they even saying? What could he possibly have to say that she'd want to hear? He'd had her once, and he'd ruined it. Burned it down. She was supposed to be done with him.

Every little touch lit me up, nerve by nerve, until all I could hear in my head was one order on repeat:

Walk the fuck away.

And then I saw it—the shift. Sevynn's eyes narrowed, disgust carved into every line of her face. She leaned in, hissed something I couldn't hear, and stood. Bag slung over her shoulder, spine steel-straight, she walked. Didn't look back.

That was all it took.

I shoved a wad of bills on the table without counting, leaned down, and pressed a quick kiss to Meghan's cheek. "Something came up," I muttered, already halfway gone. "We'll, uh... do this again sometime."

A lie. We both knew it.

Then I bolted, trying like hell to look calm while my pulse roared in my ears. My stride lengthened, zeroed in on the swish of her hair as she disappeared around the corner. Toward the elevators.

Reason told me to stop. My body didn't listen.

21 | SEVYNN

"I just want to make sure Derrick has a good wedding, Sev. It's not about us getting back together. I just want him to see that we're okay, we're healed, we're moving on—and that him and his brother should, too. I'm sorry I over reacted in your room just now."

That was the third time he'd grazed my arm. Third. I was one touch away from shoving a butter knife through his hand. My nails dug into my thigh under the table.

Meanwhile, across the room, I could feel London like a heat lamp on my skin, even if I didn't dare look at him. I didn't need to. I already knew what he'd be seeing. Jaxon leaning too close. Jaxon smiling like he owned me. Jaxon, the same man who blew my life up, pretending to be the picture of reconciliation.

And Meghan sitting pretty at his table, probably thinking she was winning. My chest ached, a mess of confusion and fury. He kissed her. Did he take her back to his room last night? Did he—No. Don't go there. Don't.

"Do you hear me, Sev?" Jaxon pressed, his hand sliding just close enough to my wrist that I felt his pulse.

"I hear you, Jaxon." I snapped my eyes up to his, letting the ice in my stare do the work my voice couldn't. "So, what? We play the part of loving co-parents? Walk down the aisle together, dance a couple times real close? Really sell the dream?"

I didn't raise my voice, but the venom in it was sharp enough to cut.

And still, my head betrayed me. She's pretty. Of course she's pretty. Meghan's hair caught the morning light like fire — red, sleek, flawless. I bet he likes redheads. I wonder if Sarah was a redhead. I wonder if that's his *thing*.

He seemed like he enjoyed kissing her. Hell, anyone in the room could see it. His mouth on hers, slow and practiced, like he'd done it a hundred times before. And all I could think — like a sick refrain—was that it was the same tongue that had been inside me less than forty-eight hours ago. Inside me, dragging me to the edge of madness. And now it was hers. Now she had his tongue.

My stomach rolled. Did he use it on her last night? Did he take her upstairs, peel that sundress off, push her into his sheets and—
Stop. Stop.

"Sev," Jaxon's voice cut through, smug and syrupy, pulling me back to the table. "You're so distant right now. I know you say it was just for the orgasm, but we were so close last night. We were *us* again. It was my fingers you shattered on, baby."

The air left my lungs like a punch. My cheeks burned hot, shame and rage clawing at each other in my chest. He'd said it low, like a secret—like he still had that right. Like I was still his to whisper filth about.

Reduced. That's what he'd done. Reduced me to a body he

used to own. Even after everything.

I let the silence hang for half a beat, just long enough for him to mistake it for weakness. Then I leaned in, voice steady but laced with fire.

"Yeah, Jaxon. I'll play your game. For the boys. For Derrick's wedding. I'll smile, I'll stand beside you, I'll sell the picture of healed and happy—for their sake." My nails sank into my palms as I straightened. "But don't get it twisted. When this week is over, so are we. We weren't *us* last night. I've only ever given to you, Jaxon. Last night? I took. That was me. Not us."

I grabbed my bag, the scrape of the chair loud in the space between us. I half expected him to follow me, I'm glad he didn't.

My throat ached with words I couldn't give London. My eyes stung, begging me to look back at him, but I refused. Looking back would be picking a fresh scab. And God, I was already bleeding.

The elevator was open when I rounded the corner—thank fuck. I nearly stumbled inside, relief cracking through me at the thought of forty blessed seconds of silence to fall apart in. I could curl into myself, bury my face in my hands, unravel in peace before plastering it all back together in Jones' room.

But before I could even press the button for my floor, a couple stepped in.

"Twelve, please." Like I was the bellhop.

Of course the universe had other plans.

The doors were just starting to slide closed when a broad

hand shoved between them. They groaned open again—and then: London.

Before I could breathe, he was there. Taking up all the space. Stealing all the air. My back hit the wall with a thud, the vibration rattling up my spine as he loomed over me.

The couple froze. They looked like they couldn't decide whether to run or call the cops. And honestly, I couldn't blame them—it probably did look like he was about to murder me and fuck my corpse.

"Get out." His voice was gravel, gritted between his teeth. A command. He was speaking to them, but his eyes never left me.

The woman didn't hesitate. She shoved the man toward the door before he could so much as blink, maybe realizing her boyfriend was two inches taller than me and London could flick him into another dimension with one finger.

Then his mouth was on mine. It was desperate. Brutal. A crash of lips and teeth that tasted like bourbon and fury.

My bag hit the floor with a thud, forgotten, as my arms flew around his neck. He lifted me in one motion, my legs locking around his waist, his hands braced hard on my ass.

"I can't do it, Sevynn," he moaned against my mouth, breaking only long enough to drag his teeth along my jaw, down the line of my throat. His breath was hot, ragged, burning me alive.

"I don't fucking care who we are to each other."

His mouth crashed into mine again, rougher this time, his tongue claiming me like he'd been starving. My back arched against the wall, his hips pinning me hard enough that I could feel every inch of him, already straining.

"I tried—" his words tore free between kisses, broken, strained, "—tried to burn you out of my head." His teeth grazed my bottom lip, sucking it between his before dragging back down to my throat. I gasped, my fingers tangling tight in his hair, pulling him closer instead of pushing him away.

"I saw you with her." The words ripped out of me before I could stop them, jagged and sharp.

He pulled back just enough to look at me, his chest heaving, his eyes green fire. "I didn't touch her. Not the way you think. I kissed her..." his voice broke, fury aimed at himself more than me, "and it was nothing. Nothing, Sevynn. I couldn't even close my fucking eyes without seeing you."

My heart slammed against my ribs. His mouth was back on mine before I could speak, his hand threading into my hair, tilting my head just how he wanted it. His other hand gripped my ass under my dress, holding me like he'd never let go.

His forehead pressed to mine, his voice gravel and smoke. "It's you. Only you. I can't get you out of my fucking system. I don't want to."

The elevator shuddered as it climbed, but I barely felt it. All I felt was him. The scrape of his stubble against my skin, the bruising press of his body, the heat flooding every nerve until I was dizzy.

I moaned, broken and breathless, and his answering growl vibrated against my chest.

"Fuck, sweetheart," he panted, kissing me again, slower

this time, like he wanted to carve the taste of me into his bones. "I was wrong last night. Walking away. Thinking I could bury this. I can't. I can't."

The ding of the elevator as we made it to the fifteenth floor nearly undid us both. He set me down reluctantly, his hands still on me, his lips brushing mine with one last desperate press before the doors slid open.

"Tell me to stop," he whispered, voice raw, "and I swear to God I will.

My pulse thrashed. Every inch of me burned, shaking from the need clawing through my body. My hands gripped his shirt like if I let go, I'd shatter.

I swallowed, my voice barely more than a whisper, scared and certain all at once.

"Take me to your room."

His jaw clenched, a curse hissed between his teeth, and then—he lifted me clean off the floo again. His mouth slammed back into mine, all teeth and tongue and desperate groans as he carried me out into the hallway.

I didn't care who saw. Didn't care about Jaxon, Derrick, anyone. All I knew was that I needed him. Needed to burn alive in whatever this was, consequences be damned.

He pressed me against his hotel room door, kissing me like he was trying to memorize every breath I had left. His hands were everywhere—my hips, my ass, my hair—fumbling the key card until the lock finally beeped. The door flew open, and we stumbled inside, mouths still fused, his body carrying me toward the bedroom like nothing else in the universe existed.

Until the sound of a very deliberate throat clearing sliced through the haze.

London froze mid-step. His head snapped toward the living room, and mine followed—only to find two men, younger, broader, almost mirror images of him, plus a stunning teen, maybe seventeen or eighteen, sprawled with beers in hand like it was their own frat house.

I slid out of London's arms, my feet hitting the carpet as reality sucker-punched us both.

"Uh… hey," one of them said, standing with an easy grin. He extended a hand toward me like this wasn't the single most mortifying introduction in the history of introductions. "I'm Joe, London's brother. This is Marcus. And that's Sloane."

London's face went scarlet, his hand scrubbing the back of his neck like he meant to sandpaper the skin off. "Jesus Christ."

I blinked, then—because what the hell else could I do—I shook Joe's hand, then Marcus's, then Sloane's. "I'm Sev," I muttered, my cheeks burning hot enough to power the entire hotel.

"Sev," Sloane repeated, her mouth hanging open like she was auditioning for every teen movie ever made. "Londy, you have a girlfriend?"

Marcus chuckled. Joe smirked.

And then London—God bless him—snapped. "Whyyyy the fuck are y'all in my room?" His voice cracked half a pitch too high, exasperated and incredulous. "Do you three not own your own goddamn key cards? I swear to God, I need to get mine back before I commit a felony."

Joe's grin only widened. Marcus tipped his beer in salute, like this was the best entertainment he'd had all week.

"You're the only one with a couch and a kitchen," Joe said.

"And beer," Marcus added.

"Don't forget snacks," Sloane chimed in, though her eyes never left me.

Me? I wanted the carpet to open up and swallow me whole. Or maybe a fire alarm to go off so I could sprint out and blame it on fate. Anything but standing there, breathless, lipstick smudged, clearly seconds away from being railed, now being appraised by two men who looked like London on teenager setting.

London's jaw ticked, and when he spoke, it was a snarl. "Get. Out." He pointed at the door, his voice carrying that gravelly authority I'd felt at my throat just minutes ago. "And I'll have both of your nuts in a vice if you mention she was here. Especially in front of Simone."

Joe lifted his hands like a man surrendering, but his grin didn't budge. Marcus took another lazy swig of beer.

London stepped closer, shoulders squared, and his voice dropped lower, dead serious now. "I'm not fucking around. It's a delicate situation. So keep your goddamn mouths shut about it. Understand?"

Marcus smirked around his bottle. "Loud and clear. Delicate as dynamite."

Joe chuckled under his breath. "Duly noted. Our lips are sealed."

Sloane was still quiet, still watching.

London's groan was half a growl, half a prayer for patience.

The door clicked shut behind his family, finally leaving us alone. London dragged a hand down his face, exhaling like he was about to apologize, explain, maybe even talk me down.

Not a chance.

I pressed my fingers to his lips before a single word escaped, shaking my head. His eyes went molten instantly, the protest dying in his throat. Without another word, I guided him backwards, step by step until the back of his knees hit the couch. He sat heavily, still stunned, still trying to piece together what the hell had just happened.

I dropped to my knees in front of him, the carpet biting into my skin, but I didn't care. His breath hitched, chest heaving as I slowly slid my palms up his thighs, claiming.

His curse was rumbling, torn from somewhere deep. "Fuck, sweetheart..." His head tipped back against the couch, jaw tight, his hand flexing hard on his thigh like he was holding himself back by sheer will. His eyes found mine again, blazing, feral. "You want my cock in that pretty little mouth of yours?"

"Yes," I whispered, the word trembling out of me before I could stop it. "God, yes."

That was all it took. His restraint shredded like paper. One big hand cupped the back of my head, not forcing — guiding, steady, shaking with the kind of control that was about to snap. His other hand shoved his shorts down just enough, his cock springing free—hard, heavy, flushed at the tip, wet like he'd been waiting for this as long as I had.

My breath stuttered. He was... fuck, he was big. Beautiful. I still couldn't get over it, every time I see it. My mouth waters before I even touch him.

"Open," he rasped, voice dark and provocative. Two fingers slid between my lips, pressing against my tongue, slow, filthy, possessive. He watched me suck them in, my lips stretching around the length, his chest rising sharp as his thumb stroked my jaw. "Look at you. Already being so good for me."

I moaned around his fingers, heat crawling down my spine, my thighs clenching helplessly. When he pulled them free, slick and glistening, he shoved them past his own lips, sucking slow, obscene, and I nearly came right there. So fucking filthy.

My breath shook as I leaned in and wrapped my mouth around the flushed head of his cock. His hips jerked immediately, the restraint he'd been clinging to snapping loose at the edges. His hand fisted in my hair, steady but trembling, guiding me as I sealed my lips tighter around him, tongue sliding along the thick underside. His entire body jolted.

I moaned again, the sound humming against him, and the curse tore out of his chest—low, guttural, wrecked.

"Fuck, sweetheart... just like that."

I hollowed my cheeks, dragging him deeper, savoring the heavy weight of him filling my mouth. His fist in my hair tightened. I forced my throat to open, swallowing around him as far as I could take, holding, then pulling back up without gagging.

His whole body shuddered. His head tipped back against the couch, jaw tight, breath torn out ragged. "Goddamn, Sevynn," he groaned, his voice shredded with need. "You're gonna fucking kill me."

He was panting now, undone, one hand clawing into the couch cushion like he might rip it open. "That mouth... fuck. That mouth was made for me."

I looked up, caught his eyes as I took him deeper, and the sound he made—low, guttural, torn from his chest—was pure devastation. His jaw slackened, head tipping forward as his hips rocked into my mouth, shallow thrusts that had me choking on him.

"Good fucking girl," he rasped, barely breathing it, like the words were scraped raw from his chest. His grip in my hair tightened, guiding, holding, as his pace picked up. My eyes watered, spit smeared slick down my chin, but I didn't care. I wanted every inch, wanted to drown in him, and I proved it with every desperate bob, every groan vibrating against his cock.

"God, baby... fuck, I can't—" His voice cracked, ragged, unraveling. His stomach tightened under my palm, thighs trembling, his entire body strung tight. "I'm not gonna last. I'm—motherfucker, I'm—"

I moaned around him, took him deeper, and that was it. His body snapped tight, a guttural growl tearing out of his chest as he spilled down my throat. Hot, relentless, overwhelming. He tried to pull back, tried to give me the chance to breathe, but I clutched at his thighs, raking my nails down his stomach and took every drop. Swallowing. Moaning. Milking him until he finally sagged back against the couch, shattered.

His chest heaved, sweat glistening down his temples, his head tipped back. For a second, he looked stunned —like he couldn't process that had actually just happened.

Then his gaze dropped to me, lips swollen, chin wet, still on my knees in front of him —and something darker ripped through his expression.

"Fuck, Sevynn." He hauled me up with hands that shook from adrenaline and need. He sat back hard on the couch, dragging me into his lap so I straddled him, my knees bracketing his hips. His cock, still heavy and wet from my mouth, pressed against the heat between my thighs.

"I wasn't done with you," he panted against my lips, voice gravel and fire. His hands gripped my ass, dragging me tight to him as his mouth crashed into mine. It was messy, breathless, desperate.

His hips bucked once —instinct, raw hunger —and I gasped into his mouth, nails biting into his shoulders.

He broke just long enough to rasp, "Round two, baby. Right here. Right now. I need to be inside you."

22 | LONDON

When I pulled her onto my lap, she didn't hesitate—just slid her dress up and over her head, tossing it aside like it meant nothing. My breath caught. Nothing but black lace clinging to her, skin glowing under the dim light.

I leaned in, dragging my mouth over her breast, sucking her nipple into the heat of my tongue until she threw her head back with a moan that went straight to my cock. Holy shit. That sound. I'd chase it forever.

I was still iron-hard, pulsing, like my body hadn't even registered the orgasm she'd just pulled out of me. I looked down between us, at the tiny strip of lace hiding what I needed most. My fingers hooked the waistband.

"Are these a favorite?" My voice was low, barely holding together.

She blinked down, a little confused, then shook her head no.

Good.

I gripped the fabric, yanked hard, and the panties shredded in my hands. Two useless pieces. Gone.

Her gasp filled the room, sharp and sweet, as I tossed the

scraps aside. My fingers dove straight between her thighs, finding her soaked and ready, and I let out a growl I didn't even recognize as my own.

"Mine," I rasped, dragging her wetness across my cock, lining up, every ounce of restraint hanging by a thread.

"Take me," I growled, hands clamping down on her hips, dragging her down onto me in one brutal thrust.

She cried out, head thrown back, and I nearly lost it right then. Christ, the way she clenched around me—tight, hot, perfect. My hands dug into her ass, forcing her to grind down harder, faster, until every slap of her body against mine echoed off the walls.

She tried to set her own pace, riding me slow, but I wasn't having it. I gripped her hips, took over, driving her down onto me again and again until the couch rattled beneath us. She gasped, clawing at my shoulders, her nails dragging fire into my skin.

"London—" she moaned, half plea, half surrender.

"Ride me, sweetheart," I snarled, slamming her down harder, faster, until her tits bounced against my chest. "You're not stopping. You're gonna take every inch."

Her thighs trembled, her whole body quaking as I fucked her from beneath, merciless, giving her no choice but to break for me. My jaw clenched, sweat rolling down my back, but I couldn't stop. Didn't want to. I needed her undone. Needed her wrecked.

Her head dropped to my shoulder, moans breaking into sharp cries as she shattered, her walls clamping down so tight

I saw white.

"Fuck—Sevynn—" My roar tore out of me as I thrust up hard, spilling deep inside her, holding her crushed against me like I'd never let go.

Her body was still trembling on top of me, her chest heaving, her nails biting into my shoulders. I held her there, still buried inside her, forehead pressed to hers, both of us gasping like we'd just crawled out of a war.

"Holy fuck..." The words ripped out of me, hoarse, guttural. My hand slid up her back, fisting gently in her hair just to keep her close. "How am I this gone for you after only a few days?"

Her lips parted, but nothing came out. Her eyes were wide, wet, shining, like she didn't dare believe me.

"I'll never be the same after this, Sevynn," I whispered against her mouth, voice breaking. My chest ached with it, the truth tearing its way out before I could stop it. I kissed her hard, desperate, and then pulled back just enough to rasp, "I need you. Do you hear me? I fucking need you."

Her breath hitched, her nails still dug into me, and then—finally—she laughed. Not because it was funny, but because she was shaking so hard the sound just spilled out.

"London," she whispered, dragging her lips over mine, "you have no fucking clue what you've done to me. You think you're the only one laid bare here? I'm overwhelmed. You've got me so twisted up, I don't even know which way is fucking north anymore."

Her hips rocked against me, slow, needy, her forehead

pressed to mine. "So yeah," she gasped, her voice breaking with it. "I need you too. God help me, I fucking need you."

I held her face in both hands, forcing her to look at me even as her lips trembled and her body shook with what we'd just done. My chest heaved like I'd run a marathon, but my words came out steady—gravelly, but steady.

"We'll wait," I rasped, pressing my forehead hard to hers. "Until after the wedding. When the kids are back from their honeymoon. We'll tell them together. No sneaking, no hiding." My thumb brushed her wet cheek, smearing a tear neither of us noticed had fallen. "It's gonna be fine, sweetheart. I'll do whatever it takes to make it fine."

Her eyes softened, wide and glassy, and for a second the air between us wasn't sex or fire or chaos—it was the kind of raw honesty that stripped a man to the bone.

"They're gonna hate us, London."

Her voice cracked, breaking something open in my chest. She wasn't wrong. The kids—hers, mine—hell, the whole goddamn family. None of them would understand how quick this happened, how it already feels like too much to untangle.

I cupped her face harder, like I could hold her in place through sheer force of will. "Then let them hate me. Not you." My voice came out rough, jagged, the words ripping their way out. "I'll take it. Every glare, every accusation, every fucking ounce of it. You hear me, Sevynn? You don't carry this alone."

Her breath hitched, another tear slipping, and I kissed it away before it could fall.

"They're my kids too," she whispered, shaking her head

like she was already bracing for the fallout. "Derrick. Marley. Simone. We blow this up, London, we blow them up too."

"And what?" I rasped, my forehead pressing harder to hers. "We just pretend this isn't happening? Pretend I'm not already yours and you're not already mine?" My hands fisted in her hair, trembling with the effort of not shaking her. "Because I can't. I won't. I'd rather burn for it than go back to a life without you being mine, Sevynn."

"Let's give ourselves some time first," she whispered, her voice softer than the words deserved. "See what this is. If it's just two people imploding because our young-as-fuck kids are getting married, or if this is... as intense and real as it feels. Then we can decide to go for it. Tell them. Or not. I don't want to blow up their worlds for nothing."

For nothing.

Damn. It hit like a slap to the dick. My jaw locked, teeth grinding against the way those two words hollowed me out. For nothing. Like this—like her trembling in my arms, like my whole goddamn body lit up just from breathing her in—could ever be nothing.

I pulled back just enough to look at her, my chest heaving. "Sweetheart," I said, low, dangerous. "Does this feel like nothing to you?"

Her lips wobbled, but she held my gaze. "I'm trying to be the voice of reason without thinking with my lady balls."

The laugh ripped out of me before I could stop it, rough and raw from somewhere deep. "Lady balls?"

Her mouth twitched, that crooked almost-smile that undid

me worse than any moan. "Yes, London. Lady balls. Big ones. Someone around here has to keep them in check."

I shook my head, forehead dropping back to hers, still laughing under my breath. "Goddamn, Sevynn. You're gonna kill me. Right here on this couch, with your smart mouth and your imaginary lady balls."

She bit her lip like she was trying not to smile, and all I could think was *fuck reason. Fuck caution. Whatever this is, it's already bigger than both of us.*

I glanced at my watch, heart still hammering like I hadn't just been inside her minutes ago. "Well," I muttered, "we've got about four hours until the rehearsal dinner. Then it's back to pretending we don't know each other." My mouth curved slow, wicked. "So, tell me, sweetheart—can I play with your lady balls till then?"

Her laugh burst out, sharp and incredulous, head tipping back against the couch. "You did not just say that."

"Oh, I did." I leaned in, teeth grazing her jaw, voice dropping low. "You said you had 'em. I just want to give them the attention they deserve."

Her nails dragged down my chest, a shiver ripping through me. "You're out of your damn mind."

"Completely," I agreed, pressing my hips up into her, already reaching for her. "But you love it."

23 | SEVYNN

By the time I stumbled back into mine and Jones' room, I was walking like a pregnant yak. My thighs ached, my knees wobbled, and I was ninety percent sure I had beard burn on my *inner thighs* because apparently, I was today's all-you-can-eat buffet. The man had the stamina of a bull. Correction—a bull on performance enhancers. And he's older than me, so seriously, how the actual fuck.

I collapsed onto the bed in full starfish mode, thighs spread wide because if they so much as brushed together, I'd spontaneously combust. My body was humming, tender, obliterated. And yet my stupid mouth was still smiling like an idiot.

The bathroom door opened, and Jones strutted out in nothing but a towel, looking every bit as delicious and smug as he always does. He took one look at my broken post-coital corpse pose and burst into a raucous laugh that rattled the walls.

"Ohhh, bitch," Jones cackled, pointing like he'd just won bingo. "London *Baby* put in that work."

"Shut up. Just shut up," I groaned, throwing an arm over my face.

He leaned against the bathroom frame, arms crossed, towel hanging dangerously low on his hips, eyes glittering with unholy glee. "Mmm-hmm. I'm thinking... this is a six—" He tilted his head, considering me like a jeweler inspecting a diamond. "—no, wait. Seven orgasms. At *least*. Is my fuckdar still on point?"

"Your *what*?" I mumbled through my arm.

"My *fuckdar*, darling." He smirked. "It's like gaydar, but instead of spotting fellow homos, it detects how many times you've been railed into a new tax bracket."

I shot him a glare from under my arm. "You are *deranged*."

"And *right*," he sing-songed, strutting closer. "Don't lie to me, Sev. You've got the posture of a woman who was rode hard and alphabet-souped. Twice."

"Alphabet-souped?" I sputtered, sitting up just enough to smack a pillow at him.

"Please. Don't act brand new." He dodged the pillow, grinning wickedly. "London Bridges went down, full detonation domination first. Am I wrong?"

I dropped back onto the bed with a groan. "Why are you like this?"

"Because God knew you'd need me," he said sweetly, plopping onto the mattress beside me. "Now spill, bitch. Was it holy? Did you see the light? Are your ancestors clapping from beyond?"

"I've never...ever...had sex like that, Jones. It's addicting and I'm worried I'm not thinking straight. That I'm thinking..."

"With your lady balls?" he cut in smoothly, like he'd been waiting to pounce.

I groaned, covering my face with both hands. "See? Yes! Exactly. I'm worried I'm thinking with my lady balls and I'm not willing to blow up Derrick or Simmy's life for a Chicago fling."

Jones tilted his head, watching me like a cat watches a cornered mouse. "Baby, first of all, don't downgrade it to a fling when you're lying there glowing like you've been mainlined with serotonin and licked clean like a rotisserie chicken."

"Jones—"

"No. Listen." His voice dropped, just slightly. Less camp, more anchor. "You are not crazy. You're not reckless. You are a woman who finally remembered she has a body and a pulse. And maybe it's a fling. Maybe it's a forever. But don't call it nothing just because you're scared of shaking the snow globe."

My throat burned. "The snow globe is my kids' lives."

"And they'll still have those lives, Sev." His fingers brushed my hair away from my face. "You've already given them the world. You don't owe them the corpse of your happiness too. They are grown men. And that Marley baby?" He gave a little shimmy of his shoulders, eyes going wicked. "No disrespect to you, mama, but that boy could get all of this."

"Jones!" My scandalized squeak cracked out before I could stop it, and I smacked his arm.

"What?" he asked, feigning innocence, though the smirk

on his mouth said otherwise. "If he weren't straight—or, you know, your son—I'd be *ruined*. That jawline? Those dimples? Whew." He fanned himself dramatically, rolling his eyes back like he needed a fainting couch.

And then—so quick I almost missed it—his smirk softened. "Point is, you raised men who can stand on their own now. They don't need you to bleed yourself dry to keep their snow globe pretty. It's time you stop living in the wreckage of what Jaxon did and let yourself have something that actually makes you breathe again."

He gave me a look, sharp as glass and soft as silk all at once. "And from what I can tell, bitch...you breathed a *whole* damn lot today."

He gave me one last pointed look, then whipped his hair like a runway model and strutted back into the restroom. "Now get that sexy ass dressed," he called over his shoulder, voice echoing against the tile. "I am late for no one."

"Alright, people. Everyone has their entrance songs, their places, and we are five minutes from dry run. Places, people! Places!" Simmy clapped her hands like a Broadway director, and the wedding party shuffled toward their respective marks.

As we lined up near the entry doors, the room erupted in laughter.

Because strutting in, hips swaying like he owned the goddamn runway, was Jones—carrying a sparkly flower girl bucket.

"Jones, you're the sexiest flower girl I've ever seen!" I hollered across the aisle, my voice bouncing with laughter.

He took a dramatic bow, twirling the bucket like it was couture.

I turned back toward Derrick, who was grinning so wide it was a wonder his face didn't split.

"You knew about this?"

"It was my idea," he said, smug as hell. "It's gonna be epic."

The soft strains of classical music floated through the room, cueing the officiant down the aisle first. Everyone straightened, smiles polite, the picture of elegance.

Then the music *shifted*.

And not into another soft string arrangement.
Oh no.

The speakers blasted *that damn Chipmunks song*.

The very same one I'd caught Derrick and Marley howling in the hallway at four in the morning while drunk off their asses.

Marley had his arm slung around Derrick's shoulders as they strutted into the room like they were headlining a Vegas residency, mouthing the squeaky lyrics with zero shame.

"Oh my God," I muttered, covering my face with one hand as the crowd broke into laughter. "They're really doing this."

The room was roaring now, people doubled over in laughter, the Chipmunks hitting that obnoxious high note as my two grown-ass children made their grand entrance.

"Why do I even bother?" I groaned into my hands, but my cheeks ached from grinning.

The bridesmaids and groomsmen came in next, each pair armed with their own song choice. One duo twirled down to Beyoncé, another moonwalked to Michael Jackson. By the time the last couple sashayed their way in to Lizzo, the whole room was buzzing, clapping along, phones out recording every second.

And then it was my turn.

My cue hit. The speakers blared *Cotton-Eyed Joe.*

Yep. That was me. My choice. Petty? Maybe. But if I had to walk in with Jaxon, then by God, we were going to do it my way. And Derrick had laughed so hard when I told him the pick that I knew I'd made the right call.

Jaxon caught my eye from across the hall, that smug grin twitching like he wanted to say something but couldn't over the roar of fiddles and the crowd's whooping laughter.

"Ready, partner?" he mouthed.

I just smirked and lifted my skirt enough to bounce-hop into the aisle, committing to the bit. Because today wasn't about him. Or me. It was about Derrick, about Simmy, about joy.

So I bounced and clapped like I was at a honky-tonk in 1999, the crowd whistling, hollering, egging me on. And damned if Jaxon didn't join in, spinning me once, the two of us looking for all the world like we hadn't torn each other to shreds in the tabloids.

The irony wasn't lost on me. But still—I played my part. Because Derrick wanted epic, and epic he was damn well going to get.

I took my place at the front of the ballroom, still catching my breath from my *Cotton-Eyed Joe* antics, when the music shifted again.

And then he appeared.

The tiniest little man, barely more than a wobbly step away from crawling, strutted—yes, strutted—into the aisle with all the swagger of a runway model. The speakers blasted *Baby Shark,* and I swear to God the entire ballroom lost its collective mind.

He had on tiny suspenders, a bow tie too big for his neck, and the most serious expression I'd ever seen. Like this wasn't just a wedding, this was *his* moment. Each step was measured. Purposeful. A strut.

Phones shot up, people doubled over laughing, and I couldn't stop grinning even if I tried. The kid looked like he'd been training his whole life for this one walk down the aisle, chubby fists clutching that little satin pillow like it held state secrets.

By the time he reached the end, Derrick was doubled over laughing, Marley had tears in his eyes, and Simmy was clapping like the kid had just won gold at the Olympics.

And then...the moment we had all been waiting for.

The opening beat of *Nails, Hair, Hips, Heels* by Todrick Hall dropped, and we all started to scream. Clap.

Edward-McKenzie. Fucking. Jones.

He didn't just walk in—no, honey, he *arrived*. Like Beyoncé at the Super Bowl, like the Met Gala carpet had relocated to this wedding. He hit the threshold, one hand on his hip, chin lifted, and the flashes from everyone's phones lit him up like he was stepping into his natural habitat.

Every step was choreographed to the beat—hips rolling, legs slicing the aisle like it was his personal runway. He dropped the first fistful of petals with a *Salt Bae* flourish, wrist flick and all, then spun, snapped, and strutted forward, tossing flowers high like confetti.

The crowd went feral. Screaming. Cheering. Chanting in unison—"Jones! Jones! Jones!"

Derrick jumped up from his place at the front, both fists in the air, shouting over the roar: "EPIC, BABY!"

Jones pointed at him like he'd just awarded him front row at Fashion Week, then whipped a handful of petals over his shoulder with a smirk that could've killed a weaker man.

By the time Jones reached the altar, the floor was blanketed in petals, the air thick with laughter, and my ribs ached from how hard I'd been clapping and screaming.

It took a solid minute for the crowd—the rowdy fuckers—to calm down. I was the picture of elegance, obviously. I was *not*, in any way, standing on a bench yelling *"Work, bitch!"* at the top of my lungs. Definitely not. That must've been someone else.

Anyway.

Once the noise finally settled, the energy shifted. It was time for London and Simmy to take their walk.

The hush fell instantly. And then—softly, almost like a whisper—singing poured from the speakers.

"You are the sun, the moon, the stars, my love. You are the winter, the spring, the fall, my love. Whenever you are sad, my love, remember that Mommy will always be there."

A woman's voice. Beautiful. Gentle. Familiar in a way that made the air catch in my chest.

Simmy froze mid-step, her eyes wide. She looked up at London, panic and awe fighting on her face. He nodded once, his own jaw tight, and in the next breath she crumbled—bursting into tears as she threw her arms around his neck.

And then it hit me.

It was her mother. Sarah. The song Sarah used to sing to her. London had found a way to put her here, to walk with her daughter on her wedding day.

There wasn't a dry eye in the room. Not one. Guests were openly sobbing, clutching tissues, holding hands as London and Simmy made their tearful descent down the aisle.

And me? My heart split wide open. Because it wasn't just a walk. It was a resurrection. It was Sarah's presence woven back into her daughter's biggest day. It was London giving their girl the one thing she thought cancer had stolen forever.

24 | SEVYNN

Other than the chaos, the rehearsal itself was beautiful. Derrick and Simmy decided not to say their vows tonight, saving them for the morning ceremony, which somehow made the anticipation heavier, sweeter. By the time dinner was served, the whole ballroom had settled into a soft hum—glasses clinking, laughter echoing, love thick in the air.

Derrick and Simmy were stealing kisses like they couldn't help themselves, drawing playful jeers from their friends, and the glow on both their faces made it impossible not to smile.

Across the room, Meghan tried to tuck herself under London's arm. He went rigid, shoulders locked, eyes flicking straight to mine before I looked away too fast. My stomach twisted, but I shoved the feeling down. Meanwhile, Jaxon stayed tethered to me like a shadow, doing his damnedest to sell the image of "healed exes" for the sake of appearances. His hand lingered a little too long at the small of my back, his laugh a little too loud when he leaned in close, and every nerve in me screamed, *play the part, play the part.*

London's family filled the space in a way that made it impossible not to notice the difference. Where my boys and I are a compact unit, stitched together with duct tape and stubborn love, the Pierces were sprawling. Loud. Endless. He had three siblings—young, lively, their energy ricocheting off the walls—and a host of aunts and uncles who seemed to know *everyone*. His parents... oh, his parents were something else. The sweetest little people I'd ever met. His mother's thick accent curled around every word, and when her boys riled her up, she'd slip into her native tongue to curse them out while his father chuckled beside her.

They weren't old at all—clearly had London young—and Simmy had mentioned once that there were a good many years between him and his siblings. Watching them now, the youngest teasing him mercilessly, you could tell he was half father, half brother to them.

When Jaxon asked me to dance, I forced a smile and agreed. The part, always the part. His hand on mine, his arm sliding around my waist—it wasn't the pool, wasn't the chaos of that kiss he'd stolen. This was stagecraft. Polished. Polite. For Derrick. For Marley. For the families who needed to see something smooth instead of something jagged.

Still, I could feel London's eyes on me.

Every step of the dance, every polite twirl under Jaxon's arm, I felt the heat of London's gaze branding me from across the room.

"You still wear these silly things?" Jaxon asked, his smirk aimed at my noise cancellers like they were a neon sign announcing my flaws. "Eventually, you need to realize that life is noisy, Sev."

My teeth ground together, but my smile stayed plastered in place. "You know me... dramatic as ever."

He laughed, too loud, too rehearsed, and dipped me low with exaggerated flair. "Don't I know it!"

The crowd clapped at his theatrics, none of them noticing the way my jaw clenched, my nails digging crescents into his arm to keep from clawing his smug little face.

If I'd had a butter knife within reach —hell, a *rusty* one— this dance would've been cut real short.

"Simone Angelika Pierce!"

I snapped my head toward Derrick's voice just in time to see him rise from his chair, his entire face absolutely *coated* in mashed potatoes like some kind of deranged spa mask. Simmy was across the room, doubled over laughing, clapping her hands like she'd just pulled the heist of the century.

"War, baby. Oh... this is abso-fucking-lutely war." Derrick pushed back his chair with a screech and took off after her.

Simmy shrieked, darting between tables in her heels, curls flying. Half the room was already howling with laughter when Marley lunged in like a linebacker, tackling the play from the side. A slice of cake smashed against the back of Derrick's head with a wet splat.

"Motherfucker!" Derrick bellowed, spinning to glare at his brother, chocolate frosting dripping down his collar.

The whole room erupted. Aunties were shrieking, uncles were egging them on, London's brothers were standing on chairs chanting *fight, fight, fight,* and all I could do was cover my mouth because I was laughing so hard tears were already burning my eyes.

Simmy darted behind London like he was some kind of human shield. But the look on his face told me that was a fatal miscalculation. Broad shoulders squared, jaw tight, he stood in front of her like a bodyguard... until his mouth curved into a wicked grin. And then, he winked at Derrick. And I knew...

In one smooth move, London spun, catching her and hauling her against his chest. She kicked and flailed, but he had her locked down, back pressed to him while he held her wrists.

"Dad! You traitor!" she shrieked, laughter spilling out anyway.

Derrick sauntered forward, slow and menacing, like a villain in a Western. Joe, one of London's brothers, materialized at his side and offered him a plate of half-eaten food like it was a loaded weapon.

"Ricky..." Simmy's voice jumped an octave. "Baby...listen. Let's just—"

Splat.

Mashed potatoes. Gravy. Right across her face. Derrick did it slow and so damn calculated, painting her like a goddamn canvas—then leaned down and sealed it with the gentlest kiss to her lips.

The crowd lost their minds.

London released her, fist-bumping Derrick with a grin as if he hadn't just sold his only daughter out for poultry and potatoes.

And then—chaos.

Simmy lunged at London, shrieking bloody murder. Derrick chased Simmy. Marley tackled Derrick from behind. And in seconds, the ballroom was less *rehearsal dinner* and more *battlefield of carbs.*

"They're kind of made for each other," I murmured under my breath, watching Derrick and Simmy dissolve into hysterical laughter.

"Just like we were," Jaxon said smoothly, still standing at my side. His eyes locked on me with that faux-intensity I'd once mistaken for love. His fingers slipped over mine, possessive, and he leaned down to whisper something—words I couldn't even hear over the rage pounding in my ears.

But then—light.

A flash across the window. Then another. Then another.

The chaos stuttered to a halt as people turned toward the glass. Phones lowered. Laughter hushed. A low murmur rippled through the room.

There was a crowd of people blocking the road outside of the ballroom, taking pictures through the window, screaming for Jaxon.

"Uh... what's going on?" Simmy asked, her curls damp with sweat and streaked with mashed potatoes as she slipped back into the ballroom with London, Marley, and Derrick in tow.

"It's nothing," Jaxon said, his tone too casual, waving his hand like he could swat the whole thing away. "Just a few fans. News must've gotten out about us reconciling and me being here for the wedding. They probably camped out hoping for a shot."

"Reconciliation?" Marley's voice cracked like a whip, sharp and incredulous. "There is absolutely no fucking reconciliation, Dad. What are you on about?"

I shook my head, stunned, staring at him. "What *news* are you talking about, Jaxon? We aren't reconciling."

Jones was already in motion, signaling for every server and coordinator in sight. "Get security out there to calm that circus, and close these blinds!" He slipped straight into chaos control, shooting me a quick glance before striding toward the front desk.

Derrick pulled his phone from his pocket, Marley right behind him. Both froze, screens lighting their faces with the same mix of disbelief and disgust. Meanwhile, Jaxon kept right on talking, blustering through it like he could talk us all into his reality.

"Not reconciliation, per se," he hedged, smoothing a hand down his shirt like it was a press conference. "The reporters may have, ah, misquoted me."

"Misquoted you?" Simmy snapped, her voice rising with a violence. Her hands were shaking as she jabbed a finger toward the windows. "So this *news*—" the word came out acid sharp—"is *you* out there giving interviews. About reconciling. At our wedding. Tonight."

"Mom..." Derrick's face was plastered with both anger and worry, as he handed me his phone.

My jaw clenched, bile hot in my throat.

The headline screamed:

"Actor Jaxon Moore Reunited With Ex-Wife During Their Son's Wedding Weekend."

I swallowed hard, heat and nausea rising together in my chest. I scrolled down, eyes snagging on the opening lines:

"Is it true love rekindled — or a carefully staged play at optics? Sources say Calvin Klein model turned actor Jaxon Moore was spotted poolside in an intimate moment with his ex-wife, Sevynn Moore. The timing has raised eyebrows, given that Moore's current fiancée, twenty-two-year-old Jessica Hayes, is pregnant with their first child. Hayes told reporters Moore asked her to remain out of sight during the high-profile family wedding week, citing his agent's recommendation to present a 'united family front.' The rehearsal dinner is scheduled for 7 p.m. tonight at the DeFrantis Hotel's Venetian Ballroom, one of the most expensive in the city. Jaxon is reportedly set to walk with his ex-wife down the aisle, calling it a symbol of their rekindled love."

My stomach dropped before my eyes even found the photo.

There I was. Head thrown back in pleasure. Jaxon's mouth buried against my neck. The grainy, voyeuristic shot captured us in the pool, but it didn't matter how cheap the photo was — it told its story all too clearly.

The next swipe showed us at lunch, just hours ago — his fingers brushing over my arm. Another, me clinging to his back, his laugh frozen mid-shot like we were young and stupid again. Next, a kiss at the pool, his hand fisted in my hair, my mouth pressed to his. And then the last one — the kiss at the games, the one he took without my permission.

A series of moments, stacked and stitched into a lie. Together they told a story that didn't belong to me. Not love. Not a second chance. A headline.

It was all a joke to him. A trick to get me soft and pliable so he paint this picture, so he could further his career. I hear them yelling. Screaming. Derrick is angry, so angry. Simmy is, too. So many voices. So many faces.

"They just happened to 'catch' you in the pool together, and 'catch' you here tonight dancing together. Rekindled love? There's no way you're not behind this!" Derrick screamed.

No. Not here. It needs to be epic.

It was all starting to feel too much. My breaths weren't coming anymore—short, shallow, like my lungs had forgotten how. Heat prickled under my skin, crawling up my neck until my whole body felt on fire.

My chest cinched tight. The edges of the room smeared gray. Words sat heavy on my tongue, but nothing came out.

So dramatic. Can't breathe. Such a drama queen. Poor Sevynn. Poor Sevynn.

The old voices, sharp and mocking, pounded in my skull. My hand clawed at my throat, nails biting into skin, while the other formed a fist and thumped against my chest. Hard. Desperate. If my body wouldn't breathe, maybe I could drum it out of myself.

Too many voices. Too many eyes. A hurricane of sound, closing in, pressing me under.

I was floating. Untethered. The darkness pressed closer...closer—

"Back the fuck up. All of you."

His voice. Rough, sharp, cutting through everything.

London.

I wanted to sob in relief, but no air came.

"Sweetheart, breathe." Low now, steady. Commanding. Trying to pull me back, inch by inch, to the surface.

But I was already drowning.

25 | LONDON

Sevynn's body trembling was now, eyes glassy, lips pressed tight like she was holding herself together with sheer will.

My fists curled at my sides, every instinct screaming to cut through the noise, to pull her out of this storm before she shattered.

Their voices piled on, louder and louder, Jaxon's fists hitting the table to exaggerate every point he tried to make. It was all drowning her out, drowning *me* out, until all I could hear was Sevynn's shallow, ragged breathing.

The shouting was a blur. Marley's voice cracked. Ricky's fury lashed like a whip. Jaxon defended himself with that same polished arrogance that had always gotten him out of trouble. Even Simone was screaming into the void.

And Sevynn—God, Sevynn was folding in on herself. Her chest rose in shallow, panicked bursts, her hands trembling as she tried to keep pace with the words flying at and around her. Her eyes darted to the floor, to the ceiling, anywhere but on the people in this room, as if the sheer force of humiliation would swallow her whole.

This wasn't like the arcade. That had been noise. This was worse. This was her family. Her sons' voices. Her name splashed across tabloids *again*. Jaxon's betrayal. Jessica's "interview." All of it crashed into her at once.

When her hands flew up with one clawing at her throat, nails biting into skin, and the other formed a fist and thumped against her chest hard and desperate, something inside me snapped.

I crossed the distance in three strides, shoving past the shouting, crowding out Jaxon, Marley, Ricky —all of them. My hands cupped her face, warm and damp beneath my palms, her skin shaking under the weight of everything pressing down on her.

"Hey sweetheart." My voice came out low, rough, meant for her and her alone. I pressed her gently back against the wall behind the table, sheltering her with my body. "Look at me."

Her eyes snapped to mine, wide and desperate, glassy with tears that refused to fall.

"Don't listen to the noise, baby. Lock in with me." I murmured, brushing my thumbs over her cheeks, steady, grounding. "Eyes on me. Deep breaths."

She sucked in a shaky inhale, but it was jagged, broken halfway through, her chest rising too fast, too shallow. Her trembling eased just barely under my palms, but she was slipping again, her gaze darting toward the noise, toward the shadows of her sons' anger, toward Jaxon standing there like a specter of every mistake.

"Sevynn baby," I whispered again, firmer this time, thumbs pressing lightly into her cheeks as if I could hold her together. "Stay with me. Eyes on me. Just me."

Her breath hitched. She shook her head, eyes glistening, her lips forming words she couldn't get out. The humiliation, the shame, the anger—they were all choking her.

"Breathe," I urged, leaning closer, lowering my forehead to hers until there was nothing else in her line of sight but me. "In through your nose. C'mon, baby, with me. Right here."

I exaggerated the inhale—slow, steady, loud enough for her to hear—then released it in a controlled exhale, brushing her cheek with the warmth of it.

She tried. God, she tried. Her chest heaved, ribs straining, but it fell apart halfway through, her breath splintering into a jagged sob.

"Mom?" Ricky's voice cut across the room, sharp with panic.

I snapped my hand up without looking, palm open, commanding silence like it was instinct. The room obeyed.

Then my hand was back on her face, firm but gentle, cradling her trembling jaw. "Eyes on me, sweetheart. Just me. You don't need to carry their voices right now. Only mine. That's it."

Her eyes flickered, glazed and frantic, but they finally caught on mine again like a drowning hand clutching a rope.

Her hands shot up, pressing against mine on her face like she wanted to shove me away, but she didn't. Her nails dug into my wrists, frantic.

"Shhh," I soothed, brushing away the tears that finally escaped down her cheek. "You don't have to fight me, Sevynn. Just borrow me for a minute. I'll breathe for both of us until you catch up. In... and out."

I did it again, deliberate, measured. In. Out. In. Out. My own lungs burning from how badly I wanted to just scoop her up and carry her out of this circus.

Her breaths came jagged, stuttering against mine. Once. Twice. Then finally, on the third try, she caught the rhythm — just for a beat.

"That's it," I whispered, my voice breaking as my thumbs stroked her damp skin. "That's my girl. Stay with me. Deep breaths. In... and out. No one else is here but us. Just you and me."

The room had gone completely still. I didn't even register who was watching. Marley's fury, Ricky's heartbreak, Jaxon's bullshit—all of it blurred into the background.

All I saw was her—wide, drowning eyes locked to mine, chest rising too fast but starting, *just starting*, to follow the rhythm I laid down for her.

Her lips parted on a shaky exhale, and she collapsed forward against my chest. My arms wrapped around her instinctively, holding her tight, my chin pressed to her hair. "There she is. I got you," I murmured again and again, the words becoming a mantra. "I got you, sweetheart. Just keep breathing, baby."

Her face was buried in my chest, her breaths uneven but *there*. My arms stayed tight around her, shielding her from the room, from the storm, from everything clawing at her.

"What the hell is happening here?" Jaxon's voice cut through, sharp, demanding, like he had the right to ask.

I didn't move. Didn't even glance at him. My hand stayed firm on the back of her head, my chin resting against her hair as if anchoring her in place. My voice came out low, steady, edged in steel.

"Don't you fucking speak," I said, each word measured and cold. "Not one word, or so help me."

The silence that followed was instant, suffocating. I didn't have to look to know Jaxon's jaw had tightened, his chest puffed up like he was ready to reclaim ground he'd already scorched. But he didn't dare answer.

Because right now, Sevynn was in my arms. And I'd be damned if I let him, or anyone else, rip her apart again.

Slowly, carefully, she lifted her face to mine. Her lashes clumped with tears, her eyes rimmed red, but she was *there*. Present. Breathing.

"You're okay?" I asked, my voice soft now, breaking on the edges. My thumbs brushed away the damp streaks on her cheeks, and when she gave me the tiniest nod, something unclenched in my chest. I pressed a kiss to her forehead—gentle, lingering—before I forced myself to loosen my arms and let her go. "You're okay." This time more of a statement.

It felt like peeling my skin off, but I stepped back. One measured pace. Then another. Back to where I'd stood before the whole world narrowed down to her and her panic.

The air was thick as concrete. No one spoke. Not Ricky, not Marley. Not even Jaxon. The entire room was looking at us. I didn't have to see them to feel it—their gazes bouncing between us, trying to decode what had just happened, what it meant.

But I didn't look at them. Not once. My eyes stayed locked on her, steady, as if sheer willpower alone could hold her upright against the storm.

26 | SEVYNN

When London finally eased back, it felt like the floor gave out beneath me. His warmth, his steadiness—it was gone, and I was left standing in the wreckage, my skin buzzing like I'd been struck by lightning.

I wrapped my arms around myself, wishing I could fold into nothing, disappear into the wallpaper. But I couldn't. Not with every pair of eyes in the room glued to me.

Derrick's jaw was locked tight, his chest rising and falling like he'd just run a mile, like he was seconds from launching into another fight he didn't know how to finish. Marley's expression was caught somewhere between fury and confusion, his gaze darting between me and London as though he'd stumbled into a play he wasn't supposed to watch but couldn't look away from.

"Sev, honey." Jaxon's voice was syrupy soft, rehearsed, like every other time he'd tried to smooth over the chaos he'd caused. He took a couple of measured steps toward me, hand starting to lift. "Are you okay?"

His fingers had barely left his side when London's voice cut the air. "Don't you fucking *touch* her." It wasn't even loud or sharp. Just low with an authority that snapped every head toward him.

The room froze. Jaxon's hand hung in the air like he'd been caught stealing. Derrick's eyes widened, flicking between them. Marley's lips parted, silent, but his knuckles went white against his thighs.

My heart was pure voltage in my chest, pounding so hard I swore they could all hear it. Because London wasn't just defending me. He was claiming me—whether either of us wanted him to or not.

I hated them all in that second. For watching. For judging. For waiting for me to crack like some sideshow attraction. My breath hitched, shallow, and I wrapped my arms tighter around myself, wishing I could vanish into the floor.

"Breathe, baby," London said again, low and steady, like the words were meant only for me. Like he'd memorized my tells already—the tremor in my fingers, the way my shoulders locked when panic clawed its way up my throat. His voice was a tether, but the silence that followed was a noose.

"Is there...are you two?" Derrick's voice cut through the tension. He didn't finish the sentence, but the implication landed like a grenade. The room froze. My heart stopped.

"Excuse us, everyone," Derrick said, suddenly all steel and politeness. "Apologies for the commotion." He walked forward, reaching back for her. Simmy grabbed his hand and together they led the way out of the ballroom, their postures screaming authority for the crowd. Marley and Jones trailed after them, serious now.

Jaxon hovered behind me like a shadow, but London's hand pressed against the small of my back—protective, anchoring, a silent *I've got you.*

By the time we reached a small breakout room around the corner, London shut the door behind us with finality. The quiet pressed in like a weight.

"Did you plan this, Dad?" Derrick asked immediately, his voice razor sharp. "The cameras. The interviews. All of it?" His eyes narrowed, burning holes into Jaxon. "And don't fucking lie to me—because if you do, you'll never see me, or this family, again."

The words landed like a sledgehammer. His gaze snapped to me, softer but no less brutal. "I mean that with my whole fucking chest, Mom. Never again."

"Of course not, son. I would never... I would never."

Bullshit. My pulse steadied, my lungs finally catching air. Rage carried me the rest of the way.

"So, call her." My voice was flat, sharp. "Call Jessica. Right here, right now. In front of everyone."

Jaxon scoffed, his face twisting. "I'm not even going to dignify that with an answer. I'm not a fucking child, Sevynn."

"Then prove it," I shot back.

The silence stretched until Jones finally stood. He'd been leaning in the corner this whole time, arms folded, mouth a thin line—but the second he moved, the air shifted. Deadly. Final.

"Give me your fucking phone, Jax."

Jones' tone was velvet laced with steel. He peeled off his

blazer slow, folding it across the chair like he was about to model it, not maim someone. "You've got about three seconds before I fuck up this silk shirt with your blood, and trust me, bitch..." His gray eyes cut sharp as blades. "...you don't want to see me stain my Dior."

Simmy's eyes went cartoon-wide. Marley gaped like he'd just realized who Jones *really* was beneath all the glitter.

Jaxon? He laughed. One sharp, cruel puff that sliced through the room.

And then he was airborne—Jones had him by the collar, slammed back into the wall so hard the picture frames rattled. Jaxon's feet kicked an inch above the floor. His hands scrambled uselessly at Jones' wrists, face red with the sudden choke of no control.

"Hey, London Baby," Jones said calmly, not even winded, "be a dear and check this motherfucker's pocket for his phone."

London stepped in, efficient, slipping the phone free while Jaxon twisted.

"Alright!" Jaxon barked, voice ragged. "Alright—fuck, okay!"

Jones held him there a beat longer, just enough for Jaxon's face to streaked purple, then dropped him like trash. He crumpled, gasping, fumbling to straighten his blazer like he still had a shred of dignity.

The silence after was deafening. Derrick stood, fists curled tight, eyes locked on his father. Simmy's lip trembled, fury and heartbreak blending. Marley muttered, "Holy fuck," under his breath.

Jones smoothed his cuffs, the showman back in place. "Go on then. Let's hear it."

Jaxon wiped his mouth with the back of his hand, glaring at Jones like he wanted to bite but knew better. He turned to me instead, and there it was—the pivot, the excuse already forming.

"Look, everything I told you at the pool was true. I did moan your name, Jess and I did fight. When I went to the pool, the photographers were out there to catch me doing some laps. It was supposed to be a *'Relaxed and Chill Jaxon enjoying Wedding Week'* type of article. And you were there, and… what happened happened."

My stomach twisted. "So you knew they were there when…"

His shoulders sagged. "I just needed to get back in good with the fans, with the studio. If I didn't spin it, I'd —"

Jones cut him off with a flick of his hand, already turning back toward his corner, not even sparing Jaxon a glance. "Derrick, baby… he's all yours now."

And this time, Derrick didn't hesitate. He launched forward, and the crack of Derrick's fist against Jaxon's jaw rang out like a starter pistol. The sound was sharp, electric, shattering the thin veneer of civility we'd been clinging to.

Jaxon went down hard, stumbling back into a chair that skidded against the floor and nearly tipped with the force of his fall. The thud echoed through the room, reverberating in my ribs.

For a heartbeat, no one moved. The silence was almost louder than the blow.

Simmy's hands were over her mouth. Marley's jaw was locked, eyes blazing, his whole body taut like he wanted his own turn. Jones looked perfectly composed, smoothing the lapel of his blazer as if he'd planned the choreography. And me? I just stared at Jaxon, sprawled and dazed in that chair, finally knocked off a pedestal he never deserved.

The silence stretched so tight it buzzed.

London was the only one who moved. He walked to the door, calm, intentional, and pulled it open with a controlled click. His voice was even, almost polite, but it cut sharper than any punch.

"Best you be leaving now, Jaxon."

He rubbed his jaw, eyes flicking between each of us—me, his children, London, Jones. Looking for sympathy, for some sliver of the old power he used to wield. He found nothing but steel and silence.

When he finally pushed to his feet, the scrape of the chair against the floor was the loudest sound in the room. No parting words. No swagger. Just silence, and what little was left of his dignity, as he walked out.

"Motherfucker..." Derrick muttered, shaking his head like he could rattle the rage loose. Then he crossed the room in two strides, his hand closing around mine, pulling me up and into his chest. His arms locked around me, lifting me clean off the floor. "I'm so fucking sorry, Mom. We never should've invited him. I'm so sorry."

The sound of his sobs against my neck shattered me. He was twenty-three, a grown man, but in that moment he was twelve again, back to being my boy who needed me.

"You have nothing to be sorry for, baby," I whispered fiercely, holding his face in my hands when he set me down. "If anything, I'm sorry your night wasn't the epic one you wanted."

He huffed a laugh through the tears, wiping at his eyes with the back of his hand. "Mom... I've been wanting to punch Dad in the mouth since the first tabloid. That was about as epic as it gets."

27 | *LONDON*

I'd seen a lot of things in my life—steel beams bending in storms, men break under pressure, cities rise from nothing but dirt and blueprints. But I'd never seen anything like this.

Ricky, towering over his father after he clocked the living shit out of him, eyes blazing with a fury that left no room for argument. He looked nothing like the boy I'd first shaken hands with. He looked like a man forged in fire—and in this moment; he wasn't Jaxon's son. He was Sevynn's.

And God, the pride that ripped through me nearly buckled my knees.

I watched Sevynn's lips part, trembling, her hands twitching uselessly at her sides. She wanted to stop it, to soften the blow, because that's who she was—always carrying the weight of everyone else's choices. But I couldn't move. I couldn't look away. Because the boy she'd raised was defending her in a way, no one ever had.

I swear to God, I almost clapped. Almost threw my fist in the air and shouted, *That's my boy*. But he wasn't mine. He was hers. Every ounce of that strength came from her.

And as Jaxon fell back, silent for once in his smug, shallow life, I felt something heal inside me. The grief that had carved me hollow for years eased, just enough for breath to fill the space it left behind. In that moment, I knew that I wanted to spend the rest of my life loving and protecting her with that same ferocity.

I opened the door, told him it was best he get on about his fucking business. And when it shut behind him, the quiet that settled over the room was worse than the shouting. Heavy. Knowing. Because now it was just us—and the real inquisition was about to begin.

I'd basically laid claim to Sevynn in front of a hundred people. Talked her down from panic like she belonged to me. Baby. Sweetheart. Pressing my mouth to her temple, brushing her tears away with my thumb. How the fuck do we explain that away? To them, to ourselves, when on paper we're strangers—almost in-laws at best.

Her eyes flicked to mine through the chaos. Wet, shattered, but lit with something dangerously close to fear. Not fear of me—fear of what we'd just exposed. And I knew in my chest, in my bones, she felt it too.

"Okay, okay," Simone cut through the silence, clapping her hands like she could physically snap the tension. "Clearly there is uh... another conversation that needs to be had here." She slid closer to Sevynn. "Are you okay? Really?" She caught Sevynn's hand, squeezing it tight.

"Yes, love. I'm okay. I promise." Sevynn's smile was watery, brittle, but it held.

Simone's eyes narrowed. "Dad was able to talk you down

from a *pretty severe* panic attack."

She didn't phrase it as a question, but the implication was a loaded gun sitting between us all.

"He did, yes." Sevynn's voice cracked, but she managed to meet my eyes for a half-second. "Thank you, London."

Marley snorted, arms crossed, eyes bouncing between us like he was clocking a tennis match. "For fuck's sake, I can't do this the roundabout way. Is there something going on between the two of you? That was kind of...intimate out there."

Ricky's jaw flexed, his hand dragging over his mouth. He didn't say anything yet, but his gaze was locked on Sevynn, steady and unblinking, like he was already bracing for answers he didn't want.

And Jones—of course, Jones—finally leaned back in his chair with a sigh so theatrical it rattled the damn walls. "Well," he drawled, gray eyes glittering like knives, "I don't know about y'all, but I'm *dying* for this tea. Come sit on my lap, Marley baby. I need to be held."

"Goddamnit, Jones," Marley muttered, storming to the other side of the room, cheeks red as hell.

Interesting.

"Mom?" Ricky's voice cut in—low, but edged like he was bracing for impact.

I shifted beside her, straightening in my chair. My forearm brushed hers. She was vibrating beside me, and I wanted to steady her, shield her, anything.

Jones arched a brow, smirk sharp enough to cut glass.

"Tick-tock, Sev. Don't keep your children—or my very neglected gossip palate—waiting."

Simone swatted at him without looking away from us. Her eyes were locked on Sevynn, laser-sharp.

"Mom, just be honest," Ricky said again, jaw tight. "What's going on?"

The room shrank smaller, tighter. Too quiet.

She tried to laugh, thin and shaky. "Honest? About what, exactly? That I had a panic attack and London happened to be there to help me?"

"Uh, no." Marley cut in, eyes flashing. "Honest about the way he called you *sweetheart* and *baby*, like he's been doing it for years. Honest about the way you two looked at each other like—" He broke off, dragging his hands down his face. "I don't know. Like more than this."

My jaw clenched. I was ready to step in, take the hit, shoulder the fire. "Guys...listen—"

Her hand shot out, gripping my thigh. Stopping me cold.

"Yes." The word ripped out of her, raw, quiet, undeniable. My heart slammed once, hard. Her hands were shaking. So were mine. "Before we knew who we were to each other," she whispered, voice cracking. "Yes."

The silence after was brutal. Ricky's jaw locked so tight I swore I heard the grind of his teeth. Marley muttered a stunned, "Holy shit," dragging a hand down his face.

Simone didn't move. She just *looked* at us—sharp, unblinking, like she could peel the truth out of our bones.

My throat burned. I forced myself to speak. "We agreed nothing could happen. Not once we knew. Not with you all caught in the middle."

Heat crawled up my chest, suffocating. I raked a hand over the back of my neck, the other over my mouth, and when my eyes found Sevynn's, I knew. This was it. Make or break.

The silence stretched until it snapped.

Simone's eyes dropped—to my hand. The one resting against my jaw. Her gaze froze there, wide. Then she stood so fast her chair screeched against the floor, and in two steps she was at my side, clutching my hand like she couldn't believe it.

"Dad," she whispered, her voice trembling. "You took your ring off? When? I didn't even notice."

My chest cracked. The words came rough, stripped bare. "The day I met Sevynn, babygirl." Her eyes searched mine, wet and wild. "For her," I rasped. "I took it off for her. I had to."

Before I could get out another word, she was closing the distance over to Sevynn, wrapping her arms around her so tight, it shocked a gasp out of Sevynn's chest.

"Thank you," Simone whispered into Sevynn's shoulder, her body trembling. "Thank you."

When Simone finally pulled away, her face blotchy and tear-streaked, she didn't hesitate. She turned and rushed into my arms, wrapping me up like she couldn't get close enough. I folded instantly, burying my face in the curve of her neck, shoulders shaking as my tears slipped free.

"Oh my god, I've cried so much today already!" She said,

sniffling, making her way back over to sit next to Sevynn. "Tell me *everything*."

"Not everything, babygirl," I teased.

"Uhmm—*ewww*." Simone wrinkled her nose, dragging out the word.

"I second that," Ricky muttered, but there was the tiniest curve to his lips.

"Third." Marley raised both hands like he was swearing in to testify.

"Yeah...yeah. Let's hear it people."

"All right, children, calm down." Sevynn gave them all a look that was equal parts Mom voice and playful surrender before turning back to Simone. She squeezed her hand.

"London and I only met this week. It's not some wild, crazy, swept-up romance, so there's not much to really tell."

She paused, cutting me a glance and smirking through the remnants of tears. "Maybe a little."

"Oh. My. God!" Simone squealed, smacking her palm against her knee, her whole face lighting up.

I groaned, rolling my eyes heavenward.

"He took me out on a date within a couple hours of meeting me," Sevynn went on, her voice threaded with mischief, "to the arcade of all places."

"Dad!" Simone gasped, looking at me with mock outrage.

"What?!" I lifted both hands, shrugging like I was innocent.

"She'd never been to one!"

Her laugh broke free, soft but real, and something in my chest healed at the sound.

"And that's where we'll end this story," Sevynn cut in quickly, her tone final, like she'd just slammed a door.

"Mom!" Ricky nearly shouted, his eyes bugging out as he pressed a hand to his chest in full-on mock horror. "Did you have a...a one... night... stand?"

"Hell *yeah*, she did!" Jones clapped. "Now, who wants details?"

"NO!" Sevynn, Marley and Ricky yelled in unison.

"Prudes."

Simone with her hand still covering her mouth at the question darted to me. I froze under her stare. "Dad. Did you —?"

Christ. My face burned. "Can we *not* do this right now?" I groaned, pinching the bridge of my nose.

"Confirmation received!" Marley crowed, throwing both arms up like he'd just scored the winning touchdown.

Ricky muttered something that sounded a hell of a lot like, "Unbelievable," but I caught it — the twitch at the corner of his mouth. He wasn't nearly as pissed as he wanted to look.

Sevynn straightened, her shoulders squaring like she'd just decided she was done being the punchline. "You know what? Fine. I'll own it. I have spent enough time today being embarrassed."

I turned my head toward her, eyebrows climbing, curious where the hell she was about to take this.

"It wasn't a one-night stand." She declared. That earned her a room full of stares. Mine included. I felt my head tilt, trying to make sense of what she was doing. "It was an all-night, all-morning....and a few other times stand."

"Mama, *nooo*," Ricky groaned, dragging a hand down his face before gagging theatrically. "No. Don't say that." He jumped up and down, like a todder having a tantrum. "Don't *say* that!"

"I'm never using that term again," Marley muttered, "because, holy shit, my brain is now permanently scarred."

"My lap is still available, Marley baby." Jones taps his thighs and Marley dismisses him with a flick of his wrist.

Simone just sat there, mouth slack, eyes glazed, like she'd just dissociated straight out of the small room and into another dimension. My poor kid.

And me? I was trying not to laugh. Trying. Failing. Because Sevynn, with her chin tilted high and that little fire in her eyes, was worth every ounce of this chaos.

"Dad?"

"Yes, baby girl?"

"You're officially uninvited from the wedding. Marley, do you want to walk me down the aisle tomorrow?"

"*Hell* yeah, sis!" Marley shot up so fast his chair scraped the floor, bouncing on his toes like a kid about to hit recess. "Beyonce? NSync? Bobby Brown? What are we doing?"

I blinked. "And why am I uninvited?"

"Because I want to get married without *gagging*, Father." Simone rolled her eyes with precision only a daughter could perfect, then immediately softened as she turned toward Sevynn. She leaned in, taking her hand in hers like it was the most natural thing in the world.

"I'm so glad I met your son," Simone said, her voice steady but shimmering with emotion. "He's the *greatest* thing to ever happen to me, and that's because of who you are as a mother."

Her words hung there, luminous, like she'd just handed Sevynn a piece of her heart. I watched Simone's throat bob as she glanced down at Sevynn's hand, still clasped tightly in hers, and the tears that had been threatening finally spilled over, unchecked. A soft sob escaped her as she rubbed the bridge tattoo on Sevynn's wrist.

"Oh my god." She whispered. Her eyes flashed up to mine, then back to Sevynn's wrist. What's this tattoo of?" She asked, tracing her fingertip gently along the ink.

Sevynn lifted her arm slightly, smiling faintly. "It's the Tower Bridge."

"In London?" Simone asked, her brows furrowing, almost like she already knew the answer.

Sevynn nodded. "I got it when I was there for work. I was just...taken by it. Not sure why. But it always stuck with me — the strength of it, the beauty of it. Reminded me a lot of my boys."

For just a beat, Simone's tearful gaze flicked to me again. A fleeting glance, but sharp enough to cut me open, before she turned back to Sevynn. Her bottom lip trembled, but her voice was sure when she spoke again.

"But more than Ricky," Simone said shakily, "I'm a big believer in fate. I think I was meant to find *you*. That *we...*" Her chest rose on a shaky breath, then steadied. "...were meant to find you, Sev."

The room fell into a silence so tender it almost hurt, as if everyone there felt the gravity of what had just been said — even if they didn't understand it.

And in that moment, I wasn't an architect, or a widower, or even a dad fumbling his way through this wedding week. I was a man standing in front of two women who had wrecked me in entirely different ways — my daughter and the woman I couldn't stop wanting — and I knew I'd never be the same again.

Then she stood, radiant even through the tear stains, as Ricky and Marley both leaned down to kiss their mom on the cheek. Marley immediately mussed her hair, earning a sharp swat and a mock glare from Sevynn.

"You never needed to hide, or ask our permission to see each other," Simone said softly, her eyes flicking from me to Sevynn with startling clarity. Then she turned toward Ricky. "Right, baby?"

Ricky nodded without hesitation. "One hundred percent."

"So, whatever this is — you have our blessing. I want Dad to be happy, and Ricky needs you to be happy. He worries about it. It keeps him up at night, thinking you're not." Her voice wavered, but the conviction in it was steel. "So, please. Be happy. Both of you."

Then she did something that rooted me to the spot. She took Sevynn's hand, lifted it gently, and pressed a kiss to the bridge tattoo on her wrist. My brow furrowed, confusion pulling at me, because I knew there was meaning there I didn't understand.

But before I could ask, Simone gave Sevynn's hand a final squeeze and stood tall, like she'd just made peace with something far bigger than me.

"Boys," she declared, pointing toward the door like a general rallying her troops. "Time to drink our feelings away in shots. TO THE BAR!"

"TO THE BARRRR!" Ricky echoed, grinning.

I barely had time to breathe before Simone bounded across the room, launching herself into my arms. Her legs dangled, her arms wrapped tight around my neck, and her whisper cut through everything:

"She's it, Dad. She's the one Mom promised she'd send to you. The London Bridge—just where Mom said it would be. Right on her wrist."

And just like that, I nearly broke. My chest caved, my throat burned, and I had to set her back down before I lost it completely.

She'll have a bridge, like your daddy. A London Bridge, right here.

Her eyes, filled with tears and certainty, locked on mine as she nodded like she'd just handed me the truth of the universe. Then, word for word, she repeated what Sarah had said all those years ago:

"You'll see. One day, you'll see. It's fate."

The tears came. Hot. Unstoppable. And hers matched mine.

"I love you, Dad. See you in the morning?"

I nodded, swallowed hard, managing a rough laugh. "So I can still walk you down the aisle? Haven't been banned yet?"

"You'll do," she teased, her smile wobbling through the tears.

"I love you, baby girl," I rasped, my voice breaking all over again.

Ricky was next, hugging me with a grip I hadn't felt from anyone except my brothers—solid, grounding, fierce. Marley followed, awkward as hell but still tugging me in for a quick hug before tapping my bicep with a playful punch. He immediately winced, shaking out his hand like he'd just slammed it into a brick wall.

"Dude, you're like fucking steel," he muttered, flexing his sore fingers while squeezing my arm like he needed proof. "What do you even lift?"

I snorted, shaking my head as Ricky groaned.

"For fuck's sake, stop feeling up my father-in-law, Marley."

Marley only grinned, rolling up his t-shirt sleeve and flexing like he was auditioning for a protein powder commercial. "Just making sure this man's worthy of my mom."

Jones, of course, couldn't resist. "You can feel me up, Marley baby. I'll show you mine if you show me yours."

"Stop flirting with my son, Jones," Sevynn snapped, half-exasperated, half-amused. "He's too young for you."

"He's ten years younger than me, darling. That's prime trope material."

"And I'm straight, goddamnit."

"Keep telling yourself that, Marley baby."

"Good God," Ricky muttered, pinching the bridge of his nose. "Walk, idiots."

"See you in the morning, Mom."

"Later, peeps."

"Take care of my girl, London Baby."

And then they were gone. Just like that, the noise evaporated, the chaos swallowed by silence.

I barely had time to close the door before Sevynn was on me—launching herself into my chest, slamming me back against the closed door. Her mouth crashed to mine with a force that felt less like a kiss and more like a storm breaking loose, all teeth and tongue and desperation.

She reaches behind me, fumbling with the door and finding a lock to secure our privacy.

Her fists tangled in my shirt, dragging me closer, her other hand tugging hard at my hair until my head tipped back. "I need you, London." The words were ragged, torn straight from her throat, her breath hot against my lips.

"Fuck, baby," I groaned, gripping her waist as I hauled her higher, her legs locking tight around me. My hands slid down, palming greedy handfuls of her thighs. I turned us and pressed her hard against the door.

"I don't care if it's reckless." My mouth crashed into hers again, hungrier. "I don't care where we are."

Her whimper undid me. My teeth grazed her lower lip as I whispered against her mouth, "You're fucking mine, Sevynn."

I kissed her harder, rougher, each press of lips a demand, each drag of tongue a vow I couldn't take back.

"Say it." My voice was gravel, my chest heaving as I pinned her tighter against the door. "Right fucking now. Say it."

Her nails dragged down the back of my neck, her body trembling in my arms. I pressed harder into her, the solid weight of the door at her back, my need for her a living, breathing thing between us.

"Say it," I growled again, my mouth trailing fire along her jaw, down to her ear. "Say you're mine, Sevynn."

Her head fell back, a gasp ripping out of her. "Yours, London..." My name was broken, almost a sob.

"Fucking mine," I bit out, sucking gently at the pulse hammering in her throat. My thumbs dug into the softness of her thighs where I held her pinned. Her hips rocked against me, the friction making my vision blur.

My hands slid inside her pants, sliding two fingers inside her wet heat. She moaned into my mouth, her body bowing into me, chest heaving.

"Good girl."

She shuddered at the words, a violent, full-body tremor that had her clenching around my fingers—a tight, wet promise of what was to come. Her head fell back against the door with a soft thud, her eyes squeezed shut.

Then her lips were at my ear, her breath a hot, broken whisper that seared straight into my soul. "I want you. Right now, London. *Please*."

That single, shattered *please* was the final blow. Sanity evaporated.

My mouth crashed against hers, our breath mingling in ragged, shared gasps. The world outside this door ceased to be. There was no noise, no thought, only the desperate press of her body against mine and the bruising, hungry kisses we traded—each one a punctuation mark in a sentence of pure need.

I fumbled with my belt and fly, my hands clumsy with urgency. I shoved my pants and briefs down just enough to free myself, my cock springing out, hard and aching, the tip already slick with need. I slid her pants and panties to the floor, exposing her. The scent of her arousal, sweet and musky, filled the air between us.

I hoisted her again against the solid wood of the door, my hands gripping the soft flesh of her thighs, spreading her wider. I lined myself up, the head of my cock nudging against her slick heat, and with a guttural groan, I pushed inside.

The fit was so fucking tight, a burning, silken friction that stole the breath from my lungs.

"Fuck. Oh, fuck," she cried out, her voice breaking on the words. I covered her mouth with mine to swallow her cries before hotel security came banging on the door. Her inner muscles fluttered around me, trying to adjust, pulling me deeper. "This... you're so *deep* like this." Her breaths were uneven gasps against my mouth.

I pressed her harder into the door, my body pinning hers, and began to move with a relentless, grinding rhythm. I rolled my hips, seeking that perfect angle, and found it when she arched off the door with a shattered silent cry. Her head tipped back, a beautiful line of surrender, her lips parted and her eyes clenched tight.

"Look at me," I demanded, my voice a savage thing. I forced my forehead to hers again, my breath shuddering against her sweat-slicked skin. "Sevynn, I need you right here with me. I need to see you."

Her eyelids fluttered open. Her eyes were flames, pupils blown wide with pleasure, wild and unfocused until they locked on mine. And in that searing connection, something fundamental in me shattered.

My control snapped.

I drove into her harder, faster. My pace became frantic, desperate, a piston-like rhythm that slammed her against the door with every thrust. The sound of our bodies meeting, skin slapping against skin, of her ragged cries and my own harsh grunts, was the only music left in the world. Her nails scored my shoulders, biting deep, the sharp pain only fueling the fire. I could feel the coil of her orgasm tightening around me, her body clenching and grasping, trying to pull me even deeper inside her.

"Yes—fuck—*London*—" The way she screamed my name, a half-moan, half-desperate plea, was my undoing.

"That's it, baby," I grit out. "Give it to me. I want to feel all of it. Now. *Come for me.*"

The command, voiced against her skin, was the final trigger. Her body went rigid in my arms. A broken, keening wail was torn from her throat as her climax ripped through her, a violent, crashing wave. Her inner walls convulsed around my cock, a series of frantic, milking spasms that dragged me over the edge with her.

With a final, savage push, I buried myself to the hilt and followed her into the abyss. My own release was a white-hot explosion, my roar muffled against her neck as I emptied myself into her, pulse after pulse, until I was spent, shaking, and utterly consumed.

For a long moment, we stayed like that, pinned together by gravity and aftershocks, our harsh panting the only sound in the sudden, deafening silence. When it finally ebbed, when the world slowly started to stitch itself back together, I pressed soft, desperate kisses along her jaw, her cheeks, her trembling mouth. My voice was hoarse, ruined, but gentle.

"Mine," I whispered one last time, forehead pressed to hers. The silence held—thick, perfect—until the sharp rap on the door shattered it.

"Hotel security!"

28 | SEVYNN

"What's next?" I asked, my voice muffled against his chest, my bare leg hooked over him like I couldn't stand to let go. My fingers traced lazy lines down his abs, memorizing every ridge. "What happens when Chicago is over?"

After we left the hotel's security office—basically *bribing* our way out of getting arrested—we made our way back to London's room and tore into each other again, and again. Now we were wrecked, spent, tangled in damp sheets. The high was fading, but the realization was beginning to creep in: we'd be leaving Chicago in just less than a day.

His laugh was low, rumbling beneath my cheek. "Sweetheart, Chicago isn't the end of anything. It's just where the fuse lit."

He tipped his head to look at me, green eyes sharp in the dim light. "You're in Raleigh, I'm in Durham. I'm riding home on your plane. Driving you back from the airport. Carrying your bags inside. Then, you'll give me a tour of your home, so that I know exactly where to fuck you first. I'm thinking the walls, then the kitchen counter. Then the shower. And every damn corner of your house until I've ruined you for anywhere else. That's my plan."

He smirked, thumb brushing over my jaw, but his voice softened. "Then we figure it out. Because I'm not letting this be a fling. Not you."

My breath caught, heat licking down my spine. "That's... detailed," I murmured, trying for teasing, but my voice wobbled.

"Detailed?" He grinned, dimples cutting deep. "Baby, that's me being restrained."

I shifted, dragging my fingertip absently over his chest, not meeting his eyes. "What about your home? Don't you... want to go back there? Or when will you?"

His brow arched, but I kept talking, words tumbling faster than my brain could catch them. "I mean, I'm not asking you to stay with me or anything. God, no. It's just—I have a big house, way too big, honestly, and there's plenty of room. Not that it matters, because I'm sure you have a big house too, not that big houses matter." My cheeks burned. "It's just... we leave in less than twenty-four hours, and I don't know where you stand with everything."

I trailed off, cheeks burning, suddenly very aware of how unsexy it was to ramble about square footage and luggage logistics after the sex marathon we'd just had.

He let out a low chuckle. "Are you done?" His voice was low, patient, but edged with amusement. "Because I don't want to interrupt your nervous word vomit."

My head snapped up, scandalized. "Word vomit?"

One brow arched, his dimples nowhere in sight. "That's what it was, sweetheart. Adorable. Terrible. But adorable."

"Yes, I'm done. Yes, I'm nervous."

He rolled over in one smooth shift, pinning me with his weight, spreading my legs with his thighs until I was caged under him. His palms pressed to the mattress on either side of my head, his gaze locked down on mine. The room stilled. My pulse rioted.

"Where I stand with everything," he said, voice rough, "is this. And I want you to listen to every word so there's no mistaking me."

Silence. His stare didn't waver.

"Nod for yes, sweetheart."

I nodded, throat tight.

"Good." His breath skimmed my cheek. "Here's where I stand. My house? It's just drywall and dust. A vacant, empty reminder of a life that's long gone. I don't even sleep in the bedroom—I crash on the couch, bury myself in work. That place isn't home. It hasn't been for years." He shifted closer, the weight of him pressing me deeper into the sheets. "But the second I saw you—rhinestone Kindle, milking smut, ridiculous cloud-face slippers—you were home. You. No rhyme. No reason. Maybe fate. Maybe Simone's right and Sarah had a hand in it. I don't give a damn what the explanation is. What I know is this: since that moment, it's been you."

My breath hitched, tears pricking.

He leaned down until his forehead pressed to mine, his words vibrating through both of us. "So I'm telling you now. This is it for me. Crazy or not. And in one year, I'm going to ask you to be my wife. If I thought you wouldn't bolt the second I pulled out a ring, I'd be on my knees right now." His jaw flexed, his whisper scorching. "That's where I am with everything. Am I clear?"

I nodded again, trembling.

"Good." His mouth brushed mine, reverent and brutal all at once. "Because I'm not leaving your side unless you tell me to. I'll have a toothbrush and a razor in your bathroom before the sun sets tonight. I'm not letting you go, Sev. Not now. Not ever."

"I love you, London." I interrupted before he could say anything else. My voice cracked, but I didn't care. "I'm not a reckless person. I never have been. I'm type A down to my bones—planner, scheduler, lists for my lists. My life has always been...neat. Controlled." I laughed once, watery. "And this entire week? It's thrown me off balance in every possible way. But through all of it, there's been one constant."

My fingers traced the line of his jaw, trembling but sure. "You. I think I've loved you since you fumbled your way through that ridiculous flirting in the lounge. Since the arcade, when you knew exactly what to do to pull me back from the edge. Since your mouth found the scar on my neck like it was something holy. Every kiss, every touch—you've unmoored me in ways I never expected to feel, never even believed I *could* feel."

I shook my head, breath catching. "There's no rhyme or reason to it. And maybe I don't need one. So in one year, I'll say yes. In six months, I'll say yes. Hell, in six minutes I'd say yes. Because you're it for me, too. Whatever this is...it's already everything."

His eyes shone above me, wet, unguarded, and then his tears spilled—hot and startling against my cheek. He kissed me so deep my toes curled, my lungs burning with the force of it. When he pulled back, his forehead pressed to mine, his voice was trembling. "I love you, Sev. Marry me. We can't wait as long as you want, but I need to put a ring on your finger as soon as we get back to North Carolina."

My laugh broke on a gasp. "Oh my *god*, London! It's too soon! Are you crazy, we barely know ea—oh, *fuck*!"

Because before I could finish, he slammed inside me in one hungry thrust, stealing the breath from my chest.

A rasping groan tore from him, raw, primal. "Hmmm. Fuck, sweetheart—you're already clenching, and I just got here." He drove deeper, harder, his forehead pressed to mine, his breath shaking. "What were you saying?"

"London—" My voice cracked, strangled between protest and plea.

"That it's too soon?" Another punishing thrust. "That I'm crazy?" His hand gripped my chin, forcing my eyes open, forcing me to *see* him as he pounded into me. "Maybe I am. But you love me. Say it again."

"I—oh god—I love you!" The words poured out of me, half scream, half sob.

"That's my girl." His mouth crashed against mine, teeth, tongue, everything, devouring me. He didn't let up, his hips a merciless rhythm, his cock stretching me, filling me so deep I swore he was breaking me open. My nails raked his back, dragging furrows down muscle and scar alike, clinging like he was the only thing keeping me alive.

"You're mine," Every thrust punctuating it, branding me from the inside out. "And I'll ask you a thousand fucking times until you finally say yes."

"London!" My body arched, trembling, the orgasm already tearing up my spine like fire.

His hand slid down, thumb circling my clit, cruel and perfect. "Come for me, sweetheart. Right now. Say yes when you do."

I shattered. Violent. Guttural. My scream ripped the air apart as I convulsed around him, trembling so hard I thought my body would break. My "yes" was a sob, every emotion hitting me at once as he fucked me through it, never easing, never letting me down.

And then he snapped, rutting into me hard enough to rattle the bed against the wall.

"Fuck, Sevynn—*fuck*—" He came with a roar, burying himself so deep I swore he carved his name into my bones. His whole body trembled, brutal shudders rolling through him as he spilled into me, forehead pressed to mine, his lips mouthing something I couldn't hear.

We collapsed together, sweat-slick, shaking, gasping like survivors of a storm. His arms locked tight around me, possessive and unyielding, even as his breath hitched with laughter.

"We're fucking insane," he rasped, pressing his mouth to my temple, his voice hoarse and raspy. "Insane. But I think I love you."

I choked on a laugh, still trembling, my fingers clutching his shoulders. "You better. Because I'm pretty sure it doesn't get any better than this."

EPILOGUE

Marley

The first thing I felt was pain. Skull-cracking, brain-melting pain. The second was the Sahara in my mouth. The third was... regret. Big, neon-sign regret.

"Fuck, shit," I groaned, throwing an arm over my face. The faint glow through the curtains was too bright, the sheets too warm, the world too fucking loud for someone who clearly died at the bar last night and was resurrected with a hangover. I was praying for death or at least a gallon of water. That's when I heard it—a deep, raspy groan that was sure as fuck not mine, and from somewhere *way too damn close.*

My stomach dropped straight through the mattress. Slowly... and I mean so fucking slowly, I turned my head. And my soul left ejected from body.

"Holy shit."

Edward-McKenzie Jones. *Yes, that* Jones, my mom's flamboyant, dramatic, chaos-incarnate best friend; was sprawled across the bed next to me.

Naked. *Naked I say!*

His damn skin practically glowed against the sheets, long hair fanned across the pillow in these glossy, unfair waves, like he'd just shot a goddamn shampoo commercial.

And then I realized something else.

I was naked too.

My whole body went rigid. "JONES!"

He groaned, rolling onto his back. "Ahhh, fuck. Why are you yelling, dammit?" His voice was raspy, sleep-heavy, unfairly deep—like sex and gravel rolled into one.

And holy *fuck.* His dick was hard. And… *pierced*?

Cue the fucking *PANIC.* I was in a hotel room with my mom's naked best friend, and he was sporting a full-on Prince Albert display of morning wood like it was goddamn show-and-tell.

"What the fuck did you do?" My voice cracked, heart battering so hard I was half-convinced it might rip through my ribcage.

One lazy gray eye cracked open, bleary but sharp enough to make my soul sweat. He tilted his head, hair sliding over his face like he was *posing,* even half-dead from tequila. "Sweetie, judging by the way you're clutching that sheet over a very sexy and very naked body, I'd say the better question is what did *we* do?"

Complete system malfunction. Sparks. Smoke. Static. "No. No, no, no. That's not—this isn't—"

He studied me, head tilted, like he was trying to solve a riddle. So am I, dude. Samesies. Shit.

Finally, he sighed, dragging a hand through his hair before reaching blindly for the glass of water on the nightstand. His throat worked as he drank, and I hated myself for noticing.

"Relax," he muttered, setting it down. "You're adorable when you panic, but it's too early for melodrama." He cracked the faintest grin. "That's my job."

"Jones!" I hissed, heat crawling up my neck. "Did we—did you—*DID WE*—"

He cut me off with a lazy grin, licking a drop of water from his lip. "Marley Baby, if I'd had your ass last night, you wouldn't be walking right now."

"Then why the fuck am I naked?" I demanded, sheet clutched tighter.

He shrugged, completely unbothered, arm thrown behind his head. "You stripped. Something about 'sheets are lava' and then you passed out face first on my thigh. Romantic, really."

He reached over to the nightstand, his abs constricting with every movement, and a line formed of muscle formed along his side as he stretched over.

Stop looking at his fucking body, you idiot!

He grabs his phone, unlocks it and starts playing a video, tossing it over on the side of the bed I'm standing on.

"I want to stay in your room, Jonsie. Everyone is going to a room with somebody, and no one is in my room."

I'm telling him, clearly drunk off my ass. I look up at him, and he's watching me with a smirk.

"Fine, but I don't have sex with drunk straight men, Marley baby."

"Did you all hear that? He calls me Marley baby!" I'm yelling

into the camera as I hold the phone too close to my face. Then I pan the camera back over to Jones, and he's watching me with a hunger in his eyes. The camera keeps rolling as we get to his room. It's mostly of my feet, then his, then mine again, me singing a chipmunk song. When he closes the door, I sit the phone down and start undressing. I can't see myself undressing because the screen is dark. But Jones is telling me NOT to undress because he doesn't want my mom to kill him. But I do it anyway.

"You realize you're standing in my room with a hard cock right now, Marley baby?"

"Yes."

"Do you want to sleep on the couch? I'll get you some sheets."

"Couch sheets are lava. I'm going to bed with you."

"I'm not having sex with you, Marley."

"Don't you find me attractive? I find you so fucking attractive, it makes my head spin."

My mouth drops, and I look back up to Jones, and he's still looking at me, watching.

"Let's get some sleep, baby boy." I grab the phone and start talking into the camera again. *"I'm going to sleep in Jones' bed naked, with a hard dick. I wonder if I can get him to suck it...or if he'll let me suck his."*

I close the video so fast my finger is a blur. I toss it back on the bed. "Ohhhohkayyyy. So, I was very, very drunk. I am *so* sorry. I'll get dressed and leave now. So, so sorry."

"Don't look so scandalized, Marley Baby. You'll get used

to waking up next to me, eventually."

"I'm never drinking again."

"Sure you are. But for now—you still have a champagne toast to give, Best Man. Better go get yourself dressed before I steal the spotlight."

Find out if Jones finally gets his 'Marley baby' in Book Two of The Reckless Hearts Series, "To The Best Man…"